HIDDEN THREADS

HIDDEN THREADS

A Virginia Davies Quilt Mystery
Book Eight

By
David Ciambrone

Names, characters, businesses, places, events, and incidents are either the products of the author's imagination or used in a fictitious manner. Any resemblance to actual persons, living or dead, or actual events, is purely coincidental.

No part of this publication may be reproduced, stored in a retrieval system, or transmitted in any form or by any means, electronic, mechanical, photocopying, recording, or otherwise, without the written permission of the publisher.

Text Copyright © 2022 David Ciambrone

All rights reserved.
Published 2022 by Progressive Rising Phoenix Press, LLC
www.progressiverisingphoenix.com

ISBN: 978-1-958640-21-0

Printed in the U.S.A.

Book and Cover design by William Speir
Visit: http://www.williamspeir.com

ACKNOWLEDGMENTS

Writing is a solitary affair, but, any author will also tell you their writing depends on a host of others who have provided needed information, ideas, inspiration, critiques, just plain support when we needed it and someone to listen when things go array. To this end, I'd like to thank the following people and groups for their support bringing this book to life.

The Williamson County Coroners critique group for their sound critiques and support.

My great publisher Amanda M. Thrasher and editors at Progressive Rising Phoenix Press, LLC. Without them, this book would not have seen the light of day.

The San Gabriel Writer's League mystery critique group.

My wife Kathy for her support, wonderful ideas, and the quilt that was used on the cover for the story.

CHAPTER 1

Exhausted, and not just a wee bit disgusted, Virginia Davies-Clark crammed the pencil inside her blonde topknot, tossed a wadded-up paper into her trashcan, plopped into the soft leather of her office chair, and studied the map on the wall across the wide expanse of her new oak desk. *That was a hell of a meeting, and the director still insists I can't kill, stuff, and display the accountants in a museum diorama. I thought Accountosaurus Rex would be a cute name for the display. Of course, he wouldn't let me do it in the past, either.* Her thoughts were interrupted by a phone call. *Now what?* She answered briskly, "Hello?"

"Is this Ms. Virginia Davies?" asked a woman's voice.

Still irritated, Virginia responded tersely. "Yes."

"Virginia, you may not remember me, I'm Gail Knight. I was a professor of yours when you were at the University of California at Irvine."

Virginia thought for a second, then relaxed. "Yes, of course I remember you, Dr. Knight. You taught the basic programming course I took. You made the subject interesting and fun, especially with your stories about when you worked at Microsoft in its early days. It's been a long time. What can I do for you?"

"I've retired and just purchased the *Circle A* ranch, or farm, or whatever they call these huge parcels of land in Texas," said Gail.

"You did? Where in Texas?"

"Near Georgetown. I understand you live nearby."

"Yes, I do. You bought a ranch? What are you going to do with a ranch?" *How does a retired professor buy a large ranch on her retirement pay? Savings maybe?*

"Live here. I'm going to start renovating it."

"How big is this huge parcel of land exactly?" *To someone from Southern California, over an acre is big.* Virginia leaned back in her chair.

"Three hundred and eighty acres," said Gail. "The buildings are solid and livable but are dated and need renovating."

"That is big. I have a friend who did a renovation of a ranch house a couple of years ago. I could introduce you to her. She's got a list of good contractors, and my husband is an engineer, so maybe he could help."

"That would be great. Your husband is an engineer?"

"Yes. He's a professor of mechanical engineering at the University of Texas in Austin."

"Oh, yeah, I remember now, you married Dr. Andy Clark. You were dating him at UCI. He was a professor of mechanical engineering and the faculty advisor for the engineering student club on campus, wasn't he? They published a glossy monthly *Playboy*-style magazine to raise money, and they raised a lot of money with that magazine."

"Yes, that's my Andy." *I guess everyone who went there then remembers. Computer science was in the engineering department, of course she'd remember that.*

"So, what are you doing now?" asked Gail.

"I'm a curator at the San Gabriel Museum in Georgetown."

"Good for you. Are you still quilting?"

Virginia grinned. "You remembered that? Yes, I'm still quilting and I'm a member of the Main Street Quilt Guild in Round Rock, Texas." *Why all the questions? Where is she going with this?*

"Good. You see, I need a quilter's advice. I would love to get together with you if you have some free time."

"How about lunch tomorrow?" asked Virginia.

"You're on. Where and what time?"

"Noon at the Longhorn Steakhouse in Wolf Ranch shopping center? It's on Highway 29 just off the 35, or the I35 as they say outside of California," said Virginia.

"I know the place. But I have to make a confession," said Gail.

Virginia picked up a pen and clicked the top a couple of times. "What's that?"

"Like I said, I need some help, and I remember people around UCI saying after you graduated you were some sort of investigator."

Oh, boy. Virginia sat straight in her chair. "I do stumble on some... problems once in a while that I've been helpful in resolving."

"What kind of problems?"

"The occasional issues with quilts, antiquities, robberies, pirates, smuggling, murders—"

"Perfect!"

"Perfect?" Virginia knitted her brow. "Murder is perfect?"

"Yes... er... no. The problem is, I have a mysterious issue with the place I just bought. The *Circle A*. And I want to give you an old quilt to evaluate that supposedly has something valuable hidden in it. It's from my newly acquired ranch."

Mysterious issue with a quilt and ranch? Virginia leaned on her desk.

"Is the old quilt related to your... *Circle A* ranch problem?"

"Yes. When I realized I had questions about the quilt, I asked around about who to talk to regarding a mystery surrounding an old quilt, and everyone I spoke to in the quilting community told me to see you. They said you were the expert at investigating this sort of thing and that you do it all the time. Imagine my surprise when I realized I knew you from my class back in California."

"What does the... problem consist of, besides the quilt?"

"Possible illegal antiquities, maybe smuggling, maybe some murders, and ghosts."

CHAPTER 2

At noon the next day, Virginia and Dr. Gail Knight slid into a booth in the Longhorn Steakhouse. Gail, with graying hair and wire-rimmed glasses, looked at the menu, then glanced around. "I like the ambiance. This looks like an upscale Texas steakhouse, but with great prices."

"The food is good, too." Virginia ordered two iced teas from the server and examined the menu. "Now, before she comes back, what is this problem you're having with ghosts?"

Gail sipped her tea. "Let me start with a little history, then we'll get to the problems and the quilt I brought for you to examine."

"Okay."

"I retired, as I told you. California is extremely expensive, and the place is... well... not what it used to be. I wanted to move to someplace less expensive and still sane. I've always wanted a farm or ranch. So, I purchased a ranch called the *Circle A* near Georgetown and moved there. I'm getting ready to do some renovations to it."

"You already told me that."

"Right." Gail pushed her glasses back up her nose. "I bought the ranch from the niece of First Lieutenant Robert Cumo of the U.S. Army 3rd Infantry Division. He was a veteran of the battle for Rome, such as it was, during World War II. Lieutenant Cumo lived on the *Circle A* since he returned from the war in 1945 until 1990 when he died at age 97 from complications from an old war wound. That and old age. His niece lived there after his death and sold it to me due to financial problems and issues with the ghosts."

"That's a lot of information about the niece's uncle. Strange she'd mention all that."

"It's important to why she wanted to sell the ranch, besides her money problems. And there are the ghosts."

Virginia took another drink of her tea then leaned forward. "Ghosts. Got it. Go on."

"Visitors and neighbors have talked of floating lights, shadowy figures, and poltergeist-style sightings for over sixty years."

"What did his niece say?"

"She thought her uncle left Italy after the war with a few valuable souvenirs from Rome and maybe the ghosts want the souvenirs returned."

"Valuable souvenirs? Like what?" asked Virginia.

"Like art and antiquities."

"Interesting. What kind of art and antiquities?"

"I'm not sure."

"Does his niece think he brought the looted artifacts to the ranch?"

"His niece and someone else thinks he did. Since I purchased the ranch, I've noticed a few of the floating lights and shadowy figures around at night. Then there are the holes."

Virginia straightened when the server arrived to take their order. The women paused their conversation to order food. Once the server was gone, Virginia asked, "Holes? What holes?"

"Someone's been digging holes around the ranch and filling them back in. I don't know what to make of them."

"Someone looking for the… treasure maybe?" Virginia raised an eyebrow. "Is there a pattern to the holes?"

"Not that I've noticed."

"How does the quilt fit into this?"

"Cumo's niece said when her uncle died, he told her there were clues to the whereabouts of the… antiquities hidden in the old quilt. But his mind was pretty well gone by the end. She wrote it off as the rambling of a terminally ill old man. After the war, Cumo wasn't a healthy man and suffered from respiratory and neurological challenges for years. She looked at the quilt anyway and couldn't see anything. So, I thought maybe a quilter might be able to find whatever might be there. That's when I contacted you."

The server brought them their lunch.

While eating Virginia asked, "Do you have any ranch hands? Are you raising cattle or something?"

"Yes. There are a few men who take care of the ranch and the cattle. I've got Black Angus cattle. I need to keep the cattle, so I keep my Ag property tax exemption. If the cows go so does my exemption, and the property value assessment and taxes would go up, way up. So, I went from being a computer science professor to a cattle rancher."

"You've got a big ranch. Do you know anything about ranching?"

"Not much, but I'm learning. Fortunately, I've got a grad student from Texas A&M in College Station who is helping me run the ranch as part of his doctoral dissertation on range management. He's a nice young man. His name is Anthony Morena."

Virginia put down her sandwich. "How'd you find him?" *Italian?*

Gail chuckled. "He came with the ranch. I've been to A&M and talked to his Ph.D. advisor. The professor thinks highly of the lad and says he is trustworthy, a good student, resourceful, and a hard worker. So far, he's been right."

"How long has he been working at the ranch?"

"About a year and a half."

"How about the ghosts?" asked Virginia as she took another bite of the sandwich.

"At first, I figured they had some natural causes or were the product of overactive imaginations." Gail hesitated, leaned forward, then spoke in a hushed tone. "But now, I've seen some."

"You've got me intrigued. What do the ghosts look like?"

"A few wore World War II army uniforms, others looked like Roman soldiers. They were spooky. They were not completely solid, more semi-transparent, and they wavered as they moved."

"Did they talk?"

"Talkative ghosts? No, they appeared to be looking for something and didn't notice I was around," said Gail.

"Where did you see them?" asked Virginia.

Gail nibbled at her hamburger. "The apparitions come and go. Usually I see them outside, near one of the barns or one of the out-buildings. Sometimes a couple of ghosts will walk through walls in the house going from room to room. A few have been spotted in the basement."

"You have a basement?"

"Yes. I was as surprised as you are," said Gail.

"A friend of mine has a ranch and her house has a cellar." Virginia finished her burger. "Do they show up any place else?"

"Yes. There are manifestations in various locations out on the ranch."

"Do you have any springs or creeks on the ranch?" asked Virginia as she took another bite of her sandwich.

Gail frowned. "Yeah. There are some creeks and I do have a couple of nice springs and a few large ponds. Why?"

"Do the ghosts appear near the springs?"

Gail knotted her brow in thought. "Yes. Sometimes. Is that important?"

"I don't know. Just asking."

Gail twisted slightly and held up a cloth bag. "While I still remember, here's the quilt we talked about." She opened the bag and showed the design to Virginia.

Virginia took the bag holding the quilt and set it on the seat next to her and glanced inside. "I like the bright colors and the stars. The fabric separating them is interesting. I'll start examining it tonight. On the phone you also mentioned illegal antiquities, smuggling, and murder, as well as ghosts. How do they fit together?"

"The smuggling was probably how Cumo got the illegal antiquities, which his niece thinks may be on the *Circle A*, into the country after the war. In the past sixty years, five people have disappeared, apparently searching for the treasure. One was found dead on the ranch near a spring."

"Someone on the ranch found the body?"

"Yes. Cumo's niece owned the ranch then. She told me about the dead guy. A ranch hand found the body. The sheriff said it was suspicious but couldn't see any sign of injury. They did an autopsy and found his heart stopped but they couldn't figure out why. The ME didn't find any physical reason or poison, but he didn't know what specifically to look for either. The man was healthy until he dropped dead. It's still an open case, but I don't think anyone is actively investigating it anymore."

"When did he die?"

"Sometime in the mid-nineties."

"Was there a search for the other missing people?"

"I think so. As I understand it, reports of the disappearances were made to the authorities. I don't know exactly what the sheriff did back then. I heard five men just disappeared. Puff. Gone. They vanished a few years apart. The niece thinks they were murdered, but I wasn't the owner of the *Circle A* then."

Virginia sat back in the booth. "So, over the last sixty or so years, we've got five missing men, possibly murdered, and one dead man whose actual body was found, and he died of a mysterious cause. There are ghosts of Roman and World War II soldiers searching for something, maybe a treasure consisting of artifacts of some type smuggled out of Rome after World War II, and a quilt with something hidden in it."

"Don't forget the floating lights and holes mysteriously dug and filled back in." Gail leaned forward with an expectant look. "Do you think you could help solve this mystery? Will you?"

Virginia bit her lip, then nodded. "I'll look into it. I've got a couple of friends who I would like to have help if that's okay with you."

Gail raised her voice in excitement and flailed her arms drawing attention from nearby tables as she spoke. "Yes! Great!" She looked around at the staring people, hunched down, and blushed. "Sorry. I'm so excited."

Virginia chuckled, "I noticed."

"When can you start?"

"I'll get to that in a second. Dr. Knight, I know solving mysteries isn't in your wheelhouse, but did you happen to notice if you were followed here or if you've been watched since you purchased the ranch?"

"Huh? Ahh… no. I haven't been looking for anyone following me. Why?"

"There are two men sitting in a booth just down from us against the far wall who have taken an inordinate amount of interest in us."

CHAPTER 3

Virginia sat at a conference table in her office at the San Gabriel Museum with two of her friends who, at a glance, seemed to be opposites: Dr. Terry Sorensen looked more like an auburn-haired young soccer mom than an anthropologist and archeologist working at the museum, and Natalie North was a petite, but curvaceous, blonde former Hollywood actress known for occasional controversial and exhibitionist behavior. Despite their apparent differences, both women had worked with Virginia before on cases involving old quilts. They listened to the story Virginia told as they examined the notes she had provided of her conversation with Dr. Gail Knight. Dr. Knight's quilt lay spread out on the table.

Terry sat back and shook her head. "That's quite a tale, and with all the stuff about ghosts, maybe Natalie should consider making it into a movie."

Natalie smiled. "It does have a cinematic quality to it, doesn't it?" She looked at Virginia. "What are you going to do about it?"

Virginia took a breath. "What *we* are going to do is look into it."

Terry shook her head. "I figured as much. You're going to have your cat examine the quilt, like you usually do, right?"

"Yes, Leo gets a shot at it. That cat finds the darnedest things. But I think we need to put all this in perspective."

Natalie picked up her spiral notebook she had been writing in. She glanced at the others. "I'll act as recorder for this motley group. Let's start at the beginning. First Lieutenant Robert Cumo served in the battle for Rome in World War II. According to his niece, he is rumored to have looted valuable art objects and other antiquities while there. He also found a way to hide them from the Italians and the army. Then he supposedly packaged them and returned to the states with his ill-gotten gains. He most likely used military transport to avoid U.S. Customs, probably through the Port of New York. Then, with the war over, he's discharged or resigned his commission. He now somehow gets his... his stuff away from the army and transports it to Texas without being detected. He then buys a ranch, with what money we don't know, and then becomes a cattleman. The alleged treasure disappears. Then bring on the ghosts, hole diggers, missing and dead men, and of course the quilt."

Virginia leaned back and crossed her arms. "You summed it up pretty succinctly."

Terry fiddled with the edge of the quilt. "What did the Lieutenant do in the army?"

Virginia uncrossed her arms, leaned forward, and looked at her notes. "He was a logistics officer."

"So, he made things move," said Terry.

Virginia and Natalie stared at her.

"Military logistics people package, move, ship, and store hardware, food, equipment, weapons, and other things. They move people, too. That's what they do. We have people like that here at the museum."

"You're right, we do have logistics people," said Virginia. "Only our people wear a multitude of hats. Anna and Frank do purchasing, arrange for shipping and receiving of artifacts, move items to displays, and along with the curators, keep track of our inventory."

"Cumo would know how to move not just army gear, but his loot as well," said Natalie. "He'd be familiar with U.S. and Italian Customs regulations and procedures, too."

Virginia nodded. "It seems like the Lieutenant had the tools and knowhow to do the job right under the army and customs folks' noses."

Terry shuffled the papers in front of her then looked at Virginia. "Any idea as to what constitutes this lost treasure... besides it being art and antiquities?"

Virginia looked up from the quilt. "No. We need to do a search and see what may be missing from museums, art galleries, and homes that was reported in the forties, especially in Rome and Italy."

"Yeah, I can get on that. But there were some art and antiquities that were most likely not reported as stolen because they were stolen by someone else in the first place," said Terry. "These will be a little harder but not impossible to get leads on."

Natalie frowned. "How are you going to locate all this? I just googled it, and I'm not impressed with the amount of information that's on the Internet."

"There are other online databases to use besides Google. I'll use connections in various academic institutions, archeological, anthropological societies, and art circles, and then I'll check with my less than honorable contacts."

"Less than honorable contacts?" asked Natalie.

"Don't ask." Terry raised one eyebrow in a questioning slant, then whispered, "Would you like to buy a real Egyptian mummy?"

Natalie made a sour face. "Yuck. No thanks."

Virginia tugged the quilt closer and examined part of it. "From the type and design of the fabric and the quality of it, I'd say this quilt was most likely made in the mid-fifties. My dear cat, Leo, and I will examine it in more detail later." She sat back. "Terry, you're going to do your search to determine, if possible, what the lieutenant may have removed from Rome. I'm going to examine the quilt. Natalie, I'd—"

"You want me to explore the *Circle A* ranch because I own one and would be more likely to spot something out of the ordinary. I also know a lot of the male ranchers, and they like to talk to me."

"Yes. And I want you to meet Gail Knight. She's an interesting woman. I'd like to get your take on her."

"Isn't she your friend?" Natalie tucked a piece of blonde hair behind her ear.

"Yes. She was a professor I had at the university. Interesting lady. See how much she'll spill to you. If you engage her in conversation, she may tell you something she forgot to mention to me or is hiding."

"Hiding? Okay."

"When can you ladies start?"

Terry took a breath. "I can have some preliminary information in two days."

Natalie shrugged. "See if you can arrange my visit to the ranch for tomorrow morning. I'll talk to some neighboring ranchers, too. I should have an idea of the layout of the ranch by the time Terry's done. Talking to the ranchers will take a little longer."

"I'll call Gail as soon as we're though. One more thing, a couple of men were watching Gail and me at lunch. She may be under surveillance. Keep an eye out."

Terry and Natalie nodded.

Natalie leaned forward. "I think we need to come up to speed on life in the forties and fifties and maybe the sixties. Being aware of the culture, and what the times were like back then may help us determine what happened. I think the three of us have some understanding of the seventies and on already."

A frown creased Terry's forehead. "Why would that be important to this case?"

Virginia's chair squeaked as she leaned back. "The forties and fifties were a lot different than today. They didn't have computers, and TV was new. Radio was big then. Color movies were new. There were cultural differences then as well. To a point, even quilting was different. Just after the war, there was a big transition going on in the country. Foreign trade was different, and that may shed some light on the Lieutenant's possible means of getting the artifacts into the country undetected. Natalie's right. We need to put the theft and possible smuggling into the context of the times.

Natalie leaned forward. "From now on... let's meet at my house. This is off the books for the museum, and using their facility might be a conflict. My house is big enough to use as headquarters."

Virginia smiled. "That's nice of you, Natalie. Your offer is accepted. Getting up to speed on the forties, fifties and sixties is a good idea as well. I'll take a crack at the forties, you two split up the fifties. Let's gather up our notes, and I'll take the quilt. You already have the pictures of it, and we'll meet at Natalie's home in two days after our preliminary work is complete. Is seven in the evening, okay?"

They all agreed.

Virginia watched the women leave, then called Gail Knight and arranged for her to meet Natalie the following morning. She leaned back in her high-backed leather desk chair and stared at the ceiling in thought. *Because there is the possibility of looted art and artifacts from Rome involved, I'd better call my other boss at the Smithsonian Central Security Service. Senior Special Agent Tom Mason will probably want the three of us to do this investigation as SCSS special agents. He'll activate us from reserve to active-duty agents. My real boss here at the San Gabriel Museum, Dr. Doverspike, will love the new grants he'll receive to compensate for Terry and my active-duty assignments. I'd better talk to him first. I'll ask Tom to have the Smithsonian do a search of lost or stolen World War II treasures from Rome, too.* Virginia glanced at her notes then chuckled. *I know who to call about the "good old days."* She picked up her desk phone and dialed. When answered on the third ring, Virginia said, "Dad, I have some questions about when you were young, and I need to hear about what grandpa did during the war."

CHAPTER 4

Virginia drove home from the San Gabriel Museum with the quilt and found her husband, Andy, and cat, Leo, enjoying a TV show. She snuggled next to Andy on the couch and said, "How was the university today, professor?"

He held up his hand, "Just a minute, this is when Amy Winslow identifies the killer."

Virginia turned her attention to the TV. Andy and Leo were watching Mystery 101 on the Hallmark Movie and Mystery Channel. She looked at her cat. Leo sat on the edge of the couch cushion mesmerized by the show. She leaned into Andy. "Leo likes this show? There aren't any animals on it."

"He loves mysteries and likes the lead character, Amy Winslow. He's been sitting here with me watching it since it went on. I think Leo knows who the culprit is."

"Right. Leo's now a detective? He's a cat. Okay, Sherlock, where are you taking me to dinner?" She jerked as Leo let out a loud meow and pranced around. "What happened?"

"Amy identified the killer and Leo had figured it out."

Virginia eyed him skeptically. "Right. Leo solved the murder. Maybe a short side trip to the little hospital across town is more in order than dinner. I understand they have nice air-conditioned rooms with soft padded walls in restful colors and comfortable white long-sleeved jackets that tie in the back to wear. I hear Thorazine comes in strawberry flavor now." Virginia looked at her cat. "They may have a jacket his size, too. You two could be roommates."

"Come on... you know he likes to watch movies."

"Yeah, Animal Planet, Puss-in-Boots maybe, Scooby-Doo for sure. But mysteries?"

"He likes mysteries. You do know Scooby-Doo is a mystery series."

"Yes, I know they're mysteries." Virginia sighed. "But Leo's a cat."

"Did you know Leo likes watching my Charlie Chan, Murder She

Wrote, and Miss Fisher DVDs?"

"He really watches them?"

"Yes. He'll sit on the couch and watch them for hours."

Virginia looked at Leo. "Maybe they have Thorazine in fish or chicken flavor for Leo. Do they have kitty psychiatrists?"

"I don't know. Probably." Andy switched off the TV. "How'd it go at the museum?"

"Nice save, professor." Virginia filled Andy in on the events, including seeing Gail Knight and the quilt. Leo pranced toward the kitchen.

Andy arched a speculative eyebrow. "Let me guess, you and your merry band are going to investigate this so-called lost Italian treasure and the ghosts."

Virginia gave him a smile. "You're not going to object, are you?"

"Let's see, it's got ghosts, strange lights, a lost treasure, missing persons, and a dead man. What could go wrong?"

"You forgot the quilt."

"No, I didn't. Where is it?"

"In the kitchen."

"Well, if you want me to take you to dinner, you'd better hide it. You wouldn't want anything to happen to it," said Andy. "We can discuss this over dinner."

Virginia jumped to her feet. "I'll put it away and be ready in fifteen minutes. Feed Detective Inspector Leo."

After dining and retuning home, Virginia spread the old quilt out on her cutting table in her quilt room. She stared at it. The bright, multicolored stars stood out against the black and white designed background. She turned it, folded it, and inspected the binding with a magnifying glass. After an hour she turned out the lights and joined Andy and Leo watching TV.

Andy glanced at her. "Well, did you find a map to the treasure? Does X mark the spot?"

Virginia sulked. "No."

"Want Leo to take a look?"

"Sure, why not? I struck out."

Andy picked Leo up and carried him to Virginia's quilt room. He turned on the lights and set the cat on the quilt. "Okay, Leo, find the location of the treasure."

The cat walked around on the quilt inspecting it, then curled up on it and went to sleep.

Andy pointed. "He's thinking about it."

"He's no help. It's late. Let's go to bed. Maybe I'll spot something with

Hidden Threads

fresh eyes tomorrow."

The next morning while eating breakfast, Virginia's boss, Dr. Fred Doverspike, Director of the San Gabriel Museum, called. "Virginia, thank you for giving me a heads up on your treasure investigation. Special Agent Tom Mason contacted me early this morning. We negotiated a more than generous grant to cover a lot of our new work, and besides paying for you and Dr. Sorenson, he's covering other costs here at the museum. He's even given Terry a grant for her research and field work in South Carolina, and one for you to cover your all the costs of your Navajo project. He wants you to start as soon as possible."

"I'm glad you're on board with this, Dr. Doverspike."

"Are you kidding? I think I'll rent you and Terry out to the Smithsonian as much as possible. The grants you've garnered from them have been over the top and have really been a big help to our field work, research, and displays. He also said to have you call him. He's got some information about missing artifacts and art from Rome during World War II. He did mention something I thought was funny."

"I'll call him, thanks. Wait. Tom was funny?"

"Yes. He said when he contacted your friend, Ms. Natalie North, she finagled money out of him, too. Maybe I need to hire her at the museum and rent you three out as a package. I'll have to think about that. Now go and find that treasure. Maybe you can convince the owners to loan some of it to us for a display."

"I'll see what I can do." Virginia hung up and looked across the table at Andy. "I'm on active duty with the Smithsonian Central Security Service along with Terry and Natalie. I need to call Tom."

Virginia dialed Special Agent Tom Mason's number. When he answered Virginia said, "Tom, Dr. Doverspike called me and told me the news. Thank you for the grants. He's happier than a Texas tornado in a trailer park. He said that you had some information?"

"Yes. Funding you three actually saves me money. Lower overhead and you guys, especially you, are my best agents."

"Thank you for that. But what information?"

She heard rustling of paper, then Tom spoke. "Yeah, there was a big theft of some Etruscan gold jewelry, books, scrolls, and art objects from a museum in Rome toward the end of World War II. The value of the heist in the mid-nineteen-forties, and this is only an estimate, was over ten million dollars."

"Wow!" She did a quick calculation on her iPad. "That's over one-hundred and forty-three million dollars today. If we find it, can we keep part of it? No one would miss a few million. I could open a bank account in the Cayman Islands."

"Virginia!"

"Just kidding. Can you send me a list of what was stolen?"

"Hmm... not really. The museum in question does not like to advertise that it was or may still be vulnerable. But let's simply say, it's big, it holds a lot of... stuff and only part of it is open to the public. The museum and associated library are famous. You do the math. They tried investigating themselves but back then... they didn't get very far. Officially the case is still open, and they supposedly still have someone looking into it."

"OMG. I think I know."

"Keep it to yourself for now. But you, Terry and Natalie are now on active duty. I would suggest you get some experts to help. According to rumors in Italy, the people interested in this, besides the museum owners, are wealthy and dangerous, and they have contacts in parts of the U.S. You need to solve the issues at the ranch as well. Maybe a call to the local constabulary in your neck of the woods is in order before you step on too many toes."

"Got it."

"One more thing, please keep the body count reasonably low."

"Reasonably low? Okay."

"Call me if you need help. Good hunting." Tom disconnected.

Virginia sat back and looked at Andy. "You won't believe this."

Andy buttered his toast. "What?"

"The stolen treasure came from the Vatican."

Two days later at seven in the evening, Virginia, Gail, and Terry met in Natalie's large, country-style kitchen and sat around her oversized, wooden table with their boxes and briefcases of documents, notes, and maps.

Virginia looked around the kitchen of Natalie's Victorian mansion. "I see you finished the final changes."

"Yeah, finally. It's all done. It took longer than I expected."

"You've done a great job." Virginia glanced at her watch. "I invited a guest. He has a working knowledge of the military and is an encyclopedia about the forties and fifties. He loves that time period. I thought he could fill in any blanks we may have."

Gail gave her head a shake. "Why do we need to know about the forties and fifties?"

"Terry asked the same question the other day. We need to put the theft and possible smuggling into context of the times. Things were quite different then compared to today. For example, we have technology we take for granted that they didn't have. We may find some things that will explain how the alleged crime was able to be committed and how the Lieutenant got the ill-gained goods out of Italy and into the U.S. undetected. And maybe, where he was likely to hide them."

"You have a point," Gail agreed.

Natalie rose up in her chair and looked out the window behind Virginia. "I think your friend has arrived. Who is he?"

"Captain John Steadman of the Georgetown Police Department. He's a great guy, and ladies, he's married."

Terry gave a fake pout. "In that case, send him home."

Natalie rose and walked to the front door and opened it as John was about to knock. She looked at the tall gentleman dressed in a gray Polo shirt and black slacks with a semiautomatic holstered on his hip. A police badge was fastened to his belt. "Good evening, Captain, please come in, I'm Natalie North." She stepped aside and waved him in. "We're meeting in the kitchen. Follow me." As Natalie led John through the front room and down a hall, she noticed him taking everything in. "I recently finished the last restoration projects."

"It looks great. I remember when you moved here. You made quite a... a splash in the community."

She ushered him into the kitchen. "You mean I was scandalous and terrorized the local ultra-conservative churchgoing women and busted the balls of some male contractors?"

"Something like that. But Virginia told me about you and what you were doing, and I am a big fan. Any friend of Virginia's is a friend of mine." John stopped at the side of the table. "Hi, Virginia. Thanks for inviting me." He nodded at Gail. "Nice seeing you again, Dr. Knight. Virginia gave me a briefing about the issues at your ranch."

Gail smiled. "Nice to see you again, Captain. She asked you for help? My ranch is in the county."

"Yes, your ranch is in the county, so this would normally fall in the sheriff's jurisdiction. But with the city butting up against it at the large creek at the back of your ranch, and Virginia being the federal officer in charge, the Sheriff asked the Georgetown Police to assist her with the investigation. The sheriff knows how Virginia works and was quite happy to let the Georgetown PD take the lead, and any blame, on this. John looked at Terry. "You must be Dr. Sorenson. I've heard wonderful things about you from Virginia."

"Thank you." Terry smiled. "Nice to meet you, Captain." She pushed the chair next to her out with her foot. "Have a seat and join us. We're just getting underway."

CHAPTER 5

Virginia spread her notes and pictures out on Natalie's table. "Terry, any luck with reported stolen artifacts and art from Rome?"

"The information on the Internet about stolen art and artifacts from Rome, as Natalie pointed out, is sparse and not reliable. I checked some government archive websites with limited results and then with colleagues, also with partial results. During World War II, the Nazis stole a lot of art. There is quite a bit about that on the websites. But it seems the Nazis didn't manage to get a lot out of Rome. My less than honorable contacts said there were rumors about a large heist of valuable articles at the end of the liberation of Rome, but not by the Nazis. But any real facts were lost or hushed up for some reason."

Virginia nodded "I asked the Smithsonian to see what they could come up with. It tallies with what you said, Terry. But from their information, I think the articles were stolen from the Vatican. According to the Smithsonian, the value of the alleged heist in the mid-nineteen-forties, was estimated to be over ten million dollars. The church wanted, and still wants, the theft swept under the rug."

Terry's eyes widened. "Ten million dollars? That's huge. What is that in today's dollars?"

"Over one-hundred and forty-three million dollars," said Virginia.

John leaned forward. "Why would they want something like that kept secret? That's a lot of… whatever to be stolen and then ignored."

"You want to tell the world, especially the criminal world, that one of the largest libraries and museums in the world, and belonging to the Catholic Church, was robbed, and they didn't know it until sometime later?" asked Virginia. "Their security was… weak and may still be if they don't know how they were robbed."

"Good point. They did try and investigate, didn't they?" asked John.

"Yes, but this was in the mid- to late nineteen forties. Investigation techniques and forensics weren't what they are today. The war was on or just winding down, and Italy had been occupied by Germans and then by

Americans. Confusion was the name of the game, and people did what they had to do to survive. Rome fared better than most, though. According to the Smithsonian, the Vatican still has someone investigating it." Virginia stared at her notes. "I'd better ask the Smithsonian for the name of the Vatican's investigator."

John tilted his head. "From what you said, why do you need me?"

"Because you are our *official* forties and fifties expert. I'm a historian and curator and cover a lot of areas and times, especially American History. Since the treasure was taken and hidden in that time period, we thought it would be a good idea to have a subject matter expert on the team, hence you. We tend to look at things and events through the eyes and mind of someone in the twenty-first century. To figure this case out we need to be able to see events back then and think like someone around the end of World War II up through the fifties. None of us were alive then. And you, being a local police, officer will help with getting information from the sheriff and other Texas law enforcement agencies when needed."

Natalie chuckled. "I hope you're good at looking the other way on occasion, Captain."

John frowned. "Why?"

"Sometimes we slightly bend a few laws… use them more as a suggestion… like the Texas police use the vehicle code."

"Oh, boy. Just don't commit any felonies, please."

"Ahh… we'll try not to," said Natalie with a sly grin.

John looked at Virginia. "Do you… bend a lot of… hell, never mind. Wait, how bad do you bend them?"

Terry raised an eyebrow. "Do you like pretzels, Captain?"

He rested his head in his hands. "Oh, God."

Virginia smiled. "I'm glad you're on board with us, John."

He raised his head and looked at Virginia. "Do I have a choice?"

"No."

He sighed. "Okay." He pushed a binder toward each woman. "Here are files that contain a lot of information on the timeline Virginia mentioned. It has information about the times, laws, art, music, movies, toys, homes, businesses, and what life was like back then. I included some material about how law enforcement worked then as well. It's a start. If you need more, there are references included, and you can also contact me. I hope this helps."

Terry thumbed through the notebook. "Wow. This is great. I can't wait to read it. This can help put things in perspective. Thank you."

Natalie rose from her chair. "Anyone for some wine?"

They all nodded.

Natalie returned with a bottle of white Zinfandel wine and glasses. "I got this from the Becker Winery near Fredericksburg." She poured the wine and sat.

John sipped from his glass. "Nice. I'm trying to lose some weight. This wine and your terrific baked goods are not helping, Natalie."

"No problem, John," Natalie said "Did you see the no trespassing signs posted around here? Calories aren't allowed on my ranch. I use them for target practice."

He raised his glass. "Sounds good to me."

Virginia glanced at Natalie. "Getting back to the subject, from what you said on the phone, did you have a chance to look around Gail's ranch? Find anything of interest?"

Natalie studied her notes, sat back, and nodded at Gail. "Yes, I had a chance to talk to Gail in some detail. She was nice enough to interrupt her day and take me on a tour of the *Circle A* ranch. It has a lot of open space, but there are a number of forested areas with various types of oaks and elm trees, cacti, and the occasional palm tree. Four creeks run through it as well. There are major granite outcroppings intermixed with the limestone we normally see around here. This area was seismically active tens of thousands of years ago. Hell, there's an extinct volcano near the Austin airport. I found some caves on her property. In a couple of them are holes that appear to be entrances to deeper grottos. One has water coming out. A couple of springs feed some ponds. The mysterious holes Gail showed me were hastily dug and refilled." Natalie pulled out a U.S. geological Survey map of the area and pointed. "I plotted the structures, outcroppings, caves, and holes. I thought the holes were random, but the map shows differently. The holes seem to be in an arch around the outbuildings and barns. And they are bizarre. There is more dirt in or on the filled in holes than what was removed And the new dirt isn't from the ranch."

Terry frowned. "So, someone brought in their own dirt?"

"Looks like it."

"The only reason I can think of is they wanted to have it analyzed. But for what?"

"I don't know. I took samples from the new dirt in the holes and the surrounding area for comparison."

Terry made a note. "Give them to me and I'll have them analyzed."

"Okay. When the meeting is over, I'll grab them."

Gail sat and listened then said, "What about the ghosts and strange lights?"

The women exchanged glances, then Virginia spoke. "You said they were usually seen outside near a couple of barns or outbuildings. You mentioned a couple of ghosts will walk through walls in the house, going from room to room, and you've seen a few in the basement. I don't believe in ghosts. What I do believe is someone is doing something to trick you into seeing something that appears to be ghosts. That goes for the lights, too."

Gail looked depressed. "Why is someone doing this? Are they trying to drive me crazy?"

Natalie patted Gail's arm. "My guess is someone has been quietly hunting for the treasure for years. Cumo's niece told you the history of the lights and ghosts spans over sixty years. I think your purchasing the *Circle A* ranch from Cumo's niece caused someone to be afraid you'd hear about the legend and try to locate the treasure or interfere with their search. He, or they, are stepping up their treasure hunting and trying to scare you into backing off. And, Gail, they are trying to intimidate you. The lights and ghosts may have been one of the reasons Cumo's niece sold you the ranch. They have a physical cause, not supernatural."

Virginia made an entry in her notebook. "I'd like to talk to Cumo's niece. Gail, do you have her contact information?"

"Yes. I'll email it to you," said Gail.

John cleared his throat. "I agree with Virginia and Natalie. There are people around here who are responsible for all this, Gail, not poltergeists. As part of her investigation, Virginia asked me to pull the files from the sheriff on the missing men and the dead man on the ranch."

Gail leaned toward him. "What did you find out?

"The sheriff's reports say the missing men seemed to just drop off the face of the earth. There were no forensics. No one seems to know who the men were. They used first names like Jake, Tom, Sam, Jim, and Ed. The file on them is not very big. I'm not even sure I've got all the information, but what I do have leads me to think the sheriff's office at the time had little to go on. They tried their best to locate the men but came up empty-handed."

"Doesn't that seem strange?" asked Gail.

"Not really. We're talking about five unidentifiable, unrelated people, going missing over five years' time from this ranch and others with nothing to tie the missing men together. No apparent crime committed. Back in the sixties, there was no Internet or personal computers. Only banks, some universities, and a few government organizations had computers, and they were huge, slow, and didn't have a lot of memory built in. In those days, getting information from other jurisdictions was difficult. The only way to retrieve what was available from other agencies was by knowing who to ask, or from the state police and the FBI. The information available amounted to what was reported to them, not necessarily everything. Recordkeeping was done by hand. Urgent requests were sent by teletype or special delivery US Mail. No email then. Since little was known about the men, the sheriff didn't know who to ask for information. There could still be police or missing persons records of them in a file someplace collecting dust."

"Who filed the missing person report?" asked Terry.

"The Lieutenant."

"No one else?"

"No. That could be one of the reasons the sheriff back then didn't do more investigating. With nothing to go on, no one else looking for them, and not knowing what agencies to ask for help, it's hard to justify scarce resources looking into something like this. The men may have just gone on to other places. In the forties and fifties, they would be called hobos. They'd work for a while someplace then move on. Sometimes they came back through an area again."

Virginia leaned forward. "What type of work did they do for Cumo?"

"It appears they did handyman-type odd jobs and equipment repairs for him and other ranchers around the area. No one knew much about them. They kept to themselves and just did the work requested. The landowners would pay them with cash. They didn't have bank accounts," said John. "No one knew where they lived, either."

"How about the dead man? Whose body did the sheriff have?" asked Virginia.

John shuffled some papers. "His name was Franco Volpe. Italian obviously. He had a successful, high-end, Italian restaurant in New York City for years. He came to this country as a POW in late 1943. Was held in a prisoner of war camp near Yuma, Arizona. Mr. Volpe was a cook at the POW camp and later a chef in New York. He trained as a chef in Rome before the war. After the war ended in 1945, he got permission to remain in the U.S. He gained his citizenship and moved to New York City. Married, one child. Model citizen, active in his community and church. No arrests. However, some of his restaurant patrons were high-level Mafia types. He had interesting friends. His wife died a year before he sold his restaurant and moved to Texas."

Terry frowned. "Does your report say where in Italy he's from?"

John turned the page. "Yes. Rome. Volpe moved to Texas in 1985. He died in 1994."

"What did he do in Texas?" asked Natalie.

John examined a couple of documents. "He taught cooking at a chef school in Austin. He had a sizable bank account from the sale of his restaurant in New York. He didn't need to work. So, it looks like he enjoyed his teaching job, and it gave him something to do."

"So, in 1994 Volpe visited the *Circle A* ranch and dropped dead?" asked Natalie. "What did he die of?"

"No cause of death was recorded. There were no apparent signs of foul play."

"So, he just dropped dead?" asked Virginia.

"Apparently so," said John. "They did an autopsy and found his heart stopped, but the doctor didn't know why."

Hidden Threads

"Who signed the death certificate?"

"The justice of the peace signed the death certificate and listed manner of death as unknown." John looked at the papers in front of him. "Cause of death was listed as a malformed, aortic heart valve with acute stenosis."

"Is unknown a real thing someone puts on a death certificate?" Natalie asked.

John nodded. "Yes. There are five manners of death that are used on death certificates. They are natural, homicidal, suicidal, accidental, and unknown. Cause of death is something else, in this case his heart valve caused him to die."

"That's interesting."

"Who found the body?" asked Terry.

"A ranch hand," said Gail before John could answer.

"Where, exactly?"

Gail answered with a blank expression. "I don't know."

CHAPTER 6

Natalie looked across the table at John. "Do the records show where on the ranch they found Mr. Volpe's body?"

He rummaged through more documents. "Funny, it just says he was found on the ranch by a worker by the name of Eric Bauer. No exact location and no forensic evidence were collected. Maybe that's because there was no sign of foul play. The report contains nothing else on Mr. Bauer. The report says he lived on the ranch. There was no phone number, no driver's license, no social security number. That's very strange. There isn't even a vehicle registered to him. It's like he didn't exist." John looked at Gail. "Any chance there still are files on employees from that time, like a job application or W-2s? Social Security number maybe? We could get something from them."

"Cumo's niece told me all the files were taken by the sheriff back then. Sorry."

"I'll see if the sheriff may have missed them when they were digitizing the old case files. The records could still be in an evidence box someplace. The deputies who were at the scene or investigating are probably retired. I'll ask for their contact information and follow up."

Virginia made some notes then asked, "John, what is the name of Franco Volpe's child?"

John looked at his notes. "I don't know. The sheriff should have followed up on that if for no other reason than to notify the next of kin. He would have inherited Volpe's money. I'll have someone at the station run this down, too. Again, the sheriff may have done that, but the files weren't digitized and are probably lost in an evidence box in the basement."

"While you're at it, see what you can find on Anthony Morena, Gail's Texas A&M grad student who's helping her at the ranch."

"Okay."

"I already talked to his graduate advisor at A&M in College Station," said Gail.

"I'll run a quick background check anyway," said John. "The more information we have, the better."

"I guess you're right," said Gail.

Virginia looked perplexed. "Why would Mr. Volpe sell his successful Italian restaurant after decades there and move to Texas?"

"Getting old and didn't like the weather, maybe," said John. "That and Texas has no state income tax, low cost of living, and great people. Nice place to retire. Why do people from that area of the country usually retire in Florida? Same reasons. Only we usually get them from the Dakotas, Nebraska, Iowa, Illinois, Wisconsin, and Minnesota."

Terry turned to Gail. "Gail, if you don't mind my asking, why did you come here and buy a ranch after teaching computer science in southern California?"

Gail chuckled. "Pretty much for the reasons Captain Steadman said. "No income tax, lower cost of living, nice friendly people, and better environment to live. It was great in California once, but now it's overcrowded, horrible traffic, everything is too expensive, screwy politics, homeless everywhere, and the crime rate is soaring. Texas seemed like a good idea. I've always wanted to have a farm or ranch. When I retired, I discovered I could afford to do it here. I didn't count on ghosts and some long-lost treasure being involved."

Virginia settled back in her chair. "Okay. John, see if you can find Mr. Volpe's child and where his inheritance is. I hope the county or state didn't take it. Just think of the lawsuits."

John leaned forward. "Dr. Knight, if you get any more manifestations or ghosts, please write down the date, time, location, the conditions at the time, and anything unusual... besides the ghosts. Same with the lights you mentioned. It could help us."

"Natalie gave me a copy of her map," said Gail. "I can use that to show where they appear, if they appear again."

"Virginia told me about the men she thought were watching you," said John. "If you feel threatened, call 911."

Gail chuckled. "You want me to tell a 911 sheriff's dispatcher someone or something *may* be following me?"

He stared at her. "You have a point. If you can see through your visitor, call me or Virginia, otherwise call 911."

"Okay."

Virginia looked at Gail. "I'd like Terry, Natalie and me to tour your house and basement and have you show us where you've seen ghosts and where else on the ranch the apparitions appear."

"Great. When do you want to come?"

"Tomorrow too soon?"

"No. Come about ten, I'll put coffee on."

Virginia looked at John. "You want to come, too, Captain?"

"I'd like to, but I have some police department meetings and I need to follow-up on the things from this get together. Fill me in on anything you discover. I'll call you with what I find out."

"Okay."

Natalie looked at Gail with a concerned expression. "You going to be okay at home? You can stay here."

"Thank you, but I think I'll be okay. I have an alarm system. If someone tries breaking in, I have a 12-gauge, pump shotgun I'll use." Gail smiled at John. "Then I'll call 911."

John eyed Gail. "Do you know how to properly shoot it?"

"You want to see my skeet shooting medals?"

John shook his head. "Oh, God, you too? I know these three are dangerous... now I'll need to add you to the list. Dr. Knight, I'm glad you live in the county instead of inside city limits. You'd normally be the sheriff's problem."

"Can you give John a list of the names and any IDs you have for your ranch people?" asked Virginia. "He can run a quick background check on them... just to be careful."

"Yes. I'll email the list to you tomorrow morning, Captain."

"Okay. I'll keep an eye out for it," said John. "Gail, if you're ready to go, I'll follow you home to make sure you get there safely, and make sure no one is there waiting for you."

"That would be great. Thank you, Captain."

Natalie glanced around at the group. "I think that wraps things up for tonight. I'll get your soil samples, Terry. And, John, thank you for the notebooks, joining our little group, and your help."

"You're welcome." He rubbed his forehead, "Prowlers, unique alarms, ghosts, treasure, missing people, dead bodies, an old quilt, and you ladies... this is going to get interesting." He turned toward Gail. "After I follow you home, I'm going to have a stiff drink. Maybe two."

After John left to follow Gail home, Virginia sat back in her chair. "Well ladies, what do you think?"

Terry shook her head. "For whatever reason, back when Mr. Volpe's body was found, either the sheriff didn't see fit to do much of an investigation, or from what John said, we don't have all the files because they didn't digitize them all yet."

Virginia looked perplexed. "Back then, the Sheriff may not have had a lot of experience with homicide. It was decades ago. This area was more rural back then. More farms and ranches. They probably didn't have a lot of mysterious murders."

Terry shook her head. "If the sheriff needed help with a suspected or actual homicide, they'd call in the Texas Rangers. But I think John was right. What we're missing is probably still in a box someplace waiting to be digitized."

Virginia nodded. "Makes sense. Natalie, since you are a rancher that everyone knows, you're still going to talk to the other landowners around here and get some additional information that may not be in reports, right? I'm sure you could charm anything out of them they might be reluctant to tell the police."

"Yes. I've talked to a couple of ranchers close to my place and I'll continue with those near the *Circle A* ranch," said Natalie.

"Thank you. You know, for some reason, and maybe it's just me, but some things don't add up," said Virginia.

"Some things?" Natalie chuckled. "I get the feeling there is more to this than what we've heard so far."

"I'm looking forward to seeing Gail's house, the basement, and the ranch. I don't believe in ghosts either," said Terry.

Virginia nodded. "I want more information about Franco Volpe's next of kin and the guy who found him, Eric Bauer."

Terry scribbled a note then looked up. "I'd like to know more about this legend. First, there's the stealing of the treasure, possibly from the Vatican, and hiding it in Rome. Then, moving it across an ocean on military ships and into the U.S. undetected. And lastly, getting it across the country to the *Circle A* ranch without anyone noticing. How'd Cumo do it all by himself? I know he was a logistics officer, but in reality, could he have successfully done it all alone? After all, he was a first lieutenant, not a major, colonel, or a general."

"Maybe he had help and he cheated them out of their share," said Natalie. "Maybe it's the co-conspirators or their descendants who are looking for the treasure. And to add to the confusion, Mr. Volpe was a POW in Arizona at the end of the war. Why would he be concerned about the treasure, or if Cumo actually stole it? Plus, how'd he find out about the heist or the Lieutenant?"

"We don't know if Volpe knew Cumo while he was in Rome or if he heard about the thefts from other prisoners," said Terry. "Remember, he also had contact with members of the Mafia while he lived in New York. They may have told him about the theft of the treasure."

Virginia blew a strand of blonde hair from her eyes. "Someone has been looking for this treasure for over sixty years. Who? Co-conspirators? Treasure hunters?"

Natalie chuckled. "They'd be pretty old or dead by now."

"Their descendants or modern-day treasure hunters would be alive," said Terry.

"And if the treasure is real, what did Cumo do with it?" asked Virginia. "I can't see going through all the effort to steal the treasure and hide it since World War II and never cashing it in. Who knows, maybe he did cash it in, but how, when, and what did he do with the proceeds? Lots of unanswered questions."

"I think we need to know more about Anthony Morena, Gail's Texas A&M grad student," said Natalie. "John said he'd do some more checking into his background. That may be interesting. I think we need to study the materials Captain Steadman gave us about the forties and fifties. That will give us a flavor of the times and fresh set of glasses to look at this through."

"I'll email my notes of what my dad and grandfather told me, as well," said Virginia.

Natalie glanced at her watch. "We have a lot of questions, but it's late, and I'm tired. Let's do our homework and meet again as planned."

Terry started to clear the table of the glasses and dishes. "I'll give you a hand with the cleanup."

"Thanks. Just stack them on the counter by the sink," said Natalie as she slid her chair back and rose. "I'll get to them later."

Virginia held up her hand. "One more thing, I took a quick look at the mysterious quilt. It has bright star blocks and is very colorful. First glance doesn't seem to indicate any map per se, like X marks the spot. I didn't expect it to. But I'll look closer. It was definitely made in the fifties and is not what I would have expected for a quilt of that vintage. The spacing strips between the blocks may be a hint to something. What exactly, I don't know... yet."

CHAPTER 7

The next morning at ten, Natalie pulled her white Toyota Land Cruiser, with Virginia and Terry on board, onto the long gravel driveway leading to Gail's two-story ranch house. She parked on a gravel parking area in the shade under a tall elm tree. As they climbed out of the car and looked around, Natalie said, "I explored the ranch yesterday using one of Gail's ATVs. The barns and other structures are behind the house. The mysterious holes are over there." She pointed at a cluster of oak trees. "The shimmering manifestations appear, there, near a small storage shed out back, by a well, and down by a cave with water coming out into a stream."

Virginia nodded. "Got it. I saw that you noted the locations on your topographical map."

"Yes. I got a quick tour of the main house as well," said Natalie. "I'm looking forward to seeing it in more detail today. I can tell you this, from the limited time I had inspecting it, the building is solid. The builder used a lot of oak, so by now the beams are hard as iron."

Terry stared at the cluster of oaks and elms. "Later I'd like to search that grove of trees. If there are supposed ghosts there, then there is something causing them, and it may be hidden in the trees."

Natalie glanced at the side of the ranch's main barn. "There's a van over there. Dr. Knight may have company."

"Let's go see if Gail is free or if we need to reschedule our visit," said Virginia, leading the way to the front of the house.

They walked to the front door and reached for the doorbell. Gail opened the door before Virginia could press the button.

Gail smiled and swept her arm, motioning them to enter. "Good morning, ladies. Come on in." Gail led the women into a neat, Texas-themed living room. "Please, have a seat."

Virginia glanced around. "Your house is lovely, Gail. We saw a van outside. Do you have company? We could reschedule our tour."

"It's okay, he was just a realtor. We were at the kitchen table having coffee while he told me he had an undisclosed client who wants to buy my ranch for a specific sum. It was for more than I paid for the place. But I said no. Because his car was out back, the gentleman just left out the back door." Gail shook her head. "He wasn't too happy, that's for sure."

Terry shifted to the edge of her chair. "Did he say who his client is?"

Gail shook her head. "No."

"Did he leave a card?"

"Yes." Gail pulled a business card from a pocket in her black slacks and handed it to Terry.

Terry looked at it, then said, "His name is John McCutchen. His office is in Round Rock, Texas."

Natalie leaned over Terry's shoulder. "His firm is called Grand Knights. Doesn't say what Grand Knights does. I think if he's a real estate broker, he is supposed to say so on his card."

"Can I borrow this?" Terry asked Gail. "I'd like to check up on him if you don't mind."

"Go ahead. I'm not selling the ranch, so I don't need it." Gail stood. "Ready for the ghost tour ladies?"

Gail led Virginia, Natalie, and Terry on a tour of the ranch house. In the front of the house was the Texas-themed living room with open beamed ceiling and a floor to ceiling stone fireplace with a thick oak mantel. Large windows overlooked the covered porch and front yard studded with old oaks. They proceeded down a short hallway past a bathroom to the dining room, then to the huge country kitchen and breakfast nook.

As they traveled through the rooms, Virginia noted the location of a series of mirrors. She scrutinized the crown molding around the ceilings and spotted a couple of places that appeared slightly different than the rest of the woodwork.

Next, Gail led them up a set of carpeted stairs to the second floor, where there were two bathrooms and four bedrooms, one of which Gail had made into an office. Virginia asked about the built-in cupboards in the hallway.

Gail shrugged. "Obviously, they came with the house. They're here to store linens and things. They're big enough for not just linens but for storing some of the items I brought from the university that I don't need in my office all the time."

Virginia ran her hand over the carved, stained, wooden doors. "Can I take a look inside?"

"Sure."

Virginia opened the doors and peered inside. She carefully moved the contents and smiled. "Gotcha," she muttered as she closed the doors. She turned to the others. "Gail, do you have an attic?"

"Yes. The stairs are right over here." Gail led them to another door. She opened it, revealing a set of stairs. "There isn't much up there. It can get hot, so I store most things in the basement."

Virginia peered around the door jam. "Mind if I go up?"

"No. Go ahead."

Virginia and Natalie climbed the stairs to the unfinished attic. Virginia flipped a light switch mounted on a roof support strut and motioned to Natalie. "At least we have light. You look around over there and I'll check this section."

Natalie peered at the floor. "I see someone made a plywood floor. I didn't relish stepping from beam to beam." She glanced around. "Not too much up here except some pieces of wood and a few boxes."

After a couple of minutes, Virginia called out. "Natalie, come take a look at this. It was behind those buckets."

Natalie scurried to Virginia and knelt next to her. "From the looks of it, that's some sort of... electrical control device, and that looks like a radio transceiver of some type." She pointed at a support beam. "See, there's the antenna."

"There are some wires that disappear down through a hole and insulation under the plywood," said Virginia.

Natalie pulled a pocketknife from her jeans and unscrewed the fasteners to the lid of one of the electrical boxes and peered inside. "I was right. This is a minicomputer and operational controller. That chip is a microprocessor and those are memory chips." She rose. "You thinking what I'm thinking?"

"This is the main command center for the ghosts' appearances."

Natalie bent closer and examined the circuitry. "That thing is capable of producing unusual holograms without the usual media needed to produce one. And you're right, this makes the house ghosts, and it talks to other controllers. This is the onsite ghost master station, spirit central."

Virginia climbed to her feet. "I take it that you've seen something like this before?"

"Yes. They use them in Hollywood for special effects. While on the set of a movie I was in, the FX guy setting something like this up asked me to help him."

"I bet he did. What was your costume like? What's an FX guy?"

Natalie gave a quick sigh. "If you must know, a husky mosquito could have taken off with my costume on a short runway. And an FX person is a special effects expert." Natalie rubbed her forehead. "Can I get back to my explanation now?"

Virginia waved her hand. "By all means."

"He showed me the equipment and how it worked. The holograms he made were spectacular. It was something like the Holodeck on Star Trek. I was supposed to be fighting some creatures that were holograms. That took some practice." Natalie stood and slipped her pocketknife back in her pocket. "We need to see if there are more of these outside for the external ghosts or verify this one is the main controller. If so, there will be smaller ones similar to this one and the lasers that take orders from this master station." Natalie leaned against an upright. "You thought something like this would be here, didn't you?"

Virginia nodded. "Yeah. At first, I thought it might be in the basement but if it used a radio signal to turn this controller on and off, then being up here seemed more reasonable."

"Good call." Natalie ran her hand over a wire. "It's been spliced into that electrical line. Want to kill the power to it and end the spectral visitations?"

"No. The people behind this may be able to monitor it and if it's offline, then Gail may have more trouble."

Natalie raised an eyebrow. "But they may send someone to repair it. If they do, we'd have someone to interrogate. I can be quite persuasive, especially when they think I'm going to give them a colonoscopy with a broom handle or cut off their—"

"Let me think about that."

"Party pooper."

They turned off the lights and returned to the second-floor hallway.

"Find anything?" asked Terry.

"We found spook central," said Virginia.

Gail stood in shock. "Spook central?"

"Yep. Main control center for the ghosts."

"So, you think you know how the ghosts appeared?"

"Oh, yeah." Virginia turned and headed for the hall stairs. "The ghosts have not always haunted this place, have they?"

Gail thought as they descended the stairs. "No. According to Cumo's niece, the random moving lights outside have been here since the mid-fifties, but the ghosts started to show up sometime in the mid-seventies. She said the Roman soldiers didn't appear until about 2000."

"Were there any renovations made at those approximate times?"

"Now that you mention it, yes. Cumo's niece did mention the renovations took place about those times. Why do you ask?"

"Because someone is using the ghosts to scare the occupants off the ranch." As they entered the front room, Virginia turned toward Natalie. "Can you have Jeff come out here? I think we need him to examine what we've found and do an exorcism."

Natalie nodded. "I'm sure he'll do it. He'll want to bring your husband as well."

"Good, call him."

Natalie moved to the side and quietly called Jeff on her cell phone.

Gail looked confused. "Who's Jeff?"

"Dr. Jeff Cummings is Natalie's boyfriend and he's an electrical and computer science professor at the University of Texas at Austin," said Virginia. "He happens to be an expert with holograms. I think I found out how they are being made. I'd like him to verify it."

"Holograms? I've been seeing holograms?"

"We think so," said Virginia. "Natalie identified the equipment and what it does. She's seen this kind of thing before."

Terry peered out the living room window. "How about the ghosts outside? How are those holograms formed?"

"Same as these," said Natalie. "We should wait for Jeff and Andy to examine the equipment and locations to make sure."

Terry nodded. "But if whoever is after the treasure is using technology to scare the people around here, why haven't they used it to locate the treasure? That's assuming it's here someplace."

"Because there are people around." Virginia sat on the sofa. "They can't very well dig the place up or bust holes in walls with someone living here. Dragging a ground penetrating radar or a survey magnetometer around would raise some eyebrows. You have the ranch hands who would run them off. Someone may call the sheriff. It has to be done with stealth and cunning."

Terry walked toward a window. "I'd like to see the barn, outbuildings and other places Gail mentioned ghosts have appeared."

Gail nodded. "Okay. Follow me."

They followed Gail outside and across the yard to a small, stone outbuilding. "We keep spare parts for the motorized equipment in here. The ghosts, when they appear, usually do so in front of it."

Virginia glanced around. "Do the ghosts ever go inside?"

"No. At least, not that I've noticed."

Terry walked around examining the trees, fence, and the roofline of the building, making notes. "You said there are more places they turn up, like a well or cave?"

"Yes." Gail pointed. "Let's take the ranch pony and I'll show you."

Natalie, Terry, and Virginia stared at Gail. Virginia tilted her head. "Ranch pony? We're going horseback riding?"

Gail chuckled. "No, it's a utility vehicle that holds four people and has a small platform in the back. I use it to get around on the ranch, and it's fun to drive. It's larger than the one Natalie used." She led them around the stone structure to a red barn, pulled open the doors and entered. She pointed to a side stall. In it sat a shiny, bright-green, four-seater, utility vehicle with a cover. "Pile in, ladies."

As they drove across the open ranch land, Natalie's phone rang. She answered it and spoke in quiet tones then looked at Gail. "Can Dr. Cummings and Virginia's husband come tonight after dinner to see about the ghosts?"

CHAPTER 8

At eight-thirty in the evening, Andy and Dr. Jeff Cummings came down from the attic and stepped into the living room where Natalie, Terry, Virginia, and Gail sat. The women looked at the two men expectantly.

"How'd it go, guys? What do you think?" asked Virginia.

Jeff set his large black duffle bag on the floor next to the couch and sat next to Natalie. He ran his fingers through his wavy black hair and smiled. "You were right. That was the onsite master station controlling other microprocessors that produced the holograms Dr. Knight witnessed. The smaller microprocessors, with their individual programing, operated the lasers." He glanced at Natalie. "I'm glad you noticed them. This system is exactly like your Hollywood FX guys used. They utilized multiple lasers and fast mirrors to create realistic, life-sized 3D images like the Holodeck on Star Trek, only probably with a little waviness. That's good for ghosts."

Gail slid to the edge of her seat. "Can you dismantle them?"

"Yes. Jeff removed some hardware from his bag. "This is the original master controller from the attic. I spliced in a new unit that mimics this one, but it will not activate any of the other microprocessors or lasers. That's what took us so long. I put dummy hardware on the control lines to look like the original secondary control units and lasers. The host computer, wherever it is, will not know anything is wrong. It will receive signals indicating that everything is the same, but nothing is happening. No holograms, no ghosts."

Terry rubbed her forehead. "Wouldn't the switching of units have been detectable when you did it?"

"There would have been a momentary flutter if anyone was monitoring it. But that type of thing happens with electronics and radio communications. And since it was just a quick blip and nothing seemed to change, I seriously doubt anyone, or their computer, noticed it."

"Couldn't they have used WIFI to control it instead of a radio?" asked Terry.

Jeff nodded. "Yes, it's possible. Maybe they were afraid Gail's computer WIFI would show another local hotspot and she might question it. But for now, the problem has been eliminated."

"Wonderful." Gail stood up. "How can I ever repay you, Dr. Cummings?"

"Just call me Jeff. I am happy to help."

"Okay, Jeff. Now what do we do?"

Virginia rubbed her hands together as Andy sat next to her. "Were you able to remove *all* their electrical stuff in the attic?"

"Everything but the radio transmitter and battery backup," said Jeff. "I had to leave that. The secondary systems here in the house and outside are dead. We can remove them later. Andy said you wanted the equipment we removed." He held up the large electronics box. "Besides this master unit, there were a couple of secondary items, and they are right here in my bag."

"Good. I want to send it to the Smithsonian Central Security Service and see if they can trace the equipment, or the components, to the people who made it."

"We're one step ahead of you on that, Virginia," said Andy. "We examined the equipment Jeff removed and found markings indicating it was assembled in Round Rock, Texas."

"Round Rock? Was there a name on the... the hardware that indicated who built it?"

"Yes. Inside the master control box is a small label underneath the motherboard. It looks like someone tried to remove all the product IDs but overlooked this one. They even put a coating on the integrated circuits to hide the manufacturers. They were assembled by a company called Grand Knights," said Jeff. "I never heard of them. Must be a small electronics firm of some type. Maybe they make custom computers."

Terry chuckled. "This is getting good."

Andy frowned. "What do you mean?"

"There was a guy here today who said he represented a client that wanted to buy Gail's ranch," said Terry. "She sent him away. But we have his card. He was from a company called Grand Knights in Round Rock. We thought it was fishy."

Natalie beamed, enthusiasm clear in her voice. "Road trip." She glanced at Virginia. "We go at night and wear dark clothing, right?"

"We did tell John we bent a few laws now and then," said Virginia. "If you ladies are free tomorrow, we should go there in the daytime to reconnoiter. Say... right after lunch?"

Natalie and Terry nodded.

"Good. Then, after our scouting expedition, we can investigate tomorrow night."

"What if someone is there?" asked Gail worriedly.

Natalie's face brightened. "I might get to interrogate him."

"Only as a last resort," said Virginia. She looked at Gail. "Natalie likes to use shop tools as interrogation implements." She shrugged her shoulder. "But she does get good results."

Gail glanced at Andy. "I think I'll stay home tomorrow evening."

Andy nodded. "Good call. You do not want to be in Round Rock tomorrow night with these three."

CHAPTER 9

The next day, after a quick lunch, Virginia, Natalie, and Terry drove to the tree lined street in Round Rock where the Grand Knights were located in an industrial office complex.

As they drove through the parking lot, Natalie pointed to the glass fronted office condominium. "There it is. Looks innocent enough. Let's drive around back to see what that's like."

Virginia drove slowly around to the rear of the complex and passed the back of the Grand Knights unit, then proceeded down the alleyway. Once on the street, Virginia pulled to the curb. She turned and looked at Terry and Natalie. "Okay, from our first pass, what did you notice?"

Natalie cleared her throat. "The front of the office was glass with their name printed and pictures of houses for sale on it. I spotted office cubicles, a row of file cabinets, and a few chairs near the receptionist's desk."

Terry nodded. "That's what I saw, too. But there were two security cameras: one high and to the side of the front door and the second aimed at the parking area and street. In the back was a steel door with a weird deadbolt lock and no handle. There was another security camera as well. Oh, I almost forgot. The glass windows in the front are alarmed. If they break, an alarm will sound."

Virginia ran her hand across the back of her neck and gave a low groan. "Must have slept wrong last night. I noticed the power conduit and power box for that business condo is huge. It's bigger than adjacent offices. They're doing something else besides selling real estate."

Terry opened her laptop and tapped the keys. "According to the State of Texas, Grand Knights doesn't have a real estate license. How are they selling real estate? From what we've just seen, whatever they are doing is costing a pretty penny." She glanced back at the computer. "This other state site says Grand Knights is an LLC but doesn't exactly state what they do." Her fingers raced across the keyboard. "I wish I had done this last night. It says here that John McCutchen, the guy at Gail's house, is a principal of the company and is an art appraiser. What does that have to do with real estate?"

Natalie thought for a second then smiled. "I propose we split up. Terry, you continue with your computer sniffing about them and this office complex. Virginia, you visit some of the other businesses in this complex and see what you can find out. Also, take a gander at the lock on the rear door without raising any alarms," she held her hands up in front of her, "no pun intended."

Virginia frowned. "What are you going to do?"

"As an actress, well, ex-actress, I think I'll go into Grand Knights and pretend to be a sexy, rich, California expat considering purchasing a large estate in the area. I'll take a look around and try and get a better picture of what's in there. There were two men inside and a female receptionist when we drove past. Maybe there are more people in cubicles we didn't see. There are two doors at the back of the office. One must be for a bathroom. I'll try to find out where the second one goes. The office is not deep, so there must be a lot of room behind it."

Virginia turned off the engine. "Okay, we've got a plan. Let's hop to it. Keep an eye out for anything else we may have missed or if something seems off. Also, note the locations of as many security cameras in the area as you can. Let's go."

An hour and a half later, at a coffee shop in Georgetown, Virginia, Natalie, and Terry sat drinking coffee and comparing notes. Virginia set her cup down. "Well, that steel rear door opens out, but it is pinned. If you tried to undo the hinge pins, the door wouldn't pull out. The lock is a Shi-He Chi-Me U-lock. The U-lock's obstructed keyway and key variation make it an unpickable."

Terry and Natalie exchanged confused glances. "What's a Shi-Chi-whatever?" asked Terry.

"I'll show you." Virginia drew a sketch of the face of the lock and a key, then pointed to various parts. "As you can see, the lock has sharp turns that the picks, yes, more than one, would have to make. Once those turns are made, keeping tension and working with the multiple unseen key holes would only be exacerbated by the fact that you cannot see what you are doing. This is coupled with how extremely rare this lock is. It is made and sold in China. All the trouble that the lock presents, and not knowing what the key looks like, would further confuse a thief looking to pick the lock."

"Good to know. You spotted a Chinese lock by looking at it while casually walking past." Natalie folded her arms across her chest. "You know this… how?"

"The Smithsonian Central Security Service sent me and a few other agents to a special training course at The Farm."

"Oh. The Farm. Did you stay in bunk houses and sing around a campfire with the farmhands?"

"No! The Farm is a military reservation, really an army base, in York County near Williamsburg, Virginia, where the CIA does its training. It's officially referred to as an Armed Forces Experimental Training Activity center. I've taken a number of courses there, including one that was referred to as the 'short course'."

Natalie looked impressed. "You go girl. We've got our own spy on the team. What about the electricity?"

"Yeah, about that. The power box and conduits are larger than all the others in the complex as we saw. I noted the numbers on them and called the power company. Grand Knights is pulling more power than some of the other businesses but not much. The power company said the large conduits and boxes are left over from a previous tenant. There was one more interesting thing. I could see a radio transponder antenna near the edge of the roof. I also checked with some of the businesses in the complex. They think Grand Knights is a real estate office. One reported seeing a few deliveries late some evenings from the alley in the last couple of months, but it didn't cause any concerns. They'd seen this type of thing there before."

"This coffee is strong." Natalie cleared her throat. "Okay, my turn. I went into Grand Knights' offices. It looked like a real estate office. The receptionist, Julie, was nice and directed me to a gentleman named Howard Gillette. He went over several listings in Williamson, Travis, and Bell counties. If I didn't know better, I'd think it was on the up and up. The second door in the back is also steel with a keypad lock. The door was alarmed. There were six cubicles but only two were occupied."

"Howard Gillette?" asked Terry.

"Yes."

Terry frowned and spoke as she typed on the keyboard. "I'll do a quick check on him. Did you find anything else interesting?"

"I was getting to that. There were maps on a corkboard in the rear. One was a marked-up map of the *Circle A* ranch. There were some scribbles about a cave. There was also a map of Rome and some red lines drawn on it near the Vatican."

"Marked up maps of the *Circle A* ranch and Rome?" Terry rubbed her eyes. "Interesting. Anything more?"

"Yes, pictures of Gail and Virginia pinned to the corkboard as well as books and catalogs of ancient artwork and lost treasures on a table under the corkboard."

Virginia's eyes widened. "You saved that for last?"

"Theatrics, my dear. It's all about effect." Natalie sipped more coffee.

"How about you, Terry? Anything juicy on the computer?"

"Yeah, a little," said Terry. "I just found that Howard Gillette happens to be a licensed real estate broker in Texas and Oklahoma, and he works for Grand Knights. So, I was wrong before. Maybe they can operate under his license. And, according to the FCC, John McCutchen has a radio operator's license. I also found that Grand Knights has the interest of U.S. Customs for some classified reason. I put in a call to Senior Special Agent Tom Mason at the Smithsonian Central Security Service and asked for help."

"What did he say?" asked Virginia.

"Tom told me he'd see what he could find out from Customs. But Tom said he recently discovered that Grand Knights is affiliated somehow with a shadowy organization in Rome, Italy. It's called The Pyramid Society and the person heading it is named Giulio Cesare. The name sounds phony to me."

"*Giulio Cesare* or *Giulio Cesare in Egitto* was a play written in the early seventeen-hundreds and first performed at the King's Theater in the Haymarket, London. *Giulio Cesare in Egitto* means 'Julius Caesar in Egypt'," said Natalie. She looked at her friends' questioning faces. "I was an actress and studied film, acting, and art history in college."

"It's also a very nice hotel in Rome not far from the Vatican," said Virginia.

"I agree with Terry. Giulio Cesare sounds like someone is hiding their true identity behind good old Julius Caesar," said Natalie. "Any idea who that might be?"

"Tom doesn't know," said Terry. "But the Italian police and INTERPOL have Giulio Cesare, whoever he is, pegged as an international arts and antiquities thief and trafficker and are looking for him. He's rumored to be trying to obtain stolen Etruscan jewelry, art, and some other old religious paintings. It seems he has a client who is footing the bill for their recovery."

"Recovery? I thought you said he was a thief," said Virginia.

"Who better to locate a stolen treasure than an international art and jewel thief? And it can take a thief to catch a thief. Someone is serious," responded Terry.

"The Vatican maybe?" asked Virginia. "They've got the money, and if the treasure was stolen from them, as Tom mentioned, then they have a lot to gain, and it would be a recovery."

Natalie set her empty coffee cup down. "Remind me not to come back here. I've had better coffee in... never mind. What's the Pyramid Society and Giulio Cesare got to do with our possible break-in of Grand Knights?"

"Probably nothing to help our B&E. But it is something to keep in the back of our minds for later." Virginia stared out the front window then back at Natalie and Terry. "From what we know, it seems trying to do a quick break-in and snooping around will be difficult, if not impossible. They've got security cameras, alarms, steel doors with impressive locks, and who knows what else to guard their back-room operations. Maybe armed employees. Their alarm company may send armed guards in response to an activated alarm, and the police could take minutes to hours to respond. That depends on when they were called, how close they are, and how busy the officers are when notified. Those are unknown variables, and I don't want to be there when the police arrive. I'm sure John would not approve either. We may have found out all we can, at least for now."

Natalie bit her lower lip, then gave a sheepish grin. "I know the combination to the door to the back of the office."

Terry and Virginia gawked. "You what?" asked Virginia.

"I know the combination for the lock on the steel door."

"How did you… never mind. Why didn't you say something earlier?"

"Using it seemed fruitless. We couldn't get in anyway; the door is alarmed, and I don't know how to shut that off. Then there are the security cameras, maybe other intrusion sensors, and alarms on the exterior doors and windows we'd have to get past. We'd get arrested."

Virginia sat with her eyes closed for a second, then turned toward Terry. "Terry, please find out who owns that industrial-office complex. I have an idea."

Terry pounded on the keyboard of her laptop, then looked up. "It's owned by the Earnest T. Floyd Company. They own several strip malls and office complexes. This one is managed by Harris Banks Property Management. Both seem to be reputable firms. What are you thinking?"

"Maybe we can become property management agents and need to do a facility inspection," said Virginia. "No need to worry about cameras, alarms, or steel doors with fancy locks or the police."

"You mean me." Terry slumped in her seat. "I'll have to be the property management agent. They've just seen Natalie, the men there will definitely remember her, and they have pictures of you. They haven't seen me, so it looks like I'm it." Terry closed her computer and scribbled on a napkin, then handed it to Virginia. "Here's the address and phone number for Harris Banks Property Management."

"I'll call them now to make an appointment for this afternoon," said Virginia, taking the paper. After a brief phone call to Harris Banks Property Management, Virginia stood. "Let's go ladies, we have an appointment with Mr. Harris Banks in an hour. Grand Knights won't be expecting this."

CHAPTER 10

At three in the afternoon, Terry walked into Grand Knights real estate's office and approached the receptionist. "Hello, I'm Terry Sorenson with Harris Banks Property Management. I have an appointment with Mr. Howard Gillette to do a quick property assessment."

The receptionist, Julie Newman, looked up. "Yes, he's expecting you. If you will wait a moment, I'll get him for you." She rose and went into the cubical area. After a couple of minutes, she returned with a man dressed in a pale-blue sport shirt and tan slacks.

"Hello, I'm Howard Gillette. Your property management company called and said you'd be coming. How can I help you, Ms. Sorenson?"

Terry shook his hand. "I've been tasked with doing a quick assessment of the building and how it is being used. It shouldn't take long. Offices are usually pretty straightforward."

"Is there anything in particular you would like to see?"

"Yes. We were informed that your office space is using an unusual amount of electricity."

"We are? I don't see how." He gave her a curious look. "Why would you be worried about that?"

"That raised a red flag. We are concerned about safety and fire hazards. Something might be drawing excess power that you're not aware of, like a building wiring problem. That we can get fixed before there are any issues. Or you may have something that is using more power than is normal in this type of business. It may be something simple like a bank of computer servers to tie other branches of your company together. If that's the case, then there's no problem."

"I see. I don't recall any unusually high utility bills. Well, let me show you around, and if you have any questions, just ask." Gillette motioned with his arm. "This way." He led Terry around the open office space and through the cubical areas. "That's it. As you can see, we aren't doing anything out of the ordinary."

"Yes, so far everything looks good." Terry pointed. "I see that door is for the restroom. But where does that steel door go? Your business occupies a larger space than just this area. I need to see what's back there."

"You… it is… well, it's a storeroom holding confidential information. I can't let you go back there," said Gillette.

"That must be why you have a steel door with a digital lock."

Gillette cracked a smile and nodded. "Exactly."

Terry pulled a multi-page document from her shoulder bag. "This, Mr. Gillette, is a copy of your lease. According to it, especially section 6.3.2, Harris Banks Property Management has the right to inspect *all* of this property for possible safety, fire, or health issues, without notice. We gave you notice this afternoon, and I'm here now. So please open the door and let me look inside, or you will be in violation of your lease. By the way, section 6.4.1(c) says by not letting me inspect the whole leased area, you are in violation of the lease agreement and can be evicted within 72 hours."

"I… I don't remember that… I need to contact our management first. Can you come back tomorrow?"

With her jaw set harder than granite counters, Terry said, "You, Mr. Gillette, are the broker of record for this real estate company, correct?"

"Ahh… yes."

"And you signed this lease as management, not as an agent. So, legally you are the management. Do I get to inspect the room, or do I have my company evict you?"

Gillette rubbed one temple. "I see why they sent you. You're persistent. Okay, I'll give you a quick look, but… would you really evict us if I didn't show the area to you?"

"In a heartbeat," said Terry as she stuffed the document into her bag. She followed Gillette to the steel door and waited while he unlocked and opened it.

"Okay, let's get this over with." Gillette entered the space and turned on the overhead lights. Terry followed.

Terry looked at the large open space. She heard the ballasts of the florescent lights buzz. Six desks with computers and eight tables were scattered around the room. A layer of dust covered a couple of desks. She wrinkled her nose at the musty smell in the room. Portable whiteboards with various diagrams and maps stood to one side. Eleven metal filing cabinets with books on top lined one wall. Off to one side was a table with a computer connected to a radio base station. She moved around the room toward the rear. Next to the back wall, seven computer servers sat on an eight-foot-long table. Near it, another table was set up to be an electronics assembly station. Terry noted the 63/37 solder spools, soldering irons, and associated hand tools. She frowned as she looked at a side wall. *I think the room is about ten feet narrower than it's supposed to be. That far section of the wall looks funny.* Terry stepped around the space for a couple of minutes, then turned to Gillette. "Now I see why you were drawing more electricity than other real estate companies whose offices we manage. You have more computers and servers than they do. Okay, I think I've seen enough." Terry smiled. "We're good to go." She started for the steel door.

"Is that all you wanted to see, Dr. Sorenson?" said Gillette.

Terry stopped, rooted in place. She swallowed, then glanced at Gillette. "Huh?"

"I just remembered," said Gillette excitedly. "You are Dr. Terry Sorenson, aren't you? You're the archaeologist who led the original dig in the southeast sector of the Fort McDowell Yavapai reservation in Arizona in 2019. Your findings were exceptional. If I recall, the tribe made you an honorary member."

Terry felt her heart skip a beat. "Yes, that's me. How'd you know?"

"I get the Archaeological Institute of America journal. I'm a member. Your pictures were included in the journal article about the Yavapai dig that I read. I'm sort of an amateur," said Gillette. "That and I'm from Arizona. Are you still working for that museum you were with when you did the dig?"

"Yes." She swallowed. "I still work there. This inspection stuff is sort of a sideline. Earn a few extra bucks doing inspections." She followed him out of the room.

"I understand completely. Well, I hope we passed your inspection, Doctor."

"You did. I'll fill out the inspection report this afternoon at the office. Thank you for your time." Terry turned and hurried out of the office.

Gillette watched Terry go to her vehicle and drive away. He turned and walked to his cubicle and made a phone call. "The facility inspector I told you about arrived. It was Dr. Terry Sorenson, the AIA archaeologist. She's moonlighting as a building inspector for extra money. According to our lease, I had to show her the back room. I think she was satisfied that there was nothing unseemly going on. I think I'll add her picture to the board along with Dr. Knight, Ms. North, and Mrs. Clark. I wish I knew if or how they are connected."

Terry met Virginia and Natalie at Natalie's ranch at sunset. Sitting around the living room, Terry debriefed the other women. "The front office is a subterfuge. If they sell any real estate, it's by accident. The map in the front office with your pictures has the cave with the water coming out of it circled with some notes. There are dotted lines and a note on the map of Rome, too, as Natalie noted. I managed to get into the back room."

Natalie leaned forward. "How'd you pull that off?"

"I used the fake lease I brought with me and quoted some nonexistent clauses about my being able to inspect the premises and if they didn't let me see behind the steel door, I'd have them evicted. Mr. Gillette had no idea if I was right or not."

"You're lucky he didn't want to see the lease," said Natalie.

"You're right. My gamble paid off."

"You are devious," chuckled Natalie.

Terry grinned. "Thank you. I spotted the computer and radio they are using to control the ghosts at Gail's ranch in the back room. That place *is* the ghost command central. They have computers, servers, filing cabinets, books, papers, and maps. Some were in Italian. They have a station where they have assembled electronics. There are some Archaeological textbooks there as well. One of the tables has copies of old U.S. Army files. The room was narrower than it should have been. I estimate it was about ten feet too short. There's a section of wall that is probably a secret door."

"You spotted a secret door?" asked Natalie.

"Yeah. I'm an archaeologist. I look for things that don't seem to belong or look out of place... like a secret door. Don't you guys watch *Indiana Jones* or *The Librarian*?"

Virginia sat and stared at Terry. "Yes but... how long were you in there?"

"Altogether... about forty-five minutes."

"You did great. Good for you."

"Maybe not. Gillette recognized me from a journal article. I bet my picture is now on the wall with you two."

Natalie sighed. "Okay, we know that's where the ghosts came from. But we don't know what they may have found in the cave that is marked on the corkboard."

"Yes, we do," said Terry. "In the back room, there is a similar map. It had some notes scribbled on it in Latin."

"Latin?"

"Yes." Terry pulled out a note pad and wrote, *Etruscan jewelry, es, incidentals manere, necesse map ad reliqua thesaurus,* and showed it to Virginia and Natalie. "There was another note in Italian. It said *Il Canzoniere* by Francesco Petrarca, 1470."

Virginia shook her head. "What's it mean?"

"Basic Latin to English translation is, Etruscan jewelry, art, incidentals remain, need map to rest of treasure," said Terry. "*Il Canzoniere* was the first book printed in the Italian Language."

"That book must be part of the stolen treasure. But why would the other part be in Latin? The Romans didn't write it," asked Natalie.

"Someone from a country that Latin is the official language would write it, especially to keep prying eyes from understanding it," said

Virginia. "Like the Vatican."

"Good deduction, Miss Marple," said Natalie.

"I think they found just enough of the remains of the treasure to whet their appetite," said Virginia. "I'll bet Lieutenant Cumo couldn't bring all the stolen loot to the U.S. Like we thought, it would be too hard for one person to pull off. He brought enough to finance his post war lifestyle and to lure shady investors to finance bringing the remaining treasure to Texas. Obviously to split the proceeds."

"Then why didn't he do it? Or did he?"

"According to his niece, he was not a well man. So, he had enough money from the amount of the treasure he brought to the U.S.—and managed to dispose of without raising any alarms—to live quite comfortably. Cumo may have tried to lure some shadowy people, but as the saying goes, there is no honor among thieves. He figured that out, maybe the hard way. So, he sat on what he hadn't sold off and kept the knowledge of where the remaining treasure is a secret. He may have hidden the directions in that quilt for safety."

Natalie sat back on the couch. "What do we do next?"

"Go look at that cave," said Terry.

"Right. And Leo and I need to study the quilt in more detail," said Virginia. "I think I now know where to look on it." Virginia took a breath. "I'll examine the quilt again tonight. Terry, gather what we'll need to explore that cave. Natalie, you'd better brief Gail on the latest development, and see if you can find any more details about the treasure that was believed to have been stolen from the Vatican in World War II. While you're at it, ask Gail if we can go cave exploring tomorrow."

Natalie glanced at Terry. "I sense another road trip in our future, but this time it'll be to Rome. I love Rome. I hope it includes a lot of wine."

Terry frowned. "If we live that long. Grand Knights knows who we are, and tomorrow we're going cave exploring. Anything can happen in a cave."

CHAPTER 11

Early the next morning, on Gail's ranch, Virginia and her cohorts started up the dusty incline, over an outcropping, toward the rock wall. Gail called out to her, "Watch for snakes. There are rattlers around here."

Virginia froze. "Rattlesnakes? I forgot about them. I hate snakes." She opened a bottle of water and quickly took a drink. "Too bad this isn't something stronger."

Natalie consulted her map and pointed. "The entrance should be right up there." She moved ahead of the others and climbed the rise into the jumble of rocks and boulders. "There it is." She hurried to a narrow opening in a rock formation, consulted her map, and glanced around. "There's the stream. This is it."

Terry examined the entrance. "Looks like people have been here recently. These footprints are fresh. We need to be careful, there may be someone in there, and there could be bats and snakes." Terry switched on her flashlight and pushed through the slit in the rocks. "Okay, it widens in here."

Gail, Natalie, and Virginia slipped into the cave entrance, turned on their lights, and swung them around over the cave walls.

Virginia pointed her lantern at the small stream winding around rocks. "Let's follow the water."

Terry moved ahead and slowly maneuvered down the tunnel. Gail, Virginia, and Natalie fell in behind her. They carefully walked down an inclined dirt floor of the cave and around small boulders and outcroppings. After a nine-minute hike, they entered a cavern about sixty feet long, thirty feet wide, and twenty feet high. Terry aimed her light toward the roof of the cave. She stared at the ceiling. Stalactites of varying sizes and colors hung above. Water slowly dripped from the tips. A path wound between Stalagmites and flowstone formations. "What a magnificent cave! I wonder if this path goes back to pre-Columbian days."

Virginia pointed at the far cave wall. "It looks like the stream originates in that rock formation over there. See how it pours out of openings in the sidewall of the cave and doesn't just seep? It looks like it's coming from a fault."

"Fault? We don't have earthquakes around here, do we?" said Gail.

"Normally, no. They did eons ago. There are old faults all over this area," said Virginia. "This cave, even though it's limestone, has at least this fault crossing it. There may be more." She swung her light toward a low section. "That's an igneous rock formation. There are similar formations on Natalie's ranch."

"Hey, guys, come over here," called Natalie.

Gail, Terry, and Virginia stepped around rock outcroppings to where Natalie stood. Virginia shined her light on old wood and metal cases. "Well, lookie here. Jackpot."

Natalie knelt next to a faded, olive-drab painted metal crate with stenciling on the sides. She pointed her light on the side. "It says U.S. Army."

Gail stepped closer. "Can we open them?"

Natalie yanked open the hinged fasteners on one of the metal containers, as rust settled to the floor, and pushed up the creaking lid. She peered inside, waving her light back and forth. "Not much here. There's what looks like a gold brooch in the corner and a couple of rings and what looks like a fancy gold bracelet." She retrieved the piece of jewelry and held it up in her light. "Nice."

Terry hurried to Natalie and took the item and examined it. "It's pure gold, or at least 22 karats."

Natalie looked at the piece. "That's why it isn't tarnished, right?"

"Yes. This is a sample of Early Etruscan jewelry," said Terry. "From the 7th century BC until the 5th when the civilization came to its full glory. The best pieces of Etruscan jewelry come from these times. Early Etruscan jewelry is characterized by its abundance, the highly skilled makers, and its variety. The Etruscans loved color, so they used faience, colored gemstones, and glass beads to decorate their work." She looked over Natalie's shoulder. "What else is in there?"

Natalie looked into the container. "Just some paper and a few more of those trinkets."

"Trinkets!" Terry thrust her hand to her chest. "These are priceless pieces of art from a lost civilization. Handle them with respect."

"Sorry. More gold jewelry from a long time ago. Lost civilization? What happened to it?"

"The Etruscan civilization was absorbed by the upcoming Roman civilization."

"Oh. Nice to know."

Gail moved her lantern closer to a wooden box. "Can we open this one?"

Virginia stepped to the crate and pulled on the lid. It easily slid off. She bent over and examined the contents as Gail shined her lantern inside.

"There are old wrappings, something that looks like tiny paint chips, some papers with Latin writing on them... This says *sanguis diaboli*. Wait... there is a drawing in here that looks like the pattern of the quilting on Cumo's quilt that Gail provided me. There is something in the spacing between the quilt blocks. Now I know where to look on that quilt for more information."

Terry froze. "Blood of the devil?"

"Huh?"

"That's what *sanguis diaboli* means."

Virginia rubbed her eyes. "Great. Just what we need. The devil, a stolen treasure, and some crazy people trying to find it."

Terry smiled. "You mean crazy people besides us, right?"

"Yeah."

Gail looked around. "We should get this stuff out of here and safely locked up."

"I agree," said Terry. "Can you have some of your ranch guys get these boxes out? Since there are just a few gold artifacts, we can carry them with us."

"Yes. As soon as we leave, I'll call the foreman and have the boys bring these crates and boxes to the house." She held up her cell phone. "No signal in here."

"Since they're evidence in what could be a decades old crime, I think we should secure them in a better place than your house," said Virginia. "And because these things are known to the folks at Grand Knight and possibly others, having them at your house could be dangerous."

Gail stood gazing at a stalagmite. "I guess you're right. Where could we put them?"

"I'll call Dr. Doverspike at my museum. I bet he'd let us store them there under guard."

Terry laughed. "If *you* ask him, Virginia, he'll agree to anything."

"Funny. I'll call Captain Steadman, too. Maybe we can get a police escort for the artifacts."

Natalie cleared her voice. "Artifacts are a stretch. There are some remaining items and papers but..." she glanced at Virginia's and Terry's frowns. "Okay artifacts." She climbed to her feet. "What say we go back outside, and you and Gail make your calls. We'll stand guard. Once this... stuff is safely locked up, Terry can inventory and examine it. Gail can rest easier, and I can get a drink."

Gail bent down and pulled a spiral notebook out of the crate and opened it. "This is old, but it definitely isn't ancient." She flipped through a few pages. "It's got lists and there's a notation about something... The Pyramid Society and someone called Giulio Cesare."

Virginia raised an eyebrow. "That's come up before. Whoever wrote in that notebook knows about the Society and Giulio Cesare."

Gail thumbed through some pages. "Does anyone know who Susanna Pomeroy and Margie Albright might be? Maybe they have some information we could use, if they're still alive."

Virginia stepped closer. "What else have you got there?"

"I don't know. It's got all sorts of things. Here's a listing for S&H Green Stamps. I remember those from when I was a kid. Other pages have notations and numbers next to them."

Natalie's voice perked up. "I'll be happy to investigate that notebook, especially with a strawberry daiquiri."

"What's with the drinking?" asked Virginia.

"I'm nervous. I don't like caves. You know that."

"Yeah, I know. Strawberry daiquiri it is."

Natalie turned to Gail. "About the notebook?"

"Why are you so enthused about it?" asked Gail.

"I think I know who those women are," responded Natalie. "But before I say more, I should at least read all of it."

Virginia looked skeptical. "You know who they are?"

"Yeah, Margie Albright for example. She was the main character in *My Little Margie* on radio and TV in the early 50s. Her character was played by Gail Storm."

"How do you know this?" asked Terry.

Natalie gave them an exasperated expression. "I also read John's notebook he gave us. You need to do your homework, ladies."

Virginia smiled. "You're right. I remember my father telling me about that program the other night when I asked him about the fifties. The man who played her father was Charlie Farrell. Besides being an actor, he also owned the Racket Club in Palm Springs. It was a watering hole and a place for stars to go to have fun and dry out in the forties and fifties. He was the Honorary Mayor of Palm Springs in the early fifties."

Terry and Natalie exchanged glances. Natalie turned to Gail. "Did you know that?"

"I remember some of it, now that you and Virginia brought them up." Gail handed Natalie the book. "Have fun."

Terry motioned toward the cave entrance. "Let's get out of here and get the ball rolling securing these artifacts, getting a police escort, and researching that notebook. And I'm getting hungry."

"I agree. And now with what I've seen, I can better inspect the quilt," said Virginia.

Gail smiled. "This has been interesting, and I'm feeling better about my ranch, now that you ladies have helped out and got the ghost thing figured out and stopped. What can I do?"

"Can we reconvene here at your ranch tomorrow afternoon to figure out our next step?" asked Virginia.

"By all means. I'll make lunch." Gail placed her hand against the cave wall. "Do any of you feel this place vibrating? Was that sort of a rumbling noise?"

Terry looked at the surface of the stream. Small ripples formed, then subsided. "It was a low-level shaking. Maybe the noise you heard was just some rocks moving." Dust flew into the cavern from the tunnel they had just come from. "Shit. That was either a landslide caused by an earthquake, or someone has just blown up our way out. Do earthquakes make noise?"

"Yes, earthquakes can make noise," said Natalie.

Virginia aimed her light at the surface of the water. The ripples had stopped. "That shaking could be from an explosion. Probably not a big one; it wouldn't need to be big to cause damage, especially to our way out."

Natalie shined her light toward the rear of the cavern. "Before I panic, does this place have a back door?"

CHAPTER 12

"You have the topographical map. Does it show any strange deformations indicating another exit?" Gail asked with a strained voice.

Natalie fumbled with the map, as she unfolded it while Terry held a lantern close. "No. Hell, this doesn't even show the location of the opening we came in. When I found it, I marked it on here with a Sharpie®."

Virginia skirted a large stalagmite and walked to the back of the cave. "There seems to be a slight breeze."

Terry and the others hurried to Virginia. Terry wet her finger and held it up. "Virginia's right. That means there is another opening somewhere, and maybe the entrance is not completely blocked." She held up the lantern and swung it around, then pointed. "There's a hole over there, but it's too small for us to get through."

Virginia moved to a rock pile from an ancient landslide, searching for an opening. "The breeze is coming from over here. She climbed about 20 feet of the dirt and rock incline and straightened. "There's an opening, and it looks big enough to crawl through."

Natalie climbed up the rocks and stood next to Virginia. "You might want to reconsider that idea." She pointed her light downward. "Look."

Virginia glanced where Natalie pointed. A human skeleton and shredded remains of black clothing lay among the rocks near the hole. Virginia and Natalie climbed down to the bones. "From the state of the remains and the clothes, it's decades old."

Terry climbed down the rocks, went into her professional mode, and examined the skeletal remains. "No wallet or ID. Male, between thirty and fifty, fit, Caucasian, and from his dental work, I'd say he's most likely European." Terry examined the right tibia. "He had an osteoma."

"What's an osteoma?" asked Virginia.

"An osteoma is a new piece of bone growing on another piece of bone." Terry reached under the pelvis and pulled out a gold pectoral cross. She turned it in her hands. After wetting it and rubbing off dirt, she said, "He was a priest. From the looks of this and what's left of his clothes, maybe a

Monsignor. From the notation on the back, he was a Jesuit."

Natalie frowned. "Why would a Jesuit priest be in here?"

"He was a member of a sect of Jesuits who were... the intellectual branch of the church, as well as soldiers for the church," Virginia said. "Maybe they were searching for the stolen treasure for the Vatican." She looked at Terry, who was poking at the bones. "Any idea as to how he died?"

"He was killed," Terry said.

Gail watched from the top of the rock pile. "Was he attacked by an animal? Maybe a coyote?"

Terry shook her head. "No, he was shot." She held up the skull. "See? Bullet hole entry wound. No exit wound. Probably a .22." She shook the skull. A small, mangled bullet fell out into her hand. "Yep. It's either a .22 or .25." She looked up at Gail. "His remains were not disturbed, so no coyote or other animal got him after he died."

Gail's hand flew to her chest. "You can tell all that from just looking at the remains and scraps of cloth?"

"Yes. We can determine more in my lab at the museum. But since he was murdered, he'll be turned over to a medical examiner."

"When was he killed?"

Terry fingered a piece of black cloth as she looked at the remains. "Probably sometime in the early fifties. At this point, that's a guess."

Natalie swallowed. "We're stuck in a cave with a skeleton of a priest who was murdered. Not my idea of a good day." She ran her fingers through her hair. "We need to find a way out of here!"

Virginia swung her light around. "We are fairly deep underground. I think we should go back to the entrance and see how bad the damage is and if we can get a cell signal."

Terry looked up. "I agree. Crawling through a hole in a cave, when there could be snakes and who knows what else, is not a good idea."

Anthony Morena, Gail's graduate student helping her run the ranch, called out to the five men standing nearby. "You two, start pulling those boulders away from the cave entrance. John, go get the big John Deere with the excavator attachment and get it here yesterday. Frank, go call the fire department and get rescue equipment and medics here PDQ." He looked at the men. "Move it! The boss and her friends are in that cave."

One of the ranch hands frowned. "How do you know they are actually in the cave?"

"Dr. Knight told me she and her friends were going in there this morning."

The fifth man pulled the rope tighter around the man on the ground. "What do you want to do with this guy?"

Anthony stepped to the man on the ground. "You're going to tell us why you blew up the cave entrance knowing that people were in it."

The man glared at him. "I want a lawyer."

"Lawyer? We're not the police. So, you are going to tell me why you blew up the cave entrance or suffer the consequence. We have you captive and haven't notified the sheriff. Think about that."

The man spat out his reply. "My people know where I am, and you will suffer for this."

Jim, the man guarding the prisoner, looked at Anthony. "Want me to question the bastard, boss?"

"Blasphemy!" the man shrieked.

Anthony smiled. "That's the least of your worries, pal."

"You are interrupting my work."

"Who do you work for?"

The man struggled with his bonds. "That is none of your business."

Anthony knelt next to him. "Let's see, you are trespassing, used explosives on a cave entrance trapping people inside, and may have committed murder. I'm sure the sheriff will love you."

"I don't have to answer your or his questions."

Anthony rose. "Lock this nut job in the old supply shed. Keep watch."

"Okay, boss," Jim said. "Take the… shortcut?"

Anthony smiled and nodded. "Of course." He glanced down at the man and saw something reflecting the sunlight, then pointed at it. "What's that?"

Jim leaned over the man and pulled the silver chain. A cross fell out of his pocket. "A cross?"

The man mumbled something then clinched his teeth. "Leave that alone."

"Keep it to show to Gail when we get her and her friends out." Anthony looked back at the tied-up man. "If anything has happened to any of them… we'll get a new rope." He turned back to the men pulling rocks away from the entrance. "How's it going?"

One of the men stopped, wiped his forehead with his sleeve, and said, "Slow. We need the tractor."

"It's coming. Will be here in a minute." Anthony moved closer to the rock pile. "Any sign of life inside?"

"No. But they may be a ways back. They probably don't know we're out here."

CHAPTER 13

For fifteen minutes, Virginia followed the stream and led the group toward the entrance. Once there, they examined the landslide. "Let's start pulling rocks away. Maybe we can make an opening large enough to crawl through or get a cell signal."

Gail climbed on the rock pile, put her ear on a boulder, and listened. "I think I hear something."

Virginia moved up the slope. "What is it?"

"I'm not sure. Movement and scrapping maybe. It's faint."

"Try your cell phone."

Gail pulled out her phone and looked at the screen. "No bars." She moved higher and held her phone up. "Still no signal."

Virginia eyed the stream, noting it was rapidly turning into a deepening pond against the rock pile. "That's not good."

Natalie rushed forward and looked at the rapidly rising pond. "You're right. We'd better start digging."

"Did you ever have a part in a movie where you were trapped in a cave, or room, or something?" Terry asked.

Natalie scrunched her nose. "Let me think… yes, I was trapped in a mine once."

"How'd you get out?"

"I was trapped with two men and we…" She turned and swung her light around. "What's that noise?" She pointed her light in the direction of a pool of water. "Look. The water was building up down there, but now it's quickly going down. It's rushing under those rocks. The water must have made an opening in the dirt under the rocks." She climbed down to the pond and examined the area where the water was flowing. "There's light and a small air gap at the top."

Terry looked where Natalie was pointing. "Can we get through it?"

Natalie pulled out her phone and hopped into the waist deep water. "It's cold." She bent close to where the current was the strongest and peered at the hole. "No. It's not big enough." She held the phone near the top of the water and the air gap and dialed. A voice answered. "Dr. Cummings."

Her heart pounded. "Jeff! It's me, Natalie. There's been an explosion and we're trapped in a cave on Gail's *Circle A* ranch. We need help."

"Are you hurt? How are the others?"

"We're fine. Get us out of here."

"Where is the cave? Dr. Knight's ranch is huge."

"Oh, boy. I've got the only map. No wait, it's the only cave with a stream flowing out of it. I'm sure the ranch hands know where it is."

"I'll call John at the police station and get Andy."

"I have a better idea. Call Anthony Morena first. He's Gail's graduate student helping her run the ranch. He may know where it is and be able to start the rescue before John, you, Andy, or anyone else gets here. Hurry."

"I'm on it. Sit tight."

"I'm not going anywhere." Natalie turned and grinned at Virginia, Terry, and Gail. "Help's on the way."

Gail slipped into the receding water and dialed her phone. After a couple of rings, she heard a voice. "Anthony Morena."

"Anthony! This is Gail. We're trapped in a cave and—"

"I know, Dr. Knight. I'm outside the entrance with the guys. We're trying to dig you out. I've got the big John Deere with the bucket here moving the large stones. I called the fire department, and more rescue equipment is coming. Are you okay? Is the cave stable? Do you need paramedics?"

"We're fine. The cave appears okay, except for the rubble at the entrance. Ms. North called her boyfriend, and he's getting the police."

"I tried calling you but… you being in the cave and with so much debris in the way, I couldn't get a signal. How are you calling?" Anthony asked.

"There is a new hole where the water is flowing out. It must have enough airgap to allow a weak signal. We are right behind the landslide."

"We have the person who blew up the entrance, Dr. Knight. Want me to turn him over to the police?"

"You captured the person responsible?"

"Yes."

"Wait a second. I'll ask Virginia." After a brief wait, Gail spoke. "Where is he?"

"Tied up and locked in the old tool shed."

"Good. Keep him there, and call Captain Steadman at the Georgetown Police Department. Ask him to send officers to take over guarding the person. Virginia and her friends want to… interview with the police."

An hour and a half later, Virginia, Terry, Gail, and Natalie sat on the rear bumper of a fire engine, facing Captain John Steadman. He looked at the four women. "I'm glad you're all okay. I've called the sheriff's bomb squad. They are coming as well. Did you find anything useful in there?"

Terry held up the gold cross they found on the skeleton. "Yes, Captain. We got this off a skeleton in there."

"A what?"

"A skeleton. Male, thirty to fifty, died in the early nineteen-fifties from a gunshot wound to the head. The bullet, probably a .22 is still in there with the remains. We believe the man was a Jesuit priest."

John took the cross and examined it. "You got all that from a skeleton and this cross?"

"Yes. The bones were still intact, along with a few scraps of cloth." Terry took the cross and pointed at the engraved SJ. "That means the Society of Jesus. He was a Jesuit and probably searching for the stolen treasure."

"Jesuits are priests, not cops."

"They have been almost everything to the church. They were and still are the intellectual branch, running universities, doing research, operating in parishes, and are engaged in evangelization, etc. But they were the soldiers of the church, too. In some respects, they still are. The church may have sent them instead of their police, because they can go places and do things the police can't. They can act more like undercover people or spies than the Vatican police or Swiss guards."

John looked at Terry. "I see why you're on the team, Doctor. Where exactly is the... priest's skeleton?"

"In the back of the cave. We left him there and took the cross."

"I see." John glanced at the now open cave as he fingered the cross. "I'll need this as evidence."

"Evidence? Evidence of what?" Terry asked.

"A murder."

"A murder about seventy years old. Won't that be hard to investigate? I would think a murder that old would be more in my wheelhouse than yours."

"Yes, you're right. But there is no statute of limitation on murder, Doctor. And who knows, someone may remember something. We'll examine the remains and research this cross some more. I'll contact the Bishop of the Diocese of Austin. Maybe there are church records. It's also possible the bullet may tell us something. If I can't get anywhere with it, I'll turn the skeleton over to you."

"Sounds good to me." Terry said.

Virginia rose. "Thanks for coming and having one of your officers guard the alleged bomber, John. We need to go see the man. Call me if you find out anything about our skeleton." She turned and led Terry and Natalie toward the ATV they arrived on. Gail started the engine as Virginia, Terry, and Natalie approached the ATV. Natalie and Terry hopped in the back as Virginia climbed in the front passenger seat and fastened her seatbelt. "Okay, let's roll."

Gail smiled at Virginia. "We're going to the tool shed, right?"

"You bet. I'm curious as to the reason someone would blow up the cave with us in it," Virginia said.

They bounced over the rough terrain as they maneuvered around trees and scrub bushes, toward a cluster of outbuildings in a clearing surrounded by a small forest of scrub oak, mesquite, juniper, and cedar trees. Gail pointed. "That's the one. I don't see the police officer." She raced down a slope, leaving a dust cloud behind. The ATV skidded to a stop in front of the wooden building. The women piled out of the vehicle.

Near the side of the small shed, the officer lay unconscious in the dirt. The women ran to him. Gail knelt and examined him, then looked up at Virginia and Terry. "He's been hurt. There's blood on the side of his head."

Virginia bent down. "Doesn't look too bad, but he may have a concussion. We'd better call for paramedics and tell Captain Steadman."

Gail took a deep breath. "Okay. I'll call Anthony first. The firemen who were at the cave may still be there, so maybe they can help first." She called Anthony and then 911. She rose. "Anthony sent one of the men to the front gate to lead the medics here. The firemen are coming now, along with Captain Steadman."

"Good. Stay with him. Terry, Natalie, and I will see what happened with the prisoner," Virginia said.

Terry examined the broken hasp and lock on the shed, then swung the unlocked door open and stepped inside. She switched on the lights and stared at the empty room. "Virginia," she called, "we have a problem."

Natalie stepped to Terry's side. "Where'd he go?"

Virginia moved around Terry and Natalie and peered inside. "Our attacker must have gotten himself untied." She pointed at a broken window. "He climbed through that window, knocked John out, and escaped." She went to a rectangular piece of plywood on the floor and picked it up. "The window may have already been broken. It appears this was covering it."

Natalie poked at the hasp hanging on the doorframe. "This doesn't look good, either. Maybe he just broke the door down."

"Let's see if the officer has regained consciousness and what he can tell us." Virginia walked to Gail and the police officer. He sat holding his head. "How are you doing, Officer?" Virginia asked.

He glanced up at her. "My head hurts, but other than that, I'm fine. Ego's bruised."

"What happened?"

"I thought I heard something inside. I went to the door, but then there was another noise around the side of the shed. When I turned to check it out, the door burst open, and I was struck on my head. That's when the lights went out."

"So much for interviewing our only live suspect," Terry said.

Virginia nodded. "You're right. The police won't be happy either."

Two hours later, after being assured by the paramedic that the officer wasn't severely injured, Natalie, Terry, and Virginia sat around Natalie's kitchen table sipping iced tea.

Virginia set her glass down. "Looks like we have some computer investigating to do. How are the Jesuits, the Pyramid Society, and Giulio Cesare related, and what do they have to do with the treasure?"

Natalie leaned back. "The skeleton was that of a Jesuit. From what we just saw in the cave, he may have been after the treasure. He probably would have to return it to the Vatican. It's the Pyramid Society and Giulio Cesare that I'm not sure of. It seems they have a desire for the treasure, too. Whether it's to return it to the church or keep it for themselves is the question."

Terry leaned her arms on the table. "Could the Pyramid Society be working for the church? How about the Grand Knights real estate company? Where do they fit in?"

"All good questions." Virginia sighed. "Let's split up the questions and see what we can come up with. Natalie, contact Senior Special Agent Tom Mason at the Smithsonian Central Security Service, and ask him to see what the Smithsonian can find out about the church's investigation into the theft."

"Didn't Tom say the Vatican seemed to be sweeping the theft of the treasure under the rug?" Natalie asked.

"Yes, but obviously that wasn't true. They were and still may be searching for it. Keeping a low profile in such an investigation is not a bad idea."

"Good point."

"Terry, you dig deeper into the Pyramid Society. There must be something about them out there," Virginia said. "I'll go check out the quilt again with the new information from the designs we saw and see if I can find any connection to Grand Knights real estate."

Natalie nodded. "While I'm at it, I'll try and figure out if there are any ties between the parties involved."

"Good idea. Let's reconvene here tomorrow afternoon, say one-thirty?" Virginia asked.

Terry and Natalie nodded.

"Okay. I have a feeling this is going to be a long night," Virginia said.

CHAPTER 14

Late into the evening, Virginia stood in her quilt room examining with a lighted magnifier the quilt Gail had loaned her. Leo kept putting his face in her way as he tried to study the quilt with her. She pushed the cat out of the way. "Do you mind, Leo? Andy's in his study, go pester him and leave me alone." The cat huffed and stomped out of the room. Virginia returned to the quilt and made a few sketches on a notepad while scrutinizing the fabric between the blocks. She finally straightened and stretched. "I think I've got it. Now to—" She was interrupted by the phone.

Virginia glanced at the clock above her workbench and then answered it. "Hello?"

"Virginia, this is John Steadman. I've got some news for you."

"It's eleven o'clock. Couldn't it wait until morning, Captain?"

"I didn't realize it was that late. I just got some of the information you requested when we met at your friend Natalie's ranch. Take notes."

"Since you're calling at this hour, I take it the results are important. What've you got?"

"Got paper and pen ready?" John asked.

"Yes."

"For openers, Franco Volpe, remember him?"

"Yeah. He was the POW in World War II, owned a restaurant in New York, moved to Texas, and then died."

"Right. He was also a personal friend of Lieutenant Cumo. That's why he moved to Texas when he… retired from the restaurant business."

"He was? How'd they meet?" Virginia asked

"I discovered that Mr. Cumo was a second lieutenant at the Italian POW camp in Arizona when Volpe came there in 1943. Cumo was there because he was Italian and could speak the language. They became friends. From what I was able to ascertain from the Department of Defense, Volpe told Cumo about something in Rome that got him excited."

"How did the DOD figure that out? What was it?"

"From other officers and OSS-monitored communications in the camp

Hidden Threads

between Cumo and someone in an army battalion already in Rome. Then Cumo requested a transfer to a division ready to leave for Rome. The correspondences didn't contain any hints of anything illegal or of any military interest. Just stuff about conditions in Italy, art, some artifacts, and sites to see. Cumo received his transfer to the division as a logistics officer."

Virginia frowned. "So, the army wrote off the communications and the requested transfer as routine?"

"Pretty much."

"Cumo and Volpe stayed in touch?"

"Seems so."

"Okay. What else have you got?"

"Remember the ranch worker by the name of Eric Bauer?"

"Oh, yeah, him."

"Well, in a forgotten file in the sheriff's office, and a request for information from the FBI, we found that he was suspected of being an Italian spy during World War II."

"Bauer sounds more German than Italian." Virginia chuckled. "An Italian spy in Williamson County in the mid-forties? What was he spying on, cattle or pizza? I would think, if he really was a spy, he'd operate more in Dallas, Fort Worth, Houston, or San Antonio. What's there of military interest to a spy on a cattle ranch?"

"I don't know what he was doing. A better question is what was he still doing on the ranch in 1994? Spying in the forties and ranching in the nineties? He was over seventy when he disappeared."

"Maybe Mr. Bauer was searching for the treasure. Maybe he was German, and he was searching for it for the Nazis," Virginia said.

"That's a possibility."

"Why didn't the FBI arrest him?" asked Virginia.

"Suspecting something and proving it are two different things."

"True," Virginia said. "Anything on Franco Volpe's child?"

She heard John take a deep breath and slowly let it out. "Not yet. I'll keep looking for him. If he's still alive, he would be in his late sixties or seventies by now."

"How about Anthony Morena, Gail's Texas A&M grad student?"

"So far, he checks out okay. He's from Dallas. No police record, no wants or warrants out for him," John said. "Good grades in school. Likes fishing. He is well-liked at A&M. Nothing suspicious about his finances. Pays his bills on time. No unusual spending habits. Doesn't gamble. He has friends at school and at the ranch. Seems to be a nice guy."

"Great. He's the one who led the rescue effort for us at the ranch. I'm glad he checked out."

"Me too. I liked him when I met him there. That's it so far."

"That was a lot of work. Thanks."

"One more thing. I've got an early morning meeting with the Bishop of the Diocese of Austin to discuss the body of the priest you found in the cave. I'll let you know what I find out."

"I'll pass it on to the others tomorrow. How's the officer doing that was attacked at the shed?"

"He's got a minor concussion but is doing well. The doctors have him on a medical leave for a couple of days but expect a full recovery. Thanks for asking."

"Glad to hear that." Virginia said.

"When and where are you meeting?"

"Natalie's ranch at one."

"Okay. I'll also keep looking for Volpe's child."

"Thank you, again."

"No problem. I'll let you know when I find out anything else. Good night." John hung up.

Virginia looked at her notes. *John obtained a lot of information. Now we need to figure out how it fits in. An Italian spy on a cattle ranch? Someone at the FBI must be smoking something. But if he was a spy for the Vatican and searching for the treasure, the FBI wouldn't have a clue as to what he was looking for.* She stood and padded to Andy's study and found him with Leo playing solitaire on his computer. "I see you two are having fun."

Andy glanced at her. "Yeah. But it's bedtime. Got early office hours tomorrow for my students." He turned off the computer and headed for the bedroom. "Who was on the phone?"

"Captain Steadman. He had information on things we asked him to follow up on. I'll tell the ladies tomorrow. And guess what?"

"What?"

"The quilt gave up its secrets."

"Good. You broke the code." Andy sat on the edge of the bed. "What did it show you?"

"I have a map of tunnels or catacombs in Rome and some locations of interest."

"Does it show where the tunnels are or where they start?" Andy asked.

"Partially. But now that I know the code, I can do some more work."

At one the next day, Virginia drove up the gravel driveway at Natalie's ranch and parked near the barn. As she exited the car, Terry pulled up next to her and parked her Jeep. Virginia walked with Terry toward the rear porch. "Anything on the Pyramid Society?" Virginia asked.

"Yes. I'll fill you in when we get inside, so Natalie can hear what I found out. You?"

"I decoded the quilt and got some interesting information, including a map of some tunnels or catacombs in Rome."

They entered Natalie's kitchen and spotted her setting freshly baked muffins on the table. Virginia set her backpack on the floor, next to a chair at the table. Terry followed suit. Virginia sniffed the air. "Blueberry?"

"Yes," Natalie said. "I've got iced tea, Dr. Pepper, and Coke, unless you ladies would like something stronger."

They settled around the table and took out their notes while nibbling on the muffins. Virginia looked at each of the women. "Terry, why don't you go first?"

Terry cleared her throat. "Okay, the Pyramid Society. After using all the resources I have, plus our museum, I contacted a guy at the Smithsonian, who I did a favor for a while back. He used their computer and linked into the Smithsonian Central Security Service data bases. It appears that the Vatican was more than a little angry at being robbed during the war. They sent a crack team to track the valuables and the crooks down."

"They did? Who did they send?" Virginia asked.

"They sent a special squad of Jesuits to do the detective work."

"Squad? That's a funny term to use," Terry said.

"Okay, team, group, detachment, whatever. A small unit of priests were sent."

"Why not the Vatican police or the Swiss Guard?" Natalie asked.

Terry glanced at her notes. "The Gendarmerie Corps of Vatican City-state is the police and security force of Vatican City and the extraterritorial properties of the Holy See. The Gendarmerie Corps of Vatican were reportedly not used because the robbery occurred during the war and during the Allied liberation and occupation. The Swiss Guard protect the Pope and the Holy See. They are a military organization. A complicated situation. And the items that were allegedly stolen were thought to have been taken out of Italy. So, the Vatican assembled its own PIs... a Vatican CIA if you will. The Jesuits fit the bill perfectly."

"What does this have to do with the Pyramid Society?"

Terry smiled. "I'm getting to that. The Vatican created an organization to oversee the operation. It was called the Pyramid Society."

Virginia frowned. "It still exists today."

"Yes. The search for the treasure continues but under the radar. Maybe the priest we found in the cave on Gail's ranch worked for them."

"That fits. Good work, Terry."

Terry leaned forward, snatching another muffin. "Do I get overtime?"

Virginia laughed. "No."

Natalie sipped a little tea. "Virginia, did you find out anything about Grand Knights real estate?"

"Not much more than we presently know," Virginia said. "I thought they might be a front for the Pyramid Society, but I couldn't find any connections. I even searched the SCSS databases and had their computer go through the FBI and the Treasury Department databases. Grand Knights simply appeared. I did find a money trail from them to an individual in Rome. Someone named Victor Serrano."

Natalie thought for a minute. "What do we know about him?"

"Nothing. I've asked the SCSS to check him out before we do anything. The SCSS hasn't found any traces of any of the treasure being sold either."

Natalie smirked. "Cumo could have sold pieces of it over time to private collectors or other unscrupulous characters."

"That's possible." Terry finished her muffin. "These are good." She turned to Virginia. "Tell Natalie about the quilt."

"Okay. I decoded it. There is a map of some tunnels or catacombs in Rome, along with something that appears to be special locations. It was late, so I didn't get much more than that done. I'll continue to work on it."

Natalie raised an eyebrow. "You guys have been busy. Did you hear anything from John?"

Virginia held up her hand as she swallowed her bite of muffin. "Yes." She informed them what John had told her last night.

Terry raised in her seat and stared out the window. "He may have more for us. That's Captain Steadman's police car coming up the driveway, and it looks like he has someone with him." She squinted. "It's a priest."

CHAPTER 15

Natalie jumped to her feet and opened the door for John and the priest. She ushered them into the kitchen and had them seated with the women.

Virginia eyed John. "I take it your meeting with the bishop went well."

John nodded. "Yeah. When I told him about the remains of the Jesuit priest on Dr. Gail Knight's ranch from the early fifties and what we were doing, he contacted a priest who the bishop said could be of assistance." He pointed at the priest sitting next to Natalie, sipping tea. "This is Monsignor John Copello."

The priest nodded. "Nice to meet you ladies."

Virginia looked surprised, "I didn't expect the church to want to help since they've been covering up the theft for 70 years. What changed?"

"Captain Steadman told me about your investigation. I think I can offer some insights to help you."

"Why?" Virginia gave him a skeptical expression. "The church has covered up the theft for years. What is your involvement in our little caper, sir?"

Monsignor Copello shrugged his shoulder. "You are correct. They wanted to keep it secret and try to investigate it themselves. It was during the war when things in Rome were chaotic. The return of the art and artifacts was and is the prime concern. I must admit they've had little success. When His Excellency talked to Captain Steadman, he called me. I think we can be of mutual assistance."

"You are what? A liaison person?"

"Yes and No. I am a member of the Jesuit Order and one of the Papal special investigators searching for the treasure. Right now, I'm the only remaining one in the United States. I have been instructed to work with you."

Virginia raised an eyebrow. "This is a big country. Why are you here in the Austin area, especially now?"

"There was interest in a certain ranch years ago. When nothing materialized, we switched our efforts elsewhere. But in the last month or so, we've heard rumors of some activities at the ranch that... well, intrigued us."

Virginia stared at Copello. "I see."

"Because of the Smithsonian's involvement, I can give you a name of someone of interest. He's in his late seventies now but may be willing to share what he knows with you."

"Have you interviewed him?" asked Virginia.

"Yes. Well, I, and others have tried. He won't divulge much, and I think it is because of an old land dispute in Italy years ago. He's upset with the church and... it's a family thing with him."

Virginia nodded. "You think he'll talk to us?"

Copello gave her a hopeful expression. "Couldn't hurt to try."

"Okay. What's his name, and where does he live?"

He pulled a piece of paper from his shirt pocket. "Here is his name and contact information. His name is Gino Giacopetti, and he lives in Rome."

Terry bit her lower lip. "Does the Pyramid Society still exist?"

Copello's eyes widened. "You know about that?"

"Yes." Terry leaned across the table. "Are you a member?"

He swallowed. "Yes."

"Who is Giulio Cesare?" Virginia asked.

Monsignor Copello took a breath then slowly let it out. "You are aware of that name as well... how?"

"Good detective work. We like to know who we're up against," Virginia said. "Again, who is Giulio Cesare?"

Copello pointed at the platter with the muffins. "May I?"

Natalie nodded. "By all means. Help yourself."

He reached for a muffin and took a bite. "This is good." He glanced at Natalie "Are you the baker?"

"Yes." She smiled. "Who is Giulio Cesare? It's worth more muffins, if you tell us."

Copello gave her a questioning expression. "Bribery?"

"Yes."

Copello chuckled. "At least you're honest. Giulio Cesare is the code name for the person acting as the head of our agency... the Pyramid Society." Between bites of muffin, he continued, "The post has changed hands over the decades, so we created a name for the person who is the head of the Society to use. Like M is the head of MI6 in the James Bond Movies. You don't know M's real name. Even finding out about the society is difficult, and it being part of the church makes it almost impossible. You ladies are good." He looked at Natalie. "Another muffin, *per favore*."

"Of course." Natalie slid the platter closer to him.

"Hmm." Virginia eyed the priest. *Something is fishy about this.* "Have you ever heard of someone called Eric Bauer?"

Hidden Threads

Copello wrinkled his brow in thought. "No. The name does not sound familiar. Why do you ask?"

"He worked at my friend's ranch for a long time. It's the ranch you heard about."

"I see. I have a question," Copello said. "If you are able to locate the treasure and maybe who stole it, what are you going to do with it?"

Virginia wiped a crumb from her blouse. "Return it to its rightful owner. We believe the thieves are dead. But we know there are other players besides us and the church searching for it."

Copello buttered his muffin, then smiled. "Good. I can see why the bishop wanted me to work with you." He looked down at the table, then back at the women and John. "I'm afraid, even after over seventy years, what we have isn't much."

"You think the treasure is in the United States and here in Texas?" Virginia asked.

"From what we've learned over the years, yes."

"You think Mr. Cumo was one of the thieves?"

"We believe he was, yes. We could not prove it. He may have been working with others who we have not identified."

"No part of the treasure has turned up in museums either, right?" asked Terry.

"Correct." Copello took a bite of his muffin.

Virginia cleared her throat. "Monsignor, have you ever heard of the Grand Knights?"

"Mio Dio." He choked and then crossed himself. "Grand Knights? Yes. They are a dangerous international ring of art thieves, smugglers, and dealers in stolen artifacts. The Grand Knights have been active for over forty years in Europe. They're here?"

"You betcha. And they *are* involved."

Copello flinched. "Do you know if they have located the treasure?"

Virginia waved her hand dismissively. "No. They haven't found it. They're looking at Dr. Knight's ranch, the one you are interested in. They won't find anything, except maybe a few trinkets that remain from what Lt. Cumo managed to bring here after World War II." She glanced at Terry. "Sorry, I know they aren't trinkets. They are objects of art."

"Got that right," mumbled Terry.

Copello stared at Virginia. "If it was the Lieutenant who stole them, we could never prove it. You found some of the treasure? How... how much did the Lieutenant bring here? Where is it?"

"We found a few items of the treasure. The police and my museum have what we found for investigation and as evidence. But we believe Cumo smuggled, and slowly and quietly sold off enough of the treasure to provide himself with a good life. My guess is he brought maybe a couple of million dollars or so worth to Texas. That's in 1945 dollars. Probably 15 times that value today. He most likely sold it off over time. By doing that, he didn't bring a lot of attention to himself, and the value of each sale brought him more money. And we believe he did have help."

Copello face grew pensive. "Where is the rest? Do you have any ideas?"

"Yes."

"Where?"

"We need to talk to our agency before we give out more information, Monsignor. As an investigator, I'm sure you understand."

"Yes, of course. Please keep me informed of anything new and how I can be of further assistance."

John finished his fourth muffin, then rose. "The ladies will be in touch. I'll take you back to your office, Monsignor. I'm sure your superiors in Rome will be waiting for your call."

Virginia, Terry, and Natalie watched John escort Copello to his police car and then drive away.

Terry wet her lips. "What do you think?"

"He liked my muffins," Natalie said.

"That he did. So did John," Virginia said. "I need to call Tom at the SCSS and have him check Copello out."

"You don't trust Monsignor Copello?" asked Natalie. "He's a priest."

"I know. It's not that I don't trust him, it just seems too convenient that he happened to be at the Bishop of the Diocese of Austin's office when John was there. He said to keep him informed and asked how he could be of further assistance. He didn't actually add much, except a story about the Grand Knights and the Pyramid Society. He gave up the name Gino Giacopetti pretty quick, too. And the Giulio Cesare story stinks."

Terry set down her iced tea glass. "I thought that story was off, too."

"The SCSS had a different view." Virginia frowned. "Like we learned before, the Italian police and INTERPOL have Giulio Cesare pegged as an international arts and antiquities thief and trafficker. He's rumored to be trying to obtain stolen Etruscan jewelry, art, and some other old religious paintings. It seems he has a client who is footing the bill for their recovery. Monsignor Copello doesn't seem to be trying to mislead us. His story may be correct and the Vatican misdirected INTERPOL, the FBI, and the Italian police to keep them out of it. Maybe Giulio Cesare is not with the church, but his client is the Vatican. The church could have… misdirected Monsignor Copello to keep him involved but on the sideline. Hell, even our government lies to intelligence officers."

"Maybe the bishop had the monsignor be here to see what we are doing," Natalie said. "Like Virginia, I'm being paranoid. In what we're doing it's safer to trust but verify."

Terry held up her glass of iced tea, "I'll drink to that."

"We need to watch our backs," Natalie said.

"I'm going to call Tom at the Smithsonian. No telling what they might turn up on Monsignor Copello," Virginia said.

Terry helped clear the table. "Virginia, you told Monsignor Copello you knew where the treasure is. Do you?"

"Pretty close." Virginia sat back with the last muffin and smiled. "Feel like a road trip, ladies?"

CHAPTER 16

After eating dinner at home and talking to her boss, Tom Mason, at the Smithsonian Central Security Service, Virginia phoned Captain Steadman. "John, I asked the SCSS to do a background check on Monsignor John Copello."

"Why? The bishop said he was the emissary from Rome involved with the investigation."

"Yes, but our group had some reservations about a couple of things he said."

"Getting much background from the Vatican will be hard," John said. "They do not like to give up secrets."

"I know, but we have to try. And another thing. Natalie and I are going on a field trip to locate the rest of the treasure. But, if anyone asks you, we are following up on a lead in New York City."

"New York City?"

"Yep."

"Why there?"

"That's where Lieutenant Cumo's transport landed when he returned from Italy. That's where he would have had to transfer the treasure, unobserved, from the military transport to another means of conveyance to get it here to Texas. That's where some of it may still be. Anyway, that's your story."

"That's what I'm to tell Monsignor Copello if he asks?"

"Yes. And anyone else."

"Where are you actually going?"

"Do you really want to know?"

She heard John sigh. "Probably not. You said you and Ms. North are going. How about Dr. Sorenson?"

"No. Terry's going to stay behind for now to do some investigating here. She may join us later. I'd appreciate it if you'd keep an eye on her."

"No problem. Keep in touch. Good luck."

"Thanks." Virginia hung up and headed for her bedroom to finish packing.

Hidden Threads

The next evening, at the Austin-Bergstrom International Airport in Austin, Texas, Virginia and Natalie entered the first-class line for a British Airways flight to London with connecting flight to Rome, got their boarding passes at the counter, and checked their bags through to Rome.

As they walked toward the international flights Transportation Security Administration (TSA) checkpoint, Virginia said, "When we get to Rome, we're go to La Montecarlo II restaurant and ask for the owner, Luigi Bono. He's our contact."

Natalie looked at Virginia in disbelief. "Our covert contact owns a restaurant?"

"Yes. We'll see him about everything we need."

Natalie looked skyward and held her hands like she was praying. "There is a God. I'm going to love Rome."

"Is eating all you think about?"

"No. So, our contact, Luigi Bono, owns an Italian restaurant?" asked Natalie. "Is he married?"

Virginia waved her hand. "I don't know. It's been years since I saw him."

Natalie stood with her mouth agape. "You've met him before? What's he like? Attractive?"

"Yes, we've met. And as to the rest of your questions, wait and see."

Natalie glanced around. "Do you think we've been followed?"

"No. With the roundabout way we came, and the false information I gave John, that should throw off anyone interested in us for a while."

Near the entrance to the TSA checkpoint used for domestic flights, a tall black man stood behind a sign advertising a hotel. He dialed his cell phone. "I've lost the women. They weren't at the United Airlines counter or in the TSA security line."

"You missed them? How? We know when their United Airlines flight to New York is. They had to check in," said the voice on the phone.

"Yeah, well, I missed them."

"You said they haven't gone through the TSA inspection point?"

"I'm standing right near the entrance to it, and they haven't passed me. They've just disappeared. I'm leaving. Their plane has departed with or without them."

"Okay. We'll pick them up in New York, if they land here."

"Which hotel are they staying in?"

"We don't know. But I'll have people at the United terminal at the JFK airport in New York City watching for them. When they arrive, we'll see them when they pick up their luggage."

"Tell your people in New York to be careful. They're cagey." He turned and started to walk toward the exit, when a black-haired woman in a black dress bumped into him. She smiled at him as he touched his thigh, where it felt like he had been bitten by a mosquito. "I'm sorry…" His eyes bulged as he grabbed his chest, staggered forward, knocked into a group of people, then fell to the floor, dead.

CHAPTER 17

In a throng of anxious men, women, and fidgety children, Virginia waited next to Natalie at the luggage carrousel at Rome's Leonardo Da Vinci International Airport. The hum of confused travelers, baggage handlers, and various handcarts added to the hectic atmosphere. From some distant part of the huge room wafted the aromas of various herbs and foods. Virginia watched men in suits holding leather briefcases and talking on cell phones while watching for their bags. Others, on vacation or on more casual travel, hung back, glancing between brochures and the slow-moving carousel. She looked up at the placard that said *bagaglio* sitting atop the digital sign showing which flight's bags would be on this moving belt to nowhere. No one seemed to be watching her and Natalie.

"There they are!" Virginia pointed at the two large cloth bags with bright red ribbons tied to their handles. She grabbed her suitcase and pulled it from the moving belt.

"Good, let's go." Natalie took hers, extended the handle, and started for the car rental counter.

"Where are you going?" asked Virginia.

"To get a car. Why? Wait, you did reserve one, didn't you?"

"No. We're taking the hotel limo," Virginia said. "We need to go out by the pick-up drive."

Natalie stopped. "A limo? How did you arrange that?"

"The hotel is sending it to meet us. It was arranged when the SCSS made the reservations. Before I rent a car here, I want to see if driving is still crazy, like it was when I was here before."

"Fine, but we need to see Luigi first," Natalie said with dreamy eyes.

"After we check in and freshen up, we can catch a cab to the restaurant and look like tourists. We can see him then," Virginia said. She pulled her bag behind her as she headed to the glass sliding doors leading to the roadside pick-up area. "I didn't get much sleep on the plane. Maybe a little nap would help, too."

They walked out into the sunshine by the curb, only to be assailed by men hustling rides. Virginia noticed a tall young man dressed in a dark suit and holding a large sign with "Mrs. Clark" printed in red letters.

Virginia waved at him and scooted through the throng of travelers toward him. Natalie hustled close behind. They stopped and looked up at him.

"I'm Mrs. Clark." Virginia pointed at Natalie. "And she is with me. *Parla inglese?*"

He lowered the sign. "*Mi nome...* John. *Mi scusi. Si*, I speak English, pretty good." He smiled. "Welcome to Roma. May I take your bags?"

After he placed their suitcases in the trunk of the long black limousine, Virginia and Natalie slid into the soft leather rear seats with their backpacks and pulled the door closed.

John climbed into the driver's seat and turned toward them. "I can show you a little of the city on the way, if you would like me to do that."

Virginia and Natalie exchanged glances, then nodded.

John pulled the limousine into traffic, and as if riding on a cloud, they glided through the busy streets and past historic buildings toward the hotel.

After an hour and a half, they pulled into the entrance of the Hotel de Russie. It sat between the Spanish Steps and Piazza del Popolo on the Via del Babuino. John held the car door and helped them out of the vehicle, then carried their bags to the front desk. Natalie tipped him. Virginia smiled at the desk clerk and informed him of their reservations.

"*Si, si.* Welcome. You have an executive suite. Very nice. I know you will enjoy your stay with us." He gave Virginia the registration documents, and after she signed them, he handed her two magnetic room keys. He made a gesture with his hand, and a bellboy arrived at their side as if he just materialized out of space. The manager said, "He will assist you with your bags."

"No. We can manage, thank you anyway."

"It is no problem, ma'am. It is our policy. If there is ever anything we can do for you while you are here, please do not hesitate to ask."

As they followed the bellboy, Natalie pointed. "Check out the terraced gardens. They've got rose bushes, orange trees, and pines. And listen to the sounds of the cute waterfall flowing between the nymphaeums. Nice. And I see they have a fine bar and look there, a first-class restaurant." Turning, she pointed again. "Look, the sign says, 'Butterfly Oasis—created in collaboration with WWF—is located in the Secret Garden.'"

"I hope you mean the World Wildlife Foundation and not the World Wrestling Foundation."

"Yes! You know I don't like wrestling, unless there's sex involved," Natalie said.

"Great; a sex wrestler, as well as an actress, rancher, and knitter," chuckled Virginia.

"Hey, just keeping priorities. And I'm now a quilter." Natalie noticed

Hidden Threads

the smile on the bellboy's face and decided to tease a little. "You know what they say, when in Rome, do as the Romans do, and they had some wild parties."

Virginia shook her head. "I've created a monster."

"Yes, but one that knows how to make the best of the situation."

"Right. Now can we go to our room and do the sightseeing later?" Virginia yawned. "I'm bushed."

"Party pooper."

"And, it isn't just a room, we have an executive suite," Virginia said.

"How'd we get a suite?"

"The SCSS booked it." Virginia leaned close to Natalie and whispered, "If we are to play the part of jetsetters and black marketers, we need to live like them."

Natalie shook her head and whispered, "We're black marketers and doing it on the government's nickel. Cute."

"Yes, and you've watched too many James Bond movies." Virginia punched in the floor number.

"Says who? James Bond was a cutie."

Following the bellboy, they left the elevator and found their suite labeled in polished brass. They tipped the bellboy and entered the suite. The suite was huge and had been designed in a classical, yet contemporary Italian style with classical artwork and fabrics in delicate, restful, pastel hues. Their suite overlooked the Secret Garden and the Pincio.

The suite held two bedrooms with king size beds, a living room, an office, and an extra guest toilet. The table in the middle of the living room was glass, topped with a flowing tan tablecloth. An ornate writing desk with a lamp sat against the wall between the windows. There were also two telephone lines and WIFI. They found the suite had a private dining menu, well-stocked in-room, glass-fronted bar, a snack basket, satellite television, portable hairdryer, and plenty of storage space.

The two spacious bathrooms were finished in marble with colorful mosaics and antique finished plumbing fixtures. The Italian bathroom featured Rocco Forte Collection's exclusive products, in addition to two fluffy bathrobes.

Virginia entered her bedroom and plopped down on the bed. She bounded up and down a couple of times, and then fell back. "I think I'll just stay here and let you play Nancy Drew or James Bond. I could get used to this."

Natalie stepped into her bedroom, unpacked her suitcase, and slid it into the closet. "Unpack, and then we can rest," she called to Virginia. "You want to see this Luigi guy tonight, right?"

"Yes. After we rest for a spell, we can get cleaned up and head out. I'm exhausted."

"Me too. Might as well be refreshed when we see him tonight." Natalie hopped onto her bed. "The SCSS did really well finding us a place to call home while we're here. I'm just glad I'm not footing the bill."

At six-thirty that evening, Virginia and Natalie, dressed in dark slacks and silk blouses, stood outside the hotel as the doorman waved over a small cab. They hopped into the back.

Virginia leaned forward and tried the little Italian she could remember. "*Restorante La Montecarlo Two, per favore. Quanto costa?*" Before the driver could answer she added, "*Parla inglese?*"

"*Si*, I speak little English." The cabbie pointed at the meter. "You want me to show you around city? I give you a good price."

"I bet. No thanks, just take us to the restaurant, and we'll stay on the meter."

"Okay." He flipped the meter on and, with a puff of blue smoke out the back, the car pulled out. The restaurant was a short drive. When they pulled up in front, they paid the driver and entered the establishment.

The maître d' approached. "*Buona Sera, signorinas.*"

Natalie smiled. "Hi."

He tilted his head. "*Americano?*"

"Yes. We would like a table for two, and would you please tell Mr. Bono we are here?" asked Virginia.

He looked at them with a brief frown, then nodded. "This way, please." He led them to a table near the front window overlooking the outside dining area and street. "Who shall I tell Mr. Bono is calling?"

"Virginia and Natalie."

He shrugged his shoulders and muttered something in Italian as he walked away.

Virginia ordered *pasta all' amatriciana* and Natalie ordered chicken *alla cacciatora and an antipasto.* They waited watching the people around them and outside. As they finished, a tall thin man with black wavy hair, an open-collared white shirt with gray slacks, and an olive complexion approached. He stopped at their table.

"*Buona sera*, ladies. Welcome to my humble establishment. I'm Luigi Bono at your service." He motioned to the empty chair at the table. "May I?"

Virginia said, "By all means."

He pulled out the empty chair and sat.

"I'm Virginia Davies-Clark and this is Natalie North. Our Uncle Samuel said you'd be expecting us."

Luigi nodded and waved the waiter over. When the waiter arrived, Luigi told him their dinner was on him and to take it to his office. The young man smiled, bowed at the women, and left.

Luigi turned to Virginia and Natalie and spoke in a voice those at nearby tables could hear. "If you will follow me, I'll give you a tour of my establishment while your dinner is being prepared."

Natalie put a €10 note on the table as a tip and scurried to catch up with Luigi and Virginia.

After a tour of the kitchen, bar, and outside seating areas, he led them to his office. As they entered, Virginia examined the locks on the steel door to the office and scanned the room. The walls were concrete, and from the thickness of the doorway, she guessed they were about three feet thick, probably steel reinforced. There were no windows, just a ceiling vent with heavy steel bars covering it.

After Natalie entered, Luigi closed the door and hit a button on the keypad next to it. The sound of bolts sliding and a click, followed by a red light on the pad indicated the door was secure. Luigi pointed to a couple of leather chairs near a polished mahogany desk. They took their seats as he moved behind the desk and sat.

"We are secure in here. We are shielded from electronic eavesdropping as well. Now," Luigi said to Virginia, "I'm not a native Texan."

Virginia responded, "But I got here as soon as I could."

"Good. I'm glad the protocols are done with." Luigi sat back. "Good to see you again, Virginia. It's been a long time."

"Yes, it has, Luigi. I see you're doing well."

"I do my best. Now to business. I have some information for you, and your 'Uncle' suggested I provide you both with some weapons to ensure your safety."

CHAPTER 18

Natalie steepled her fingers and leaned forward. "I have a couple of personal questions, if I may."

"Sure, what are they?" asked Luigi.

"I noticed the Italian accent kind of slipped away when we got in here. Where are you really from?"

Luigi's eyes sparkled. "Brooklyn, New York. The good old U.S. of A."

Natalie's jaw dropped. "You're kidding us, right?"

"Nope. As Virginia already knows, my family had Italian restaurants in New York for decades. Grandparents came to the U.S. from Rome." He pointed to pictures on the wall behind them. "My grandfather, father, uncles, all of them are in the business. When the CIA recruited me, they sent me here and bankrolled me to start this place. It makes a great front, and it also makes me a lot of money. So, with what I make here, and from government service, I'm planning on retiring early. That is, if I live that long."

"Wow. I never would have guessed. I see you and Virginia are already acquainted. She failed to mention that little fact before."

"Yes. She was here several years ago on another case. I gave her some humble assistance." Luigi scooted his chair back and stood. "Now for the toys Washington said I was to give you." He pressed a hidden switch on one of the bookcases. The bookcase unit swung away from the wall. A large metal shelving unit slid out containing enough weapons to start a small war. "Are you ready for some things every lady spy shouldn't be without?"

Virginia and Natalie stood and approached the huge arsenal.

Natalie stood with her mouth agape. "Holy shit! That looks like a military arsenal."

"Now, what can I get for you ladies?" asked Luigi.

Virginia touched a couple of guns. "We could use some handguns."

"Right. Here are a couple of semi-automatics I really like. Nine millimeters, black composite for light weight, slim design for easy concealment and built-in sound suppressors, no serial numbers." He took two pistols and set them on the desk. "I'll give you four magazines each and ten boxes of ammo to start." He tossed them onto the desk with the guns. "Now, how about rifles?"

Virginia looked at the assortment of weapons hanging on display. "Do you have anything with a folding stock?"

"You bet." He took a strange-looking rifle that featured a bent metal rod for a stock. "Custom built, it fires the 7.62 NATO round. Built-in silencer and I'll throw in two extra clips and four boxes of ammo." Luigi pulled a black canvas duffle bag from a cabinet under the shelves and stuffed the handguns, magazines, clips, rifle, and ammo into it. "I'll give you one of these Leopold scopes, too. That way you'll be pretty well set in the gun area."

"Thank you," Virginia said as she examined her new toys.

"You're quite welcome." He looked at Virginia and Natalie. "I'll give you two a couple of extra items that may come in handy. You can never tell what will happen."

Natalie eyed the duffle bag. "Like what?"

Luigi pulled items off the shelves, stuffing them into the bag. "Like, four carbon fiber composite folding knives that are also glare-resistant." He looked at Virginia. "What did you do with the ones I gave you on your last trip?"

"Donna and I left a couple sticking in some unpleasant men. She somehow smuggled the rest back into the States."

"I see. Good for her."

"Who's Donna?" Natalie asked.

"She's an old friend and was my partner on the case back then."

"Oh."

Luigi continued. "Here's a box of eight, small-profile, flash-bang grenades, two compact high-temperature torches for cutting metal, a bag of plastic ties in case you need handcuffs, and the latest in night vision goggles with night amplification and magnification, along with the capability to switch to IR." After placing the items in the bag, he peered inside. "Getting kind of full, I'd better get you a second bag." He pulled out another duffle bag and transferred some of the items to it. He hefted both bags. "Yeah, that's better."

Natalie picked up a bag and held it. "We should be able to handle these okay. But about the grenades. How do they work?"

"Easy, pull the pin and throw. Just don't be where they land. The flash-bang grenades will put someone out of action for a while, so toss them carefully. You have about 10 seconds after you pull the pin to get rid of it. They will blind anyone who's in the area for a while and the sound will disorient them, so get out of the area and turn around or cover your eyes and ears."

Virginia and Natalie looked at each other, then Virginia raised an eyebrow as she looked at the small grenades. "We can do that."

"Oh, I almost forgot." Luigi opened a drawer and pulled out a small box, the size of a cigarette pack. "You'll love this." He opened it and withdrew a small, folding, parabolic dish and a listening clip. "This little device is easy to use, and you can hear anything up to a mile away. The amp is inside the box. It's an improved model to the one you had when you were here before, Virginia."

"And here are a couple of new ladies' watches with all the trimmings, like diamonds etc. that two pretty lady spies would want. They also contain small lasers." He stuffed them into the bag next to Natalie. Luigi scanned the shelving. "Let's see… ah… here it is." He picked two small containers off the shelf and handed them to Virginia.

"Chewing gum?"

"Chew this and it'll blow your jaw off." He watched their expressions. "Not really. The things that look like gum are a new type of plastic explosive. They can't be set off by chewing or hitting them. The other box contains the primers. One stick can do a lot of damage."

"How do we set them off?"

"Mold the gum as you put it around or on whatever you want to destroy and stick in the primer and get away." He picked up one of the new watches. "Besides the laser, this sets off the explosives. You press this small button on the side twice. Boom! You can be up to a hundred feet away and make it work." He tossed the watch and the explosive packages into a duffle bag.

Natalie pointed at a small box resting on the bottom of the cupboard. "What are those?"

Luigi turned and gazed at the arsenal display. "Oh, those. The SCSS created them for clandestine operative use. They are canisters that shoot a solution of DMSO and Ketamine."

Natalie knitted her brows. "What do they do?"

"Terry used these little guys on our last case," said Virginia. "They'll drop a 250-pound man in seconds but won't kill him. He'll be unconscious for about four hours and have a headache after that."

Luigi nodded. "Right. They are quite effective."

"Sounds good. Can we have a few?" asked Natalie.

"Well… why not?" He placed six in each of their duffle bags.

Virginia peered into the bags. "We have enough weapons to take on a small Army."

"If we attacked France, they'd probably surrender, and we'd have our own country. Think of the food and wine," Natalie said with a faraway look in her eyes.

"You and food," Virginia shook her head as she closed the bag near her and set it on the floor, then looked at Luigi. "If we need to contact you, how do we do it?"

"I'll give you each a business card. If you call the second number, you'll get what will sound like an answering machine. Hit the pound sign and the numbers 2243. That will get me directly. The line will secure itself." He hit his head with his hand. "Oh, shit! I almost forgot."

Virginia's eyebrows went up. "There's more?"

"Yeah. Probably the most important, next to the guns anyway." Luigi opened another drawer and pulled out two cell phones and handed them to Virginia and Natalie. "These are secure, radiation hardened satellite phones with untraceable numbers. Their phone numbers are on these." He handed them two small pieces of paper with the numbers on them along with two chargers. "They're also GPS units, so I can track you if need be. And here is a miniature, solid-state, motion-activated camera. Just plug it into the USB port on your computer to download pictures and to recharge the battery." He pulled out another item and held two of them up. "Cute little buggers, aren't they?" He explained how the incendiary packages disguised as lipstick worked. Then he pressed another button under his desktop, and the unit slid silently back into the wall and the bookcase swung back into place with a clicking sound. Luigi opened his desk drawer and pulled out eight identical items. "You will love these."

"What are they?" Natalie asked.

Virginia smiled, "They look like the EMP devices you gave me on my last trip."

Luigi grinned. "They are. Well… somewhat improved since then. Let me show you how to use the new models. It's an electro-magnetic pulse or EMP drive. When you twist this little red lever and push the orange button, it sends out an EMP that will fry any electronic or electrical thing, that is turned on, within a city block radius. You can set it to go off after a fifteen second delay as well. Your phones are immune. They've been Rad hardened." The next half hour, Luigi went through the operating procedures for the special electronic equipment and weapons.

"Here are a few maps. There are road maps, tourist maps, utility maps, historic maps, and maps to the known catacombs." Luigi stretched. "I think that will do it. Anything else I can do for you?"

Virginia and Natalie exchanged glances, then Virginia said, "I don't think so. I think we are fixed."

"One question." Natalie leaned forward. "Have you heard of anyone named Gino Giacopetti?"

Luigi frowned. "Yes. He is suspected of being an international, high-end jewel thief and smuggler. He has a villa here in Rome. He is reported to be semi-retired now. Why?"

"We have information that may link him to a big museum robbery during World War II," Virginia said.

"I have a picture of him on my computer. Let me get you a photograph." He tapped keys on his computer, then leaned back in his chair. "There. I just sent the photo along with his address to your new satellite phones."

The intercom on Luigi's desk buzzed. "The meal is ready for you and your guests, Mr. Bono," said a voice.

Luigi closed the arsenal display and motioned for Natalie and Virginia to scoot their bags behind a sofa. "Anything else?"

Virginia shook her head. "No."

He pushed a button, and the door unlocked. The waiter pushed a cart with their meals on it into the office, set the table in the center of the room, and served. He then bowed out and left. Luigi relocked the door.

After finishing dinner, they retrieved the duffle bags and thanked Luigi for the weapons and the wonderful food.

"Thank you. I'll call you a cab. And call me if you need anything, okay?"

They entered their suite and placed the duffle bags in their bedroom closets. Natalie strolled out to the living room as Virginia sorted through a dresser drawer.

From the living room, Natalie called, "Want a drink?"

"I could use a glass of wine. I'm going to change, be right there."

Natalie poured two glasses of white wine and sprawled out on the couch.

Virginia came into the room dressed in a large, burnt-orange University of Texas t-shirt, picked up her drink from the bar, and slid into an overstuffed chair near one of the windows. She sipped some wine, then set the glass on the side table. "We need to get busy tomorrow."

"I know. Let's start off by going shopping. We need new clothes to pull this off, and if anyone gets curious, we are behaving like two rich girls on vacation. We can drop hints that we are also... looking for *special* antiquities. That is, after we go for a good breakfast. I think we should eat breakfast here for the first day. They have a great menu... I looked at it while you were changing."

"You and food. Any suggestions on what to do with our arsenal while we're out?" Virginia asked.

Natalie glanced toward the bedrooms. "Do you think we could get all that stuff into our backpacks?"

"Some, but probably not all of it. We can't very well go shopping with guns, grenades, and our other toys strapped to us, and I sure don't want to leave them here. They need to be safe."

"Let's try the safes in our rooms."

"There are safes in there?"

Natalie gave Virginia a haughty look. "Of course, there are safes. This is an executive suite, and there's always a safe. They're in the bedrooms under the closet floor."

"Nice." Virginia smiled. "That's why we make a good team. Let's see what will fit." She got up and closed the drapes. "I know we are up high, but you can never tell when prying eyes may be looking."

CHAPTER 19

Virginia hoisted her black bag. "Good God, this seems heavier than before." She hauled the duffel bag into her bedroom and placed it on the floor next to the closet.

Natalie climbed off the couch and retrieved hers from near the suite entrance and dragged it toward her room. "The only thing we're missing is a Howitzer." Natalie opened the safe's door, which was set in a metal ring in the floor. An electric combination pad sat nestled in the center of the door.

"Did you find your safe?" called Natalie.

"Yes, I found it. Funny, I didn't see it earlier when I hung up my clothes."

"You weren't looking for it."

"You're right." Virginia pulled her duffle to her open closet and sat on the floor. She rummaged around in the bag and removed her pistol, magazines, and ammunition. She loaded all the magazines and slid one into the gun. After pulling the slide back and releasing it, she set the safety. She heard Natalie click the safety on her own gun.

"What are you going to keep out for now?" Natalie asked.

"My pistol, a couple of extra mags, the explosive gum pack, our new watches and cell phones, an EMP device, a couple of canisters of the DMSO and Ketamine, the explosive lipstick, and the listening apparatus," said Virginia. "We need to keep the maps out for study later. I think that's it for now. You?"

"I guess I'll do the same." Natalie peered into her bag and pulled out a grenade. "I may try and see how well one of the flash-bang grenades fits into my backpack. We can carry that much without attracting attention. What about the rifle? Will it fit into the safe?"

"I'll let you know as soon as I try it."

Virginia and Natalie packed the remaining items into the two safes.

Virginia examined the folding rifle. "Looks like the rifle might make it if I unscrew the barrel." She took the rifle apart and slid the pieces into the

Hidden Threads

safe. Finally, she closed the door and entered a new combination, *leocat*, the name of her neurotic cat back in Texas, for the combination. She rose and stretched. "I'm pretty stiff and tired, even with my nap today. Shall we call it a night?"

"Yeah, I agree," Natalie said. "I'll go turn off the lights in the living room."

"Wait a second." Virginia reached into her suitcase and pulled out a white electronic device. She hurried to the living room. "Here, hang this on the hall doorknob."

Natalie walked to her and took the plastic box with the flexible half circle on top and looked at it. "Is this what I think it is?"

"Yep. It's an alarm. Just hang it on the door. Anyone fidgets with the door and that thing will wake the dead."

"Home Depot?"

"No. Target. Twenty-nine-ninety-five, plus tax. Never hurts to be prepared."

Natalie walked to the door, hung the alarm on the handle, turned it on, and returned to the room. She found Virginia looking out the window.

"Turn off the light. I think I'll try our listening device."

"Okay." Natalie turned off the lights, padded to the window, and opened it.

Virginia pulled the little box from her backpack and set up the antenna. Putting the earpiece in her ear and handing Natalie the auxiliary one, she pointed the unfolded parabolic dish at the buildings around them. Various voices chattered in Italian. She swept the area and aimed at the buildings closest to them. No voices, just the sounds from the Via Sistina below.

"Doesn't sound too bad, I guess," Virginia said. She pulled the antenna inside the window.

"They are speaking Italian. I just understand a little, so we wouldn't know if they were having polite conversation, planning World War Three, or plotting to kill us." Natalie undid her earphone and handed it to Virginia.

"Yes, but we now know how to work this thing."

"That's good. Shall we hit the sack?"

The next morning, Virginia woke with a start at the sound of voices. She sat up and listened. Natalie was talking to someone, and from the sound of the other voice, it was a man. Slipping out of bed, she pulled on a pair of shorts and slid her gun from under the other pillow on her bed. She eased to the doorway and peered around the jam. Morning sun lit the living room. Natalie, dressed in a t-shirt and jeans, sat at the glass-covered table eating breakfast. Across from her, Luigi sipped coffee. A tan, leather briefcase rested next to his chair. Virginia sighed and walked into the room. Both Natalie and Luigi turned and watched her approach.

"Good morning; want some coffee?" Natalie asked.

"You are way too chipper at this hour, and yes, I need coffee." Virginia set the gun on the table, picked up a china cup and poured herself some coffee. Adding a spoon of sugar, she plopped into an empty chair. "What have you two been up to this morning? What time is it, anyway?"

Luigi looked at Natalie and placed his cup in the saucer. "Is she always this way in the morning?"

"This is a good day."

"Oh."

"All right you two, knock it off. I'm just waking up." Virginia drank her coffee and poured some more. "What's for breakfast?"

"To answer your first question, it's eight-thirty, and," Natalie pointed, "under the various shiny metal covers are scrambled eggs, hash-browns, bacon, and toast. Enjoy."

Virginia helped herself to everything. "This is good. Room service?"

"Yeah. The staff really went all out, and you're right, it is good."

Between bites, Virginia asked, "So, Luigi, what are you doing here? It's nice to see you and all, but I didn't think the CIA made house calls."

Luigi poured more coffee and took a sip. "I like the University of Texas at Austin t-shirt."

Virginia looked down at her shirt. It hung loose and at least wasn't transparent. "Don't tell me you went to school there."

"No. But I always liked Texas, and I like the colors. Where else except Texas is burnt-orange a decorator color?"

"You're right about that. Now, we like your company and all, but why the house call?"

"You're correct, the *company* doesn't usually make house calls, but I thought you'd be interested in this." He pulled a folder from his briefcase. "Here is the information on First Lieutenant Robert Cumo, U.S. Army 3rd Infantry Division, while he was stationed in Rome during World War II and about the theft of some Etruscan gold jewelry, books, scrolls, and art objects from," he made air quotes, "a museum in Rome about that time. The SCSS sent what they could locate and requested me to do some digging as well, and then give you what we could find. We finished compiling the information last night."

"You got this fast." Virginia hefted the folder. "You did better than we did."

"Glad to help. I don't think there is much here that will help. We couldn't find anything about his off-duty time, except a few sight-seeing trips around the area with some of his fellow officers." Luigi pulled a couple of tickets from his shirt pocket. "These are for you two. They're tickets for a tour of the Vatican museums and a few other sites in the Vatican. Your scheduled time is eleven this morning."

Virginia eyed him. "You arranged this last night as well?"

"No. This morning. A guy's got to get some sleep you know. I figured you'd want to see the place where the crime was committed back during the war."

Natalie took the tickets. "Yeah, but it's changed since then."

"True, but you need to start somewhere." He rose. "One more thing. You asked the SCSS to investigate a Jesuit priest, Monsignor John Copello. The results of that investigation arrived this morning. He checked out okay. He's exactly who he says he is. No arrests and no police or intelligence agencies are looking for him. The poor guy's been trying to get reassigned for a couple of years with no luck. He's got a Ph.D. in psychology and wants to teach at the Georgetown University in Washington, D.C. It's a Jesuit university." Luigi picked up his briefcase and nodded. "I'll leave you ladies to do your exploring and shopping. Let me know if I can be of further assistance." He strolled to the door and left.

Virginia helped herself to more breakfast. "I'm glad the priest checked out. I liked him."

"Me too," Natalie said. "Maybe if we actually find the treasure, we can include him in the discovery to help him get the transfer he wants."

"I agree. And I think Luigi is right. A tour of the Vatican Museum should be first on our agenda."

"There will be a crowd. That can provide us with a cover. Tourists on a tour," Natalie said.

"Or a place for someone to get close to us without being spotted. We need to be alert."

"Good point."

"We need to get ready for our tour this morning, and we'll examine the maps later." Virginia took a bite of toast. "I want to see if anything from the maps ties to the information and diagram from the quilt."

"When we get back from the tour, and while you check the maps, I'll read the report on the Lieutenant and see who went on the sight-seeing trips with him. Maybe a name will pop out."

"We probably need to take a quick preliminary look at Gino Giacopetti's villa, too. But right now, I want to finish this excellent breakfast."

Natalie set the tickets on the small table behind her, then ate some scrambled eggs. "We might as well enjoy breakfast; it could be our last."

Virginia rolled her yes. "Being a little melodramatic, are we?"

"You never know."

CHAPTER 20

After touring the Vatican museums, the Sistine Chapel, and St. Peter's Cathedral, Virginia and Natalie walked down a bright, tree lined street to the RED metro line subway station at Cipro. On the subway, Natalie sat and said, "I heard Italian men like women, but I've been pinched six times. I may buy a suit of chainmail."

"Poor baby." Virginia sat next to Natalie on the train. "How'd you like the museums?"

"Great. The guide seemed knowledgeable enough. The art and artifacts were stunning."

"I didn't realize how big it was. The guide said there were... what...54 galleries?"

"Yes, and I wanted to see the Sistine Chapel," Natalie said. "I liked the floor-to-ceiling frescoes. Michelangelo did a hell of a job on the ceiling, especially being upside down as he painted it."

"I liked the part about that cardinal who didn't like the painting having nudes, so Michelangelo painted him into the biblical story and put him in hell. The guide said the cardinal complained about it to the Pope, but the Pope at the time liked it, so the cardinal is painted in hell. She even pointed him out. The chapel is a lot smaller than I expected, though."

"I liked the paintings in the *Pinacoteca Vaticana*. They had Raphael's Modonna of Foligno, Leonardo da Vinci's St. Jerome in the Wilderness, and others."

"The Van Goghs, Gauguins, Salvador Dali, and Picasso were a surprise. I thought they'd be in Paris," Virginia said. "I appreciated the unique collection of artistic and architectural masterpieces and the statues. The perfectly manicured Vatican Gardens were also striking, especially that Globe within a Sphere."

Natalie nodded. "The collection of Etruscan jewelry was impressive in the variety of the work, but I thought there would be more on display."

"Me, too. The guide was obviously an art expert but not a metallurgist."

"Why would that be important?"

"Normally it wouldn't be. When I asked about the gold in the jewelry, she said it was pure gold. Twenty-four karat gold is way too soft to be used for most jewelry, especially in those times. But when I examined it and saw the tool marks, I knew it was an alloy. Probably between 18 and 22 karats," Virginia said. "I have to admit, they did some fine metalworking."

"I don't think the number of karats is important to the tourists."

"You're right. Did you notice the security systems?"

Natalie knitted her brow. "I saw motion detectors and smoke alarms. The windows are rigged to detect breakage and motion, but the guide said they are not breakable anyway. I'm sure the cases for the artifacts are alarmed as well."

"The paintings are also connected to alarms, and I think I saw some lasers for use after the galleries are empty. I could be wrong, but I doubt it." Virginia tapped Natalie's leg. "Get up, this is our stop."

As they walked to their hotel, Natalie glanced around and asked, "What did you think of St. Peter's?"

"The guide said it was the largest Christian church building in the world. I believe it. It's a whole lot bigger than I imagined. The size leaves you speechless. That cost a pretty penny to construct, and I bet it's expensive to maintain."

"And don't forget what the guide said about the obelisk in St. Peter's Square. It works like a huge solar clock that marks the hours and days. Who knew?"

"You sound like an encyclopedia," Virginia said.

"Sorry. I just enjoyed the tour a lot. But I didn't see anything that would help us solve our mystery."

Natalie led the way across their hotel lobby to the elevator. "I wonder if we had any visitors while we were gone."

They ambled down the hall to their room. Natalie stopped and pulled the hidden camera from the flowerpot, where she'd hidden it earlier, and replayed the images.

"Looks like someone came to the room and then left after we didn't answer their knock." She showed the images to Virginia. "Anyone you know?"

"No."

"He didn't try and enter, and with no uniform, he doesn't seem to be an employee, so we better stay on the lookout for him, just in case. I'll download it to our phones."

Virginia opened the door to their suite and entered. Natalie followed, dropped her backpack on the floor, plopped onto an upholstered chair, and rubbed her foot. "I need to convince my feet they weren't tortured."

Virginia checked for messages and then grabbed the TV remote off the table as she sat on the couch. "Let's take a minute and relax. Might as well see what's on."

Natalie turned facing the TV. "Wow, hey, they show more skin and things than we're allowed to in the states."

"They're not as prudish over here. Most Americans are rather uptight about nudity and sex compared to our European cousins."

Natalie leaned forward, watching the screen. "I guess so."

Virginia padded to her bedroom and set her backpack in the closet. She opened the safe and withdrew the maps and the sketches of the pattern on the quilt along with pictures of it. After she closed and locked the safe, she walked back into the sitting room, sat, and spread her document on the large, circular glass table. "I need to study these and see what we come up with."

"While you start that, I'll order lunch," Natalie said.

Virginia stretched. "Why don't we go out for lunch. I saw a place a few blocks from here that had pizza."

"You just got your stuff out, and my feet hurt. How about this? We have lunch here and go out for dinner and see more sights?"

"Sounds like a plan." Virginia sorted through the papers while Natalie called room service.

After lunch, Natalie pulled the reports from Luigi from her safe and returned to the sitting room. She sat on the couch with her legs curled up under her and pulled the reports out of the large manila envelope. "I'll read the report on the Lieutenant now."

After two hours, Virginia sat back in her chair. "OMG! We've got an even bigger mystery."

Natalie looked away from the TV and the report. "What?"

"I've been trying to fit the tunnels, or catacombs, or whatever it is shown on the quilt, with the maps Luigi provided. I even tried the Internet."

"Any luck?"

"Yes, but not what I expected."

"Do the tunnels shown on the quilt go under the Vatican museums or someplace else?" Natalie asked.

"Yes, and yes."

Natalie looked confused. "Huh?"

"There are two sets of tunnels or catacombs, and they interconnect. But there's also another one shown on the quilt that isn't on the map."

"They do?" Natalie uncurled her legs. "Where do they go? There's a mystery one too?"

"One goes under the Vatican museums, like we thought. It originates near the Tiber River. The second one runs from the first catacomb to a tunnel under Gino Giacopetti's villa. The one from the quilt cuts off the catacomb under the Vatican."

"That's weird."

"Yeah, it is." Virginia poked the picture of the quilt. "We need to explore the catacombs and see about the tunnel under Giacopetti's villa."

"We need to know more about this Gino guy, too."

Virginia leaned back. "Yes, and we need to check out his villa."

"When?"

"We can reconnoiter it after dinner. Until then, we do a little background search."

"By reconnoiter, do you mean just take a look at it... like look for alarm systems, guards and stuff or... a small B&E job?"

"At this point, I think a look-see is about it. Then we use what information we have and make plans."

Natalie opened her iPad and brought up the picture of Gino Giacopetti. "He looks like an aristocrat from an old movie. You know, ascot, smoking jacket, and black wavy hair that's a little gray at the temples. Smokes a pipe." Natalie fiddled with her iPad for a few minutes. "He's in his early seventies. He's got oodles of money, well connected in Roman society, knows royalty, and... get this, he's having a society party at his villa this Saturday evening. From the pictures of his last one, all the beautiful and important people of Rome attend."

"A party tomorrow night? Sounds like we need to do our surveillance as we planned, and then buy some new clothes."

"Something sexy but still able to hide some of our new toys?" asked Natalie with a big grin. "We're going to crash his party?"

"Yes, unless Luigi can get us invitations. Things could get interesting tomorrow night."

At ten in the morning, Howard Gillette sat in his Round Rock, Texas, office cubicle, examining some documents, when his phone rang. He cleared his throat and answered it. "Howard Gillette, Grand Knights Real Estate. How may I help you?"

"Do you know where those two women from Austin went?" Gino Giacopetti demanded in a gruff voice.

Gillette stiffened. "Ahh... New York City."

"No! Not New York. Those two women are missing! And as you already know, our man who followed them to the airport was murdered. He was found at the airport with a small poisonous dart stuck in him."

Gillette swallowed. "Any word on who killed him?"

"A woman is all the *polizia* know at this point," Giacopetti said. "Maybe one of them."

"One of them? I doubt that. How is this mystery woman tied in with Virginia Davies Clark and Natalie North, or anyone else?" Gillette asked.

"*Amico mio,* that is your department. You figure it out and find them!" Giacopetti said acidly. "The women and the research at that ranch were your responsibility. So far, you've got *niente*—nothing! This level of incompetence will not continue. I understand west Texas has a lot of wilderness… *capito?* Then there is the Gulf. It has a plenty of sharks, yes?"

"*Sì,* yes, I understand." Gillette stuttered as he visualized a dusty, shallow grave in west Texas or him wrapped in chains, falling off a boat circled by not so cuddly sharks with toothy grins. "Wha… what's the time difference between Austin and Rome?"

"You need to know the time? Rome is seven hours ahead of you. And remember what's at stake, especially for you."

"I'm on it," Gillette said, his voice cracking.

"You'd better be. I have a party here tomorrow night. I want to know where those women are before the party starts. The last thing I need is to have them turn up on my doorstep unannounced." The line went dead.

CHAPTER 21

Three hours later. Virginia and Natalie set their shopping bags on the ground next to a black iron bench. Virginia leaned back and stared at the blue sky. "I'm glad Luigi told us the upcoming party requires cocktail dresses for the ladies."

"I would have been happy with a blue Oxford shirt and jeans." Natalie glanced around. "I'm too tired to try and find the subway station and this isn't a bus stop. How do you suppose we call a cab?"

"I don't know. We could call Luigi," Virginia said as she rubbed her foot.

"Some spies we are. We need to call the CIA for a ride."

"I have an idea. Let's call the hotel and have them call us a cab." Virginia used her cell phone to call the hotel and after explaining where they were, she hung up.

Natalie gave her a hopeful look. "Are they sending a cab?"

"Better. The hotel limo. It's faster and won't cost us anything," Virginia said.

"The limo? How'd you pull that off?"

"The suite we're in is a premium one, and the use of the limo for short hops comes with the price of the suite."

"Nice to know."

After a fifteen-minute wait, the black car pulled up to the curb. They hopped into the back. As the vehicle rolled away from the curb, the driver leaned back, turning his head slightly. In broken English he asked, "Where would you *signorinas* like to go?"

Natalie leaned forward. "Back to the hotel, *per favore*."

A short time later, the limo pulled up to the hotel entrance. The driver hurried around the car and opened the door for Virginia and Natalie. They gathered their shopping bags and tipped the driver.

Natalie led the way across the lobby to the elevator. "It's close to dinner time. We can take a cab to the *Piazza del Popolo*. We can eat at Rossati, then we can go play spy."

They ambled down the hall to their room. Natalie stopped and pulled the hidden camera from the flowerpot, where she'd hidden it earlier, and replayed the images. "No visitor this time."

After dinner, Virginia and Natalie took a cab to a park near Gino Giacopetti's villa. They hiked their black backpacks higher on their shoulders as they walked.

Natalie stepped faster to draw even with Virginia. "Tell me again why we're doing this. We're going to crash Giacopetti's party tomorrow night. Why do this tonight? Shouldn't we be looking for the tunnel that's on your quilt but isn't on the map?"

"Yes. But if we're going to crash the party and look around while there, it might be a good idea if we knew some escape routes."

"Good plan."

A block away, they donned navy-blue wool watch caps and strolled to the block behind Giacopetti's home. They watched each building, noting whether it was a business, apartment, or a home, the heights, and any surveillance cameras. At an alley between two buildings, they clung to the shadows close to the side walls as they neared the rear of Giacopetti's building.

Virginia pointed at the top of the eight-foot-high stone wall surrounding the rear yard. "There's barbed wire up there. And note the cameras."

"They're hiding in the bougainvillea." Natalie slipped closer to an iron gate and carefully examined it. "That thingie at the top is part of an alarm system."

"We need to stay out of sight of the cameras, but I'd love to get a look at the yard."

"Are you nuts?" Natalie turned as a panel truck inched down the alley. "Oh, boy." She pointed toward an alcove. "Better move back into the shadows."

Virginia's eyes widened. "Good plan." She led Natalie into a darker shadowed area and looked back at the alley.

They watched as the truck stopped and three men hopped off. They opened the rear doors as the driver honked the horn. The iron gate rattled as it swung open. A man carrying an MP-5 submachinegun stepped out. He nodded at the truckers and disappeared inside the gate. The men from the truck started to unload boxes of food and wine.

"Maybe we should just walk by and smile nicely," Natalie whispered.

"Good idea."

The women ambled down the alley and around the truck to the front of the villa, crossed the street, and strolled casually down the block, while taking in the front of Giacopetti's home.

Virginia mumbled, "Note the three cameras on the front? They cover the door and the entrance to the street and alley. I'm sure there are alarms on the windows and the front door."

"Probably got armed guards inside, like the guy we saw at the yard gate. That's a lot of security."

"Maybe that's because he's an international, high-end jewel thief and smuggler. No telling what's hidden inside. And speaking of the gate, I'd still love to get inside the back yard," Virginia said as they turned a corner and wandered out of sight of the villa.

"After seeing that guy with the machine gun, ain't happening. That removes the garden as an emergency exit as well. Let's concentrate on tomorrow's party and how we're going to crash it without getting ourselves killed."

"You're right." Virginia sighed. "The last thing we need is to have Giacopetti know we're here now."

"What's his connection to the old robbery?" Natalie asked. "He isn't old enough to have been involved."

"Maybe someone in his family was. From what the priest told us, he has some serious interest. It's convenient that his villa is near the Tiber River. Upstream is where the catacomb ended, and there's a tunnel under his villa that happens to connect to the catacomb."

Natalie raised an eyebrow. "Very convenient." She pointed. "The Lungotevere del Mellini is a block that away. Feel like a warm, moonlit walk along a wide, tree-lined avenue and river?"

"That would be nice. I only wish our guys could be here with us for the stroll."

They walked along the wide thoroughfare under a canopy of trees and a three-quarter moon. At a section of the low wall along the river side of the road, steps led down to the water where long, narrow, river boats were tied. Virginia and Natalie ventured down to the river's edge. They passed a few long, narrow, moored river houseboats, workboats, and floating restaurants as they moved along, examining the side wall of the embankment. After seeing nothing out of the ordinary, they stopped at the side of a moored houseboat with a middle-aged woman resting in a deckchair.

"*Buona sera,*" Virginia said.

The woman smiled and stood. "*Buona sera. Cosa posso fare per te?*"

Natalie stepped closer. "*Stiamo cercando vecchi tunnel che possano fine sul fiume. Ne conosci qualcuno qui intorno?*"

The woman bit her lip as she thought. She grinned. "*Americanos?*"

"*Sì*"

Virginia leaned toward Natalie. "What did you ask her?"

"I told her we are looking for old tunnels that may end on the river. Did she know of any around here?"

"You speak Italian? I thought you said you didn't understand it."

"Just a little. I took a year of it in college and did a couple of films here. I'm pretty rusty."

The woman said, *"C'è un vecchio tunnel a circa cento metri lungo il fiume su questo lato. È anneito con una porta di ferro. Questo è l'unico a cui riesco a pensare. Potrebbe essere un vecchia catacomba."*

Virginia nudged Natalie. "Translation, please."

"I'm working on it. Okay, she said, there's an old tunnel about one hundred meters upriver on this side. It's sealed with a locked, iron door. That's the only one she can think of. It may be an old utility tunnel."

Virginia did a quick calculation. "That's about three-hundred-feet, plus or minus a few feet."

Natalie stepped to the side of the boat. *"Ci sono catacombe che terminano al fiume?"* She looked back at Virginia. "I asked if there are there any catacombs that end at the river."

The woman shrugged her shoulder. *"Non credo. Ce n'erano alcuni, ma sono stati chiusi molti anni fa. Ce n'è uno che era accessibile nel parco lassù. Troppo pericoloso"* She pointed. *"Ma è chiuso ora."*

Natalie nodded then said, "She doesn't think so. There were some in the area, but they were closed many years ago. Too dangerous. There is one that used to be accessible in the park up there. But it's closed off now."

"Wow. Thank her, then let's go look at that iron door."

"Mille Grazie," Natalie said.

"Your Italian is rusty? You go girl." Virginia said.

They walked upriver and found a rusted, round, locked, iron gate situated in the concrete side-bank of the Tiber River.

Virginia eyed the corroded lock. "We can open this and go exploring."

"There could be rats, or bats, snakes, or other disgusting things in there. And it could be dangerous. Swamp gas maybe?" Natalie stepped back and frowned. "And I don't want to go in there in the dark."

"It lines up with Giacopetti's place. And we have flashlights."

"Yeah, and it could also be a catacomb complete with dead bodies. Flashlights?" Natalie put her hands on her hips. "I want an arc lamp. A big one."

"The dead bodies won't object. You want an arc lamp? It could set off any swamp or sewer gas. It's methane."

"Just great. Fire and you can't breathe the stuff. Good reasons to not go." Natalie eyed the lock. "Anyway, how do you propose to open it?"

"With our chewing gum explosives."

"Remember the methane? You could blow up half of Rome. And chewing gum explosives will bring every Italian cop and fire truck within miles down here. I don't want to see the inside of the tunnel, much less the interi-

or of an Italian jail. And we are in plain sight on the edge of the river. No escape route."

"The woman on the boat could identify us, too." Virginia pondered. "Okay. Maybe we could try and locate the catacomb or tunnel she said had an entrance in that park."

"Let's check it out. If that doesn't look promising, then I vote we go back to the hotel."

"Fine. Can't hurt to look."

Natalie shook as a chill ran down her spine. "I just got the feeling we're being watched. How about we make for those stairs over there and get on the road?"

The sound of multiple ricocheting bullets flying close to them, and concrete suddenly chiseled off the wall near the door, brought both Virginia and Natalie to their knees. Virginia took a breath, her heart pounding against her ribs. "We're being shot at." She yanked her pistol from her backpack.

"No shit," Natalie spat. "I didn't hear a gun." She held her pistol close.

"Probably someone using a silencer."

They bolted ahead for the stairs. Crouched, they scurried up the steps, darted across the street, and hid behind a couple of large tree trunks. Virginia peered out from behind the tree and scanned the area, then pulled back. A cloud moved in front of the moon, casting partial shadows across the serene landscape. She glanced at Natalie behind a neighboring tree. "I didn't see anyone. No motor vehicle traffic either."

Natalie looked from behind her tree. "I don't eith… wait… two men running this way near the shrubs. Weapons drawn. That's not nice. Want to discourage them?"

"By all means." Virginia leaned out from behind her tree, wet her lips with her tongue, then aimed at the closest man. Before she could fire, the man jerked to the side, dropped his gun, and tumbled to the ground crying out in pain. She stared. "What the hell?"

"Nice shot. Got him in the hip," Natalie said.

"I didn't shoot him."

"Huh?" Natalie peered around her tree and aimed her weapon. The second man, hunkering behind a bush close to his downed partner, fell through the bush onto the dirt and broken branches, screaming and grasping a bloody shoulder. She glanced at Virginia and said, "I didn't do that one either. If the shooter hit an artery, he's toast. For that matter, who is shooting?"

"I don't know, but let's get the hell out of here." Virginia looked at the park and at the neighboring building. "Those two are making enough noise to raise the occupants of the catacombs below. At least the police will find them with their guns."

Natalie glanced around. "Too much light from the streetlamps and a lot of lit windows from those homes over there to make a clean getaway. The shooter may see us as well. And with those lights coming on in those buildings, someone will call the cops. Not what we need right now."

"If the shooter was after us, we'd already be dead. He or she probably has a silenced rifle to do that and not have us hear the shots. I don't think we're the intended victims."

"You're probably right. If we were not the intended targets, then who are the guys on the ground, and who's protecting us? Targets or not, I still don't like all the available light, even if it is faint. If the shooter changes his mind, we'd be easy targets, or some well-meaning citizen, like the woman on the boat, could describe us to the fuzz."

Virginia glanced around again. "I'll drop an EMP, and then we stroll away. There won't be lights or anything for a block or so." Virginia pulled an EMP device from her backpack, set it for 15 seconds, and tossed it into the shrubbery along the winding path. As they walked away, the EMP activated its electromagnetic pulse. Everything went dark and quiet.

CHAPTER 22

Back at their hotel, Virginia and Natalie sat sipping wine in the living room. Virginia set her glass on the coffee table. "Okay, we've had quite a night. We got a look at Gino Giacopetti's place. Heavily guarded and with a lot of security equipment. People took shots at us along the river, and two men with guns came after us. A mysterious shooter shot them but spared us."

Natalie nodded. "We also found the end to the catacomb we've been looking for."

"True. But who was our angel?"

"I don't know. But it seems someone knows we're here and has us under surveillance."

"We clearly aren't operating under the radar as well as we hoped." Virginia sat back, looking out the window. "Okay, what do we know? We have a priest who gave us Gino Giacopetti's name and said the church had an interest in him concerning the theft. We've got a map showing the catacombs of interest, including a side tunnel to Giacopetti's home. We've got a section of the catacomb that is not on any regular maps but is on the quilt map."

Natalie finished her wine and set the glass down. "We've got a dead army lieutenant that was behind the original theft in 1945. We found a couple of pieces of Etruscan jewelry in the cave system on the *Circle A ranch* that was his. He probably had help that he stiffed."

"Don't forget the Grand Knights. They are working for someone. Giacopetti maybe?"

"Then there is the Pyramid Society and Giulio Cesare. Monsignor John Copello said they are part of the church, but I still have doubts." Natalie bit her lower lip. "Don't forget Franco Volpe. He had a child we can't find."

"There is the question of who Eric Bauer really was. An Italian spy working on a ranch during the World War II? Not buying it. So, we've got zilch."

"We got a nice trip to Rome." Natalie rose and paced. "But we have a tunnel off the suspected catacomb to investigate. Does it still have treasure in it or is it just another catacomb someone left off a map?"

"Humph." Virginia watched Natalie pace. "Please sit down. I can't think with you going back and forth."

Natalie plopped onto a chair. "Tell me again why we're going to crash Giacopetti's party. Couldn't we just walk up to his door and knock?"

"Going to the party unobtrusively may allow us to mingle with his associates and learn something before we actually meet the man."

"And how do we do that?" The phone on the desk rang. Natalie climbed to her feet and answered it. "Hello?"

"Ms. North. This is Luigi."

Natalie waved Virginia over and held the phone receiver so they could both listen. "What can we do for you, Luigi?"

"I heard from my contacts at the police that suddenly every light and electronic device in a two-block radius from the river near Giacopetti's home were fried tonight. And in the same location two armed men were discovered shot to death. This couldn't be your handiwork could it?"

"The dead men, no. We wanted to escape safely, so we turned off the lights." Virginia said. "Someone shot at us by the river, then we saw the two men coming at us with guns. But before we could do anything, someone shot them."

"Who?"

"We don't know."

"Okay. Right now, the cops are looking for two unidentified blonde women. Now for the real reason I called. You two are my guests at Gino Giacopetti's party tomorrow night."

Virginia and Natalie exchanged puzzled expressions. Virginia asked, "How did you pull that off?"

"I used some unsavory contacts to wrangle three invitations. I let the word out that I have a couple of lady friends who are here from America to make discrete purchases of antiquities, especially Etruscan jewelry, and art for a well-heeled customer in the States. I said you two had the authority to make the buys and would be able get the merchandise back into the U.S. undetected."

Natalie frowned. "That worked?"

"Yep. It's called greed. I'll pick you up tomorrow night at seven." He hung up.

Virginia padded back to the couch and sat. "Who would have guessed we'd get invitations? We don't need to crash the party."

"No. Giacopetti knows we're coming." Natalie sighed, "*Qui morituri te salutant vos.*"

"Those who are about to die salute you? I love your optimism and your Latin."

"Thank you. We haven't gone yet. And, anything can happen while we're there."

"Yeah, going is one thing, coming out alive is another."

At seven the following evening, the phone rang. Natalie picked up the handset and answered. "Hello?"

"This is the concierge, madam. There is a gentleman here with your car."

"What's his name?"

"Just a moment." A couple of seconds passed. "Mr. Luigi Bono."

"Good. Please tell the gentleman we'll be right down."

"Very good, madam." He hung up.

Natalie yelled at the bedroom, "Virginia, our chariot's here."

"Okay." Virginia looked around the room, picked up her purse, and walked into the living room. "I think we have everything, let's go."

Natalie placed the miniature camera inside an artificial flower arrangement on a table across from their room door. "Now we can see if we get any visitors while we are enjoying the evening."

They spotted Luigi leaning against a table in the lobby. Virginia quickly scanned the room for anything unusual or someone taking more than a casual interest in them. She sighed. That was a waste of time, most of the men stopped and stared. Natalie walked a few steps ahead of Virginia. Natalie's blonde hair bounced across her shoulders. Her black dress hung just above her knees and the V-cut bodice exposed just enough of her breasts to be enticing to any man. Virginia followed in a low cut, short, fire engine red dress that clung to her body like paint. Her short blonde hair styled in a flip moved with her swaying hips as she strolled toward Luigi. She and Natalie stopped a few feet from the grinning Luigi.

"*Buona sera*," Virginia said.

Luigi straightened up. "*Buona sera* to both of you. My God, you two look ravishing. You could stop traffic."

Natalie put her hand on her hip. "Thank you, sir. Do you think we'll get Gino's interest?"

"You'll probably get the interest of every man there, but I would be surprised if he didn't make a bee-line to you right away." Luigi motioned toward the front door. "Shall we proceed to dinner? Our car is a Steadman."

They followed Luigi out the doors to a black Mercedes limo. Slipping into the back last, Luigi slid next to Natalie and Virginia and closed the door.

Luigi leaned forward. "Isidoro's *per favore*, John."

"*Si.*" The car rolled out of the driveway and into the evening Rome traffic.

Virginia settled into the soft seat and glanced at the bar and mini fridge. "Do you own this little beauty or are we renting it?"

"Neither. It's one of Uncle's vehicles that isn't registered to the embassy and thus not traceable to it. It comes with some special features, like it's bullet proof and sound-proof. It is also shielded from electronic eavesdropping, is immune to EMP attack, can outrun most other vehicles, has special tires that won't go flat if punctured, and has some nasty defense, systems should we need them. Oh, and John works for me."

Natalie rubbed the soft leather seat. "Nice, I could get used to this."

After dinner, the limo pulled up in front of the roped entrance to Gino Giacopetti's villa. The cream and light red stucco building with a thick glass window blended in with its neighbors. Police directed traffic around the line of expensive automobiles dropping off guests. A doorman opened the limo door and helped Luigi, Natalie, and Virginia out of the car. Straightening their clothes, they strutted toward the entrance. There, a large black man in a tuxedo checked their invitations to a master list and noted the ladies' names.

They entered what appeared to be the main hall and were directed to a well-appointed, large living room, where guests milled around statues, figurines and various oil paintings displayed with accent lighting. The room resembled a museum, including the furniture. Leather couches and chairs, solid-looking wooden tables, large wood cabinets, and glass-fronted display cases holding expensive artifacts, sat strategically positioned around the room. A Victorian desk and high-backed leather chair, in the corner near the window overlooking the street, seemed to be the only things out of place. A food buffet stretched across the far wall. Soft music wafted from the string quartet playing toward the rear on a raised platform. Waiters in short white jackets offered them champagne filled flutes.

Sipping her drink, Virginia cast an eye about the room full of people wearing expensive attire. *Obviously not the 'off-the rack' crowd.* She noticed two more rooms toward the rear and doors on the right that were closed with men standing in front of them. To the right and about two-thirds of the way to the back, more people gathered. Virginia leaned toward Luigi, "How do we play this? Do we split up or stay with you?"

"I'd suggest you two wander off and leave me to the wiles of the other ladies. Then our host can scope you out. Better if I'm not there guarding the wares, as it were."

"Got it. We'll catch up with you later," Virginia said.

"Have fun. I'll keep an eye on things. Should something look wrong, I'll come and get you."

"Okay." *Nothing like walking into the lion's den.*

Natalie studied a bronze sculpture. "This label says this statue is three hundred years older than the Roman Empire. That would make it Etruscan, wouldn't it?"

Virginia looked at the brass label affixed to the bottom of the stand. "Yes, very good. Looks like I'm rubbing off on you."

"Yeah, that and I know a fellow who got an award from the Archaeological Institute of America for something or other about the Etruscans and gold, I think," Natalie said.

"Who's that?"

"My friend, Dr. Ciambrone."

"I remember him. As I recall, he really likes you. Just how well do you two know each other?"

"Quite well, matter of fact. He is a close friend."

They both jerked at the sound of a man's baritone voice directly behind them.

"*Buona sera, parla Italiano?*"

Virginia and Natalie turned to face a man about five-foot five inches tall, in a dark, pinstriped, three-piece suit with an Egyptian-cloth white shirt and red paisley tie. The cut of the suit accentuated his firm, beefy physique. His graying pencil mustache was a contrast to his slicked back, jet-black hair and his olive complexion. Virginia's eyes dilated. She recognized Gino Giacopetti.

"*Non parlo Italiano.* Just English. Sorry," Virginia said as her heart missed a beat.

Natalie leaned close to Virginia and whispered, "That didn't take long."

CHAPTER 23

"Gino Giacopetti. At your service." He bowed, took Virginia's hand, and kissed it.

Virginia smiled. "I'm Virginia Davies-Clark."

He then faced Natalie. His eyes widened. The corners of his mouth turned up into a big smile. "Who is this beautiful lady?"

Natalie took a deep breath, drawing Gino's eyes to her chest. "Natalie North, sir. I love your home."

Beaming, Gino put his arms around their backs and directed them toward the food buffet. "I'm happy you came to my home and party. I understand you are interested in obtaining unusual pieces of art or antiques for a discriminating buyer in the United States." He stopped at the table and offered them plates.

"Yes," Natalie said. She pointed to a life-size bronze statue of a woman holding a baby. "Is that Roman?"

"*Si*. Roman. You know about these things?"

"In our line of work, I must know about such things. It's the patina and the form that made me think it was Roman." *That, and Virginia explaining it to me at the Vatican Museum on a similar piece.*

"Good. Very good. Let me show you around." Gino took Natalie by the elbow and strolled off with her, waving his arms as he talked. Natalie pressed close to him and touched his arm. *He knows we're interested in buying antiquities for some rich collector. Luigi's subterfuge seems to be working. I can't tell if he's aware of who we really are or not.*

Virginia watched them go, put down her plate, then meandered to a set of unguarded double doors at the rear of the room. She stopped at a picture hanging on the wall near the door and pretended to take an interest while scrutinizing the door. Private was scribed on a brass plate on the right-hand door. There was no guard. so she thought it must be locked and alarmed.

She strolled around the room looking at the various works and noted the security set up for the area. *Cameras, motion detectors, and pressure pads under statues and weight alarms for the hanging pictures. Heat detec-*

tors. Just like what we have at my museum. Nice, but not unusual. She looked for Natalie and spotted her animatedly talking to Gino about something in a glass case. Then Gino led her toward a set of guarded double doors. Virginia took a glass of wine from a passing waiter and continued her pass around the room, edging her way toward Luigi, who was entangled with two young women.

Luigi noticed Virginia meandering toward him. He excused himself and stepped to Virginia at the buffet table. "What do you think of the villa?"

"It looks like a cross between the British Museum and an expensive bordello."

Luigi chuckled. "You have a way with words. How's the recon going?"

"So far, so good. Your deception about Natalie and me being interested in antiquities seems to be working out."

"Good. But be careful. If he's after the treasure, then he may already know who you really are."

"Keep your phone handy. If we need help, I'll call you or send a smoke signal."

"Try sending me a 911 text. Don't burn the place down sending smoke signals. The local authorities frown on that."

"Party pooper." Virginia glanced around. "Natalie's disappeared through those doors with Giacopetti. Maybe I should go find her."

"Natalie strikes me as someone who can take care of herself." Luigi eyed the portal. "And note the large guards. Obviously Giacopetti doesn't want to be disturbed. How are you going to get past them?"

"Maybe with a diversion."

"Virginia, they won't leave their posts." Luigi's eyes widened. "And what did you have in mind for a diversion… start an earthquake, a flood?"

"Of course not. I don't know what I could use. I don't want to endanger any of the guests or treasures around here. Maybe a—how do you start an earthquake?"

"You can't."

"Too bad."

Virginia's satellite phone vibrated in her purse. She discreetly pulled it out and examined the flash message. "That was fast. It… Natalie found something, but Giacopetti must have her trapped."

Luigi leaned toward her and looked at the message. "That's a 911. We need to help her."

"You get the car and be ready for a quick exit. I'll go find her. Watch for my signal."

"I can follow your phone with mine. I'll be close by."

Virginia turned away from the table, then tripped a woman in a tight, blue dress. She stumbled into the man next to her, splashing him with her drink. He caught her before she tumbled to the floor. A gentleman a few feet away rushed toward her. He pushed the man holding her and yelled something in Italian. A shouting and shoving match escalated. Virginia hurried to the guards by the double doors. "Help." She pointed. "There's a fight over there. Some of these beautiful pieces of art could be damaged."

One of the guards pushed his way through the throng of confused party goers. Virginia pulled a canister of DMSO and ketamine from her purse and discretely sprayed a little on the back of the remaining guard's hand. He gazed confused at his hand and wiped off the liquid on his pants then stumbled backward against the wall and slid down, unconscious. Virginia poked a man nearby and said, "This gentleman needs help." As the man knelt next to the guard, Virginia slipped through the doorway into a hall containing a crystal chandelier, polished French provincial furniture, and rooms off both sides. Moving down the carpeted passageway, she listened for any sound of Natalie and Gino. Halfway down the corridor, a door opened. A tall man in a dark suit stepped out and gave her a questioning expression. Virginia straightened her dress and smiled. She took a deep breath that strained the fabric of her dress across her chest then said, "*Il signor Giacopetti mi ha chiamato. Come faccio a trovarlo?*" *I hope I asked for Giacopetti and not the weather report.*

He smiled and pointed toward the stairs. "*Giù per le scale, terza porta a sinistra.*" He looked in the direction she had come from. "*Cosa sta succedendo là fuori?*"

Virginia struggled with the translation. *Downstairs and third door on the... sinistra? Oh, yeah, on the left.* She smiled at the man. *I think he asked what all the ruckus is about.* She pointed. "Fight. A guard got sick."

"*Combattere? Una guardia è malata?*"

She nodded. "Yes. *Sì.*" *I hope I got the translations right.*

He stepped around her and rushed toward the double doors as Virginia hurried to the stairs. At the bottom of the stairway, she found herself in the middle of another corridor. *Great, looks like a basement. Now, which way?* She turned left and padded down the hallway. She stopped when she heard a commotion from above. At the sound of footfalls on the stairs, Virginia ducked into a room. She froze. Natalie huddled on a couch across the room. Two large men who resembled football halfbacks in suits stood in front of her. Giacopetti sat next to her. Virginia stepped into the room. "What the hell is going on?"

Giacopetti jumped to his feet and pointed. "Grab her!"

One of the men near Natalie rushed toward Virginia and reached out to grab her.

Virginia fired the canister she used on the other guard with the remaining DMSO cocktail into his face. He stumbled then fell face down on the carpet. The second man moved toward Virginia but fell when Natalie tripped him.

Giacopetti seized Natalie's arm. She twisted away. He grabbed her again as she slid across the couch. She reached under her skirt, pulled out one of the composite knives that Luigi had given them, and sliced Giacopetti's wrist. He yanked his arm back and said something in Italian that she figured was not nice. Natalie hopped to her feet, kicked the guard trying to rise in his head, and ran toward Virginia. "We need to blow this popsicle stand."

Virginia led Natalie out into the corridor, then toward what appeared to be a back staircase. Giacopetti screamed something unintelligible at them as three men at the bottom of the stairs above raced in pursuit. The women dashed to the back staircase and scurried up. They exited the stairwell into the kitchen. The startled staff watched as they ran through and out the back door.

Virginia text messaged Luigi. *911 back gate.* The women ran toward the gate in the ivy-covered stone wall they had seen from the alley. It was locked. Virginia frantically looked around. She spotted a ladder on the ground near the wall. "We go over the wall."

Natalie heard the back door of the house bang open and the sound of men coming from the house behind her. "We won't have time. And how are we going to climb that ladder and go over the wall dressed like this?"

"Okay, plan B," Virginia said. She ran to the gate, turned on the laser in her watch and cut the lock's hasp. She stood still for a second. "Wow. That really worked. For being small, this thing has more umph than I thought."

"Admire your handiwork later. Let's go."

Virginia pushed the gate door open, as men poured out of the kitchen into the yard. Without a backward glance, Virginia and Natalie raced out into the dark alley and toward the street behind the villa. A black Mercedes limo rounded the corner and roared toward them. Virginia pulled her gun from her purse. She recognized Luigi's car and then relaxed.

The vehicle screeched to a stop and the rear door opened. Luigi stuck his head out. "Get in. We've got to go, quickly."

They jumped into the rear seat as the car sped away. The driver said something to Luigi.

Virginia glanced at Luigi. "What did he say?"

"We're being pursued." He leaned toward the driver. "Lose them, John."

"That was close." Natalie sat back on the soft leather seat and let out a sigh. "This gets better by the minute."

CHAPTER 24

Virginia attached her seatbelt, then turned to Natalie. "What happened back there? What was Giacopetti doing to you?"

Natalie turned and glanced out the rear window at a silver SUV speeding toward them. "The guy can't take no for an answer. Giacopetti knows exactly who we are. He knows we're looking for the World War II treasure. He heard about us being buyers of stolen merchandise but figured if we are, then maybe we're looking for the World War II treasure as an under-the-radar score. I encouraged him to think that. He was surprised that we were in Rome, knew about him, and had managed to get into his party."

Virginia pushed a strand of blonde hair from her eyes. "And? Why is he looking for it? Why is he concerned about us?"

"He thinks we know where the treasure is. He's had someone in Texas pursuing the treasure that was taken there by Lt. Cumo and trying to keep track of our activities, but without success. I asked who. You'll never guess who it is."

Virginia closed her eyes and gave her head a little shake. "Guessing games now? Who is it?"

"The Grand Knight Real Estate folks. I think the head honcho there is going to meet with some unpleasant people soon. Giacopetti is pissed. He mentioned something about concrete and the Gulf of Mexico."

"That's not good. Did he say why he's so hell-bent on locating the treasure?"

"Yes. It seems his father and another guy helped Lieutenant Cumo obtain certain works of art from the Vatican without its permission. They were to split the bounty three ways and enjoy the rewards. Only Cumo stiffed them."

"Giacopetti is still holding a grudge about his father being cut out of the treasure?"

"You bet. These Italians hold grudges for generations, or so I'm told."

"Why now?" Virginia asked.

"Because there are now others who want the treasure and are not prone to share. And he knows the church is still hunting for them."

"Did he say who they are?"

"No. But when he mentioned the treasure, he momentarily looked… like the cat who ate the canary. Something's up."

"You got some good information out of him. He actually told you all this without you inflicting pain and with your clothes on?"

Natalie grinned. "Yep. I have my ways."

"Why the 911 call? What was he going to do to you?"

"He figured because we were in Rome, we were on to something. He's unnaturally nervous. Who knows, maybe he already has the treasure. He was going to have his goons extract the information from little ole defenseless me. Then he was going to have you captured and see what he could get from you, too. That's when you barged in."

"Barged in? I was coming to save your ass. You defenseless? Are you kidding?"

"I had him right where I wanted him, talking. And his henchmen had the collective IQ of a turnip." Natalie chuckled. "But thanks for the fourth down assist."

Luigi cleared his throat. "As much as I hate to interrupt this interesting little discussion, we still have a problem. That SUV is still behind us and gaining."

Virginia turned and stared out the window. "Can't we shake him?"

"We can outrun him, but not in the heart of the city. Streets are too narrow, too many traffic lights, cars, police, and there are a lot of pedestrians."

"Then we need to get creative. What kind of countermeasures do you have on this heap?"

"Heap? It is a state of the art—"

"Yeah, yeah… state of the art you aren't utilizing. What have we got to play with?"

Luigi wet his lips. "Smoke, oil slick, spikes dropped from the back to shred tires, and a combination smoke-gas compound guaranteed to cause you to vomit violently. And of course, we can drop an EMP device or shoot through gunports."

Natalie eyed Luigi. "And just why do we still have him on our tail? Use all of the countermeasures… except the EMP or shooting stuff."

"That would alert the police."

"That would also save our asses. Do it!" Virginia said.

Luigi leaned forward and said something to the driver.

"I know just the road, sir," The driver said. He accelerated and swung the car into an empty, narrow alley and carefully slipped between buildings. "Now, sir?"

Luigi nodded to the driver. "Let it rip."

The driver opened a lid on the center console and rapidly pushed several buttons.

Virginia, Luigi, and Natalie looked out the back window and watched. Smoke quickly obliterated the view, but the sound of the pursuing vehicle colliding with obstacles, tires blowing, and people in distress told them what had happened.

Virginia turned, sat back, and sighed. "At least we didn't hurt anyone besides them."

The driver exited the alley onto an avenue and turned up the police scanner. In a minute, calls for police and medical assistance and a description of a mysterious black vehicle with a partial license number that caused the incidents was broadcast. The driver turned with a big grin. "I'll rotate the license." He pressed another button, then melted them into traffic and drove toward Piazza del Popolo.

Virginia looked at Luigi. "Rotate the license?"

"The police have a description of this car and a partial license number. But the license number they have won't do them any good. We now have a new one. Our vehicle is like many others in Rome. We are now invisible. The car the police are looking for disappeared."

Natalie nodded. "Nice. Can I take this thing home when we're done in Rome?"

Luigi chuckled. "I'm afraid not, Ms. North. Uncle Sam would not take kindly to my giving it to you. Sorry. Anyway, you have a lot of playthings I already gave you."

Virginia glanced out the front window. "Where are we going?"

"We're taking a roundabout way back to your hotel," Luigi said.

Virginia opened the little bar and pulled out a beer. "Lookie here, Shiner Bock. I can use this about now. I see you stock this... beautiful machine with fine Texas beer."

Luigi smiled. "Glad you like it. From what Ms. North said, Giacopetti will be after the two of you. What are your plans?"

"Not sure right this minute. Natalie and I will go over what information we've got and what she learned tonight, then strategize a plan for the next few days. It will include exploring the catacombs we found." Virginia watched as Natalie mixed a small bottle of rum with orange juice and drank it. "That went down fast."

Natalie nodded. "Yeah, my nerves just got the message about what we've been doing and are staging a protest."

Luigi looked behind them. "No one following. You two need to be very careful. Giacopetti will be searching for you and will also be on his guard. Then you have your guardian angel who shot those men last night to think about."

"We'll be ready," Virginia said.

Natalie finished off another drink. "We have a saying where I come from. Never give your opponent a break unless it's his legs."

Luigi shook his head. "Oh, God. You two can't leave a trail of blood, dead bodies, or broken limbs across Rome."

"You're right." Virginia finished her beer. "Someone will definitely notice."

CHAPTER 25

The next afternoon, Virginia turned to find Natalie looking peaked. Her shoulders sagged, and her backpack hung limply from her hand as they walked into a shop near the Spanish Steps.

Natalie stepped to the counter and asked in a low voice, *"Dov'e il bagno?"*

The woman pointed to a sign on the opposite wall.

Natalie turned her head and looked in the direction the woman pointed and nodded. *"Grazie."* She looked at Virginia. "Go on ahead. I'll catch up in a few minutes."

"Are you okay? Do you need some water?"

"Yes, but I think I need to take a potty break and freshen up or I'm not going to make it. My kidney just floated past my eyeballs." Natalie shuffled toward the restroom. Returning, she found Virginia studying her hand drawn map. "What are you doing?"

"I think I found a way into the catacomb we're interested in that won't draw attention to ourselves."

"This doesn't involve hiking all over Rome, does it?"

"No, not all over Rome. We aren't that far, and there are shops along the way."

"Shops? Okay, lead the way, but slowly."

They wound through narrow streets cramped by three-and four-story white and pink buildings with iron balconies. Massed flowers spilled down like pink and white waterfalls as they entered an area near the Vatican. Down a couple of streets, clotheslines stretched between buildings on the second and third floors held garments swaying in the slight breeze. The ribbon of building was cut by a wandering path of greenery, including pink geraniums, palm trees, ilex, and oleander. The street was busy, with small canopy-covered booths displaying various religious items, clothes, jewelry, and trinkets. The narrow walkways between the booths were crowded with shopkeepers, hawking their wares and browsing tourists.

Virginia jostled people as she moved between the booths with Natalie behind her. "Looks like market day."

Natalie grabbed Virginia's sleeve and stopped at a stand. "Look at these necklaces. They are beautiful." She picked one up and held it up to Virginia. "Don't look now, but see that pretty, brown-haired woman with the black glasses, red pullover top, and jeans three stalls behind us, trying to look interested in that awful hat?"

"Yes, I see her. Isn't she one of the women at Gino's party? She spent a lot of time examining the artifacts in one of the larger display cases."

"I think so. She's taken quite an interest in us. Shall we lose her?"

"Let's."

They hurried through the crowd, moving people out of their way as they went. The residents, who seemed tired of being hassled by the two American women, hindered the woman following them. Virginia and Natalie turned down an alley. Two men, weating tight jeans and black t-shirts, leaned against a parked vehicle. The men straightened up, crossed their arms, and blocked the tiny road.

Natalie stopped. "Not again!"

Virginia sighed. "Looks like we have a problem."

"Yeah. Two of them and maybe a third, if the woman in the market catches up with us."

Virginia reached under the back of her blouse. "Luigi did say our pistols were silenced, didn't he?"

"Yep. Just a popping sound. Think we'll get to try them?"

"I hope not, but get ready." Virginia strutted toward the men with Natalie moving to her left side a few feet away. Her right hand held at the small of her back.

"*Per Favore*, move out of our way," Virginia said.

The man with long, black hair down past his shoulders pointed at Virginia. "No. You give us what you have in those bags."

Natalie straightened to her full five-foot height. "Like hell we will! Now move your sorry asses out of our way."

"Big talk from such a short woman." The other man pulled a knife with a long shiny blade. "Give us the bags."

Virginia and Natalie drew their pistols. Virginia stepped forward. "Drop the knife, and get lost, before we really get mad."

The knife wielding man lunged toward Virginia, screaming something in Italian.

Virginia fired twice. One shot hit the pavement near his feet. The second one tore through his lower pant leg, causing a red stain to spread on the fabric. He stumbled; his face contorted in pain as his leg buckled under him. He dropped the knife and fell to the pavement, grabbed his leg, and rolled around, rapidly rattling off words Virginia and Natalie didn't understand. The other man lifted him up and supporting him under his shoulder, hobbled down the street, away from Virginia and Natalie. As they lumbered away, the long-haired man yelled something over his shoulder at them.

Virginia looked around, then retrieved the two bullet casings the gun had ejected. "No point in helping the police. Let's get out of here before the cops arrive."

Natalie picked up the knife and joined Virginia walking down the alley. "Good shot, Annie Oakley. I'm usually the trigger happy one." She examined the knife. "Think they were Gino's men?"

They strolled down the road to a wider street and up a slight hill. "No. I think they were cheap crooks, who saw two tourist women and tried to rob us." She glanced at the blade Natalie was holding. "Nice knife."

"Yeah. Looks like quality, and an expensive piece. He's not going to like the fact that he lost it, especially to two women."

"I don't think he liked being shot, either."

Natalie tossed the knife into a dumpster. "Are we heading for the hotel now?"

"We should, before that woman in the market catches up or we have any more shootouts. We can come back here later. The entrance to the catacomb isn't far."

"I doubt we'll have any more trouble. Let's take a quick look at the catacomb."

"I thought you were tired. Anyway, we have reservations for dinner and need to get cleaned up."

"Reservations? Dinner? Why didn't you say so before?" Natalie glanced at the buildings. "Which way to the hotel?"

As they turned onto a narrow road, a small truck passed, then stopped in front of them.

Virginia stopped. "You had to jinx us, didn't you?"

"It's part of my charm."

The brown-haired woman from the market hopped out and strolled toward Virginia and Natalie. They pulled their pistols. The woman stopped in front of them and smiled. "You are Virginia Davies Clark and Natalie North, correct?" she said in English.

Virginia swallowed. "Yes; who are you?"

"A friend. Let me move the truck, then we can go to that restaurant over there, have coffee, and talk."

"Why should we go with you? Do you work for Gino Giacopetti?"

The woman laughed. "Giacopetti? Gracious me, no."

Virginia and Natalie watched the woman park the truck halfway down the block, near the restaurant. Virginia mumbled, "I think we need to keep our weapons handy. No telling who might be with her or following."

"Way ahead of you," Natalie said as she walked toward the restaurant.

Outside the restaurant, there was an open-air seating area protected by large ceramic pots with miniature orange trees, roses, rosemary, bergamot, shaddock, and other brightly colored flowers. There they found the brown-haired woman sitting at an iron table under a red umbrella. She waved them to the table. "Please, have a seat."

Virginia and Natalie took the chairs opposite her. Virginia leaned forward. "Who are you, and what do you want with us?"

"And how do you happen to know who we are?" Natalie asked.

The woman motioned for the waiter. "*Tre caffè, per favore.*" After he stepped away, the woman smiled. "I am Dr. Camella Pisciolo. I am an archeologist. I work at the Vatican, on loan from the Smithsonian." She reached for her purse and stopped when Virginia slid her hand into her backpack. "I'll move slowly." Camella removed her wallet, opened it, and displayed her Smithsonian credentials.

"I'll need to verify this," said Virginia. She pulled out her sat phone and called Tom Mason at the Smithsonian.

Agent Mason answered his phone. "To what do I owe this call before my morning coffee, Virginia?"

"Oops. I forgot about the time difference. Good morning, Tom."

"Yeah, good morning. Okay, what can I do for you? You're not in jail, are you? You two haven't managed to kill anyone yet, have you? You haven't set Rome on fire I hope."

"No. But I need to verify someone's identity. She says she works for the Smithsonian."

"Oh? Who?"

"Dr. Camella Pisciolo."

"I know her. Just a minute; let me check her whereabouts." She heard typing on a keyboard. "Yes, Dr. Pisciolo is an archeologist we have on loan to the Vatican. She is quite attractive, as I recall. Her male colleagues miss her. She's working on some artifacts from the U.S. that may actually be Roman," Tom said.

"Someone brought them to the U.S.?" asked Virginia.

"Yeah. The Romans. Ask her who her favorite football team is. And ask her, if the California State Polytechnic University at Pomona played football against USC, who does she think would win?"

"Why?"

"Just ask."

Virginia looked at Camella. "Who's your favorite football team? And if Cal Poly, Pomona played football against USC, who do you think would win?"

"I like the Green Bay Packers. And there would be no game. Cal Poly doesn't have a football team."

Virginia spoke into the phone, "She said—"

"I heard her. Send me her picture from your phone."

"Okay." Virginia snapped a picture of Camella and forwarded it to Tom.

"Yes, that's Camella." She heard Tom sigh. "Tell her that her colleagues here are depressed that she's still in Rome and they miss her."

"Okay. Thanks, Tom." Virginia disconnected. She smiled at Camella. "The Smithsonian says you're for real. Now what's this little meeting about?"

Camella's face darkened. "Locating the Vatican treasure that went missing during World War II, and keeping you two alive."

CHAPTER 26

The women stopped talking until the waiter served their coffee and withdrew. Then Virginia leaned on the table. "Why are you concerned about us locating the Vatican treasure and keeping us alive? I'd think you have more than your share of issues with what Tom said you're working on."

Camille sipped her coffee. "My project and what you are searching for are related."

"Huh?"

"That was my response, too, when I heard about it." Camille shifted in her seat. "I'm investigating some Roman artifacts discovered in a cave in the Catskill mountains of New York. They had been buried there for close to a couple of millennia. The Smithsonian determined they are real, what they are, and how long they were there by various scientific tests. There're more in Wisconsin and Texas near where you're from. Unfortunately, some made it back to Italy, and a few were sent to the Vatican Museum for study. This opened a bag of worms."

"I bet. But what does it have to do with the missing Etruscan treasure?"

"During my research, I stumbled upon some information related to the Vatican stolen treasure and something else that belonged to the church."

Natalie set her cup down. "I bet they are pissed that the treasure was stolen."

"You could say that. They assigned one of the churches oldest secret societies to investigate and retrieve it."

Virginia sipped her coffee. "I know I'm going to be sorry I asked… but who is it?"

"It's called the Pyramid Society. Its leader is known as Giulio Cesare. That name is used by all the society's leaders. The actual identity of the head person is known only to the Pope, a couple of cardinals, and a bishop in Rome. It is very hush-hush," Camille said. She finished her coffee.

"Why is it so secret?"

"According to rumors, and what little I could get from some of the Vatican security people and a priest friend, over the past centuries it has functioned as a spy organization, conducted assassinations, clandestinely obtained various items the church wanted, and much more."

"What do they do when not chasing stuff, killing, or spying?" Natalie asked.

"No one will openly say for sure. But they have you two in their sights."

"They know about us?"

"Yes."

"Why are they interested in just us?" Virginia asked as she sipped the last of her coffee.

"You are seeking something they want. And no, not just you. Gino Giacopetti has managed to get their attention, and they think there is another person or organization involved."

"We figured there may be someone else after it. Okay. The church wants their treasure back. They have wanted it for over seventy years. But why use the secret society?"

"Because a secret the church was keeping got inadvertently stolen, along with the Etruscan treasure. That's why they didn't call in the various police agencies. They are keeping the search in-house."

"What is this big secret the church is concerned about?" Virginia asked.

Camille shrugged her shoulders. "I don't know."

"How did you find out the Pyramid Society is interested in us?"

"Well, it's complicated."

"Uncomplicate it," Virginia said.

Camille took a breath. "It has to do with me working for the Smithsonian, the Roman artifacts I mentioned that were in the U.S. long before Columbus or the Vikings get there, your involvement with your friend's ranch, the treasure, and my friendship with a certain… church person who would like to meet you."

"Cloak and dagger stuff? A mysterious church person wants to meet us? Really?" Natalie shook her head. "We're not going to like this, are we?"

Camille smiled. "Would you like to meet the bishop who is involved with the Pyramid Society and is one of its overseers?"

Virginia's eyes widened. "Sure. You know who he is?"

"Yes."

"What exactly does he want to talk to us about? How does he know Natalie and me?"

"He knows you work for the Smithsonian Central Security Service, and he believes you will be discreet and will help the church. He knows you are not in this to keep the treasure for yourselves. A couple of days ago, he came to me and asked that I set up a meeting. He didn't want to do it directly, due to all the secrecy stuff around the Vatican, the society, and his need to stay in the shadows. As to the topic, I don't know."

Virginia frowned. "Are you serious?"

Camille nodded. "Totally."

"He trusts you as well?"

"Yes. Are you interested?" Camille asked.

"Are you sure this isn't a setup?"

"Around the Vatican, you can be *sure* of two things. First, when the Vatican does something, there is always a benefit for the church. Second, love is a word seldom used at the Vatican. Is it a setup? No."

Natalie rubbed her forehead. "If we say yes, how will it play out?"

"If you agree to the meeting, he will come to you."

"Do you trust him?" Natalie asked.

"Better question is, can we trust him?" Virginia asked.

Camille sat back. "He said to ask you how you two managed to shut down all the lights and electronics near the river the other night."

"He knows about that?" Virginia jerked up straight. "The church protected us?"

Camille smiled. "Two shots took out the men chasing you with guns that evening."

Virginia looked at Natalie, then back at Camille. "You're right. Okay, in that case I guess we should meet him."

Camille pulled out her cell phone and sent a text. She glanced around, then stood as a priest stepped out of a gray Fiat parked at the curb.

Virginia and Natalie turned and gasped.

Monsignor John Copello strolled to the restaurant and smiled at the women. They noticed his black suit now had purple buttons and a purple sash with fringe. He wore a purple skullcap over his graying hair and a Pectoral cross suspended from a gold chain. They rose.

Virginia cleared her throat. "You're a bishop?"

"Nice to see you again, ladies. I'm sorry for the subterfuge back in Texas. It was necessary. But I am glad to see you both. And yes, I am a bishop." He turned to Camille. "Thank you for setting this meeting up, Camille."

Camille nodded, then looked around. "This isn't exactly clandestine, Your Excellency."

"This is the last place anyone would look for us." Bishop Copello gestured toward the chairs. "Please sit. We have some things to discuss."

Virginia swallowed. "I have a question. Back in Texas, did Captain Steadman know you're a bishop?"

Bishop Copello nodded. "Yes. I'm sorry. I briefed him and then swore him to secrecy. My mission was secret. The last thing I needed was for the Bishop of Austin or any church leaders to know I was really a bishop from Rome. That would cause a lot of protocols to be observed, and my mission to be compromised. The fewer people who knew, the better. Your police captain thinks very highly of you, Virginia."

"I'm going to have a talk with the captain when I get home." Virginia looked at her coffee cup. "I think I need something stronger than coffee."

Bishop Copello waved the waiter to the table. *"Vi preghiamo di portarci una bottiglia del vostro miglior vino bianco."*

Camille smiled. "He just ordered us a bottle of their best white wine."

"This is one of my favorite haunts. Their wine list is first class." Bishop Copello patted his stomach. "The linguini with meat sauce is outstanding. Would you like to try some?"

"Yes." Natalie sat back, casually leaned toward Virginia, and whispered, "Something seems off."

Virginia gave a slight nod.

CHAPTER 27

An hour, two bottles of wine, and small orders of linguini with meat sauce later, Bishop Copello nodded to each of the women. "Well? What do you think?"

Natalie used the cloth napkin to wipe her mouth. "Superb. I see why you like this establishment. How's the pizza, and do they deliver?"

"Good and yes. They use fresh ingredients and Italian cheeses."

"I've died and gone to heaven," Natalie said.

Virginia slid her dish back. "Very good. But it is getting late, and we haven't discussed why you wanted to talk to us."

Copello wet his lips. "I know you two met Gino Giacopetti and his henchmen. I also know that there were two men gunning for you the other night. The treasure hunt has heated up."

"Did the Vatican protect us the other night?" Virginia asked.

"We have many organizations within the church, and we have… relations with others as needed. We thought you two needed some assistance and asked a certain party to provide it."

Virginia closed her eyes in thought. *In today's world, I don't think the church would hire contract killers. So, something is wrong with his story.*

Natalie frowned. "Camille mentioned a church secret that was… accidently stolen along with the treasure. Was it an accident or was it the target of the theft?"

"Because it never turned up, we think it was taken by mistake."

Virginia leaned forward. "What is the secret?"

Bishop Copello fingered his pectoral cross. "From what Camille said about you two, what we gathered from the Smithsonian, and what I learned from visiting you in Texas, I feel that I can trust you."

Virginia and Natalie nodded. Virginia shifted in her seat. "What's this secret you want back?"

"Do you remember the stories about Mary Magdalene?" asked Bishop Copello.

Virginia frowned then brightened. "Yeah. She was a companion of

Jesus when he was alive and when he was crucified. Dan Brown wrote a book with her as the subject. So did other authors."

"I heard the church finally said she was not a prostitute," Natalie said.

"Yes. You are both right," Bishop Copello stated.

Natalie leaned forward. "So, what's the big secret? She didn't exist?"

"No. She existed. There are actual records of her existence."

"There are? Okay, so she was real. She was a friend of Jesus. What's the problem?"

Bishop Copello sat back. "The problem with the old church stories, especially about saints, is that they are muddled. A lot of the early saints never existed or were real people, but the stories got enhanced by the simple way of people telling and retelling stories about them back then. The church, in the early years, made the saints because they helped foster the building of the faith. We now require more solid evidence to make someone a saint."

Virginia twisted her back then asked, "What's that got to do with Mary?"

"There are all sorts of stories about Mary Magdalene. After two thousand years, trying to weed out the truth from the fiction is difficult. Starting in early High Middle Ages, writers in western Europe began developing elaborate fictional biographies of Mary Magdalene's life, in which they heavily embellished upon the vague details given in the gospels. For example, early depictions of her are that Mary was a wanton woman and she had been possessed by seven demons. In the first century, demons were widely believed to be the cause of physical and psychological illness. Because Mary is listed as one of the women who were supporting Jesus's ministry financially, she was considered to have been relatively wealthy and literate. The places where she and the other women are mentioned, throughout the gospels, strongly indicate that they were vital to Jesus's ministry. All four canonical gospels agree that Mary Magdalene, along with several other women, watched Jesus's crucifixion from a distance. Texts portray Mary Magdalene as an apostle, as Jesus's closest and most beloved disciple, and the only one who truly understood his teachings. In the Gnostic texts, or Gnostic gospels, Mary Magdalene's closeness to Jesus results in tension with another disciple, Peter, due to her sex and Peter's envy of the special teachings given to her. The Gospel of Philip's text, where she is described as Jesus's companion, as the disciple Jesus loved the most, and the one Jesus kissed on the mouth, has led some people to conclude that she and Jesus were in a relationship. Some fiction authors, like Dan Brown, portray her as the wife of Jesus."

"So? What's this secret you are afraid of? Did she marry Jesus?"

"No. At least that's the church party line. To be honest, no one actually knows. The thing we are after is a document that the church believes was actually written by Mary Magdalene. In it, she describes her true relationship with Jesus and the torment of demonic possession and the horrors of the seven exorcisms that didn't work. She then details what Jesus did to cure her and rid her of the demons," Bishop Copello said.

Virginia frowned. "That sounds like a good thing. Why hide it?"

"Because she had a mental illness and was not demon possessed. Jesus gave her counseling and some... concoction to take. It improved or possibly cured her condition. He didn't do an exorcism. She was so grateful, that she provided him funding and became a devoted follower and companion. The document was supposedly penned in her later years and describes where she wanted to be buried when she died. This is not exactly church doctrine."

Natalie shook her head. "That doesn't seem worth hiding. Jesus did something good for her." She raised an eyebrow. "You know where she's buried?"

"I agree. But there are those who do not relish this getting out. They prefer the miracle approach. Mary plainly states that Jesus didn't do an exorcism or miraculously cure her. And she became very close to him. And to answer your question, yes, we know where she wanted to be buried. An expedition was sent to the location, and there were partial skeletal remains of a female from that time buried there. Was it really Mary Magdalene? We don't know."

Natalie looked hopeful. "Can't you use DNA, like in the cop shows?"

"The investigators did collect some viable sample material, but with all DNA testing, you need something to compare it to," Bishop Copello said. "We don't have anything else from her, or know of any descendants, so there's nothing to compare."

Virginia shrugged her shoulder. "Her document makes Jesus sound more real. He cared for her and helped her. I think the hiding of this document is a little silly."

"There are always people with different views and agendas. But whatever the real facts are, the church wants it back, that is, if it still exists. If not protected correctly, it may have disintegrated by now."

"That would solve your problem." Virginia looked up at the sky, then back at Bishop Copello. "If it is still intact, you want it before someone finds it, figures out what it is, and either puts it on Facebook or writes another book like Dan Brown's."

"Yes. If you locate the treasure, we would like you to return it and the document, if it is still with the other artifacts. The Church, through our Society, will provide you with all the information we have and support you in any way we can."

"You have more resources than we do, and you couldn't find it. What makes you believe we will?"

"Because you, Virginia, and your partners, have a history of locating lost treasures and solving mysteries. You can go places, do things, and obtain information that we cannot. You do not stop where others might. And the church needs and trusts you."

"Is the church, through the Pyramid Society, going to also continue its investigation?" Virginia asked.

"Not directly. We would like to work with you, that is, if you agree."

Virginia rubbed her forehead. *Of course they're not. Why get in our way when we can just lead them to the treasure? I didn't buy Pyramid Society and the church being together before; now I'm really not buying this church and Pyramid Society thing. Something is haywire.* "When can we get the information you have?"

"Tomorrow," Bishop Copello said.

"Including about a Jesuit priest who went missing in Texas while looking for the treasure in the 1940s?"

"Yes. We had a priest there back then. He thought he found it on the ranch owned by Lt. Cumo. But he disappeared."

Virginia grinned. "We found his remains in a cave on the ranch that contained a couple of artifacts. The priest was murdered."

The bishop's face went white as he grabbed his crucifix. "Murdered? How?"

"Yes. He was shot in the head."

"Do the authorities know who did it?"

Virginia took a breath and slowly let it out. "I'm sorry. No. We recently discovered the remains and called the police. But he was killed over 75 years ago. Maybe Lt. Cumo shot him. There were others, including the church, who were looking for the treasure. We think he found part of it and was killed for his discovery. But, like I said, we don't know who did it."

"I see. I will try to determine his identity, so we can notify his next of kin and close his records in the church," Bishop Copello said. "We'll hold a Mass for him."

"We'd like to attend, if that would be possible," Natalie said.

"That would be nice. Thank you,"

Natalie finished her glass of wine. "Does *Etruscan jewelry, es, incidentals manere, necesse map ad reliqua thesaurus* mean anything to you?"

Bishop Copello regained his composure. "Yes. It means Etruscan jewelry, art, incidentals remain, need map to rest of treasure. Why?"

"That line was in a notebook owned by a group in Texas, hunting for the treasure. They worked for Gino Giacopetti."

Copello swallowed. "I see."

"It was obviously written in Latin. Either they copied it, or it was written by someone who knows Latin. Maybe someone from the church?" asked Natalie.

"I doubt it. I will investigate and let you know."

"Okay. How do we get the information from you?" asked Virginia.

"Camille will deliver it, if that's okay with you."

Virginia smiled. "That would be great."

"So, you *will* work with the church on this matter?"

"Yes. But we do the investigation my way."

Bishop Copello beamed. "I expected you to say that. You have a deal, Virginia. We can also run interference with any local authorities for you, if necessary."

"Okay. Good." Virginia turned toward Natalie, who was quietly talking on her satellite phone. Natalie disconnected and looked at Virginia with a horrified expression.

"What's wrong, Natalie?" Virginia asked.

"That was Special Agent Tom Mason at the Smithsonian. Jeff is in the hospital in Austin. He's in emergency surgery. Something about his liver. From what Tom said, Jeff's in serious condition."

"You need to go home and be with him."

Copello frowned. "Is this Jeff a relative, Ms. North?"

"He's my boyfriend and a wonderful man. We've been talking about getting married."

"Then I agree with Virginia. You need to be with him. The treasure has been missing for over seventy years; it can wait a little longer."

"Virginia can stay and continue investigating." Natalie took a deep breath. "Tom, he's our boss at the Smithsonian, has arranged to fly me home first thing in the morning. My British Airlines flight leaves at 8:05 am."

Copello held up his hand, then pulled out his cell phone and talked in rapid Italian. He disconnected and smiled. "I'll have a car at your hotel at five in the morning."

Natalie sat with a tear in her eye. "I need to go through immigration, customs, check my bag, get my boarding pass, and—"

Copello reached across the table and patted Natalie's hand. "Relax, Ms. North. I have arranged everything. You will be taken there by Vatican police and a representative of the church. You will have no problem with traffic or anything else. Our representative will have what you need and will get you to your flight without any problem, I promise." He turned to Virginia. "Will you be getting another partner?"

Virginia shook her head. "I don't know. I'll call our boss tonight and see if Terry... Dr. Sorenson, can join me."

"You don't need to call him. I'm sure he is busy."

Virginia stared at the bishop. *Why doesn't he want Terry to join us?*

Natalie frowned as she read a message on her phone.

Copello continued, "If you need any assistance, you may call upon Camille. I know she would be willing to help you. I think she is somewhat bored with her present assignment, and she loves a mystery."

"That would be great," Virginia said.

Natalie slipped her phone closer to Virginia and tapped the table with her finger. The message on the screen read, *Don't react. We need to go now! We have a big problem. Get Camille, too.*

CHAPTER 28

Virginia slid her chair back. "We need to get going, if we're to get Natalie ready for her flight in the morning. Her packing will be interesting considering everything she's purchased." She glanced at Camille. "Can you give us a lift back to our hotel in your truck?"

Camille nodded. "Sure." She turned to Bishop Copello. "I'll see you tomorrow at the lab as usual?"

Copello rose. "Yes, my dear. That would be fine." He looked at Natalie. "I hope your boyfriend will be okay. I'll pray for him."

Natalie smiled. "Thank you."

Virginia and Natalie climbed into Camille's truck, holding their backpacks and packages. Natalie looked in the empty bed of the truck. "Why can't we just put the stuff in the back?"

"Gypsies and thieves. You could lose everything at a stoplight," Camille answered.

"Oh."

"Can I ask why we left so… abruptly?" asked Camille as she drove into traffic. "You haven't driven until you drive in Rome. It's insane."

"Try Mexico City." Natalie took a breath. "How well do you know Bishop Copello?"

"I met him at the Vatican. He came to my research laboratory," Camille said.

"Known him long?"

"Six to eight weeks or so."

"Have you been to his office?"

"No. Why all the questions?"

"Because he is not who he says he is," Natalie stated.

Camille jerked the wheel, then straightened the truck on the road. "What? I met him at the Vatican. He's a bishop."

"How many nuns, brothers, priests, monsignors, bishops and cardinals do you see at the Vatican normally?"

Camille licked her lips. "Quite a few."

"Do they wear name badges or other IDs?" Natalie asked.

"No. Only in certain areas. Where are you going with this?"

"Our Bishop Copello is a fake. He's not a monsignor either."

Virginia shifted in her seat. "Is he even a priest? Is there a John Copello who is a priest?"

Natalie shook her head. "No, he's not a priest. But there is a real Monsignor John Copello. He's a member of the Jesuit Order and has just started teaching at Georgetown University in Washington, D.C. It's a Jesuit university. He got his transfer."

"Then how did the faux Monsignor pull off the visit with the Bishop of Austin?"

"Must have used fake credentials, copied from the real Monsignor John Copello. A quick check by the bishop's office, if they even did it, would turn up the real guy, and thus make the imposter seem genuine. No one used fingerprints. The fake Copello probably used a forged Vatican photo ID."

Virginia flexed her fingers. "Tom Mason sent you the information?"

"That was what his call was about. He tried your phone, but it went directly to voice mail. Must be off."

"How did Tom figure out he was a fake?"

"When you sent him Camille's picture, you also captured the bishop's face in the Fiat parked behind her. Facial recognition software IDed him as suspicious. Tom ran a check and said he wasn't the real deal. The real Monsignor John Copello has no idea who he is. The folks at the SCSS are trying to figure out his identity."

Virginia glanced at Camille. She looked shaken, her face drawn and glum.

Camille turned a corner, then said, "I'm so sorry. I thought he was who he said he was. There are a lot of priests and bishops around the Vatican. Is any of this real?"

Virginia looked out the rear window, then at Camille. "Yes. The treasure we are searching for is real. The church and others are after it, too. The shooting of the two men in the park was very real. But I don't think the church is behind it. That doesn't make sense. They would not have been responsible for the murder of the men."

"How about the story about Mary Magdalene?"

Natalie held up her phone. "I texted Tom at the Smithsonian about the Mary Magdalene story. I just got a text message back. According to his contacts at the Vatican, that little tidbit is true. The document in question is real but not well known outside of the Vatican. It is still in its protective case at the Vatican Museum. No one there now thinks it was taken with the treasure in the forties. He also said not to trust anyone but the three of us and our special contact."

Camille shuddered, then asked, "Is your boyfriend really in the hospital?"

"No." Natalie glanced at her watch. "About now, he's teaching a class at the University of Texas at Austin."

"Oh."

Virginia turned slightly to face Camille. "You look a little under the weather. You okay?"

"Not really." Camille shook her head. "I was taken in. I thought that someone wearing bishop's clothes at the Vatican would be a real bishop. I feel so stupid. I'm not good with people, and this shows why. I'm too gullible. I believed the Mary Magdalene story and that Natalie's boyfriend was in the hospital, too. Then this elaborate scheme that... I somehow got... hell, I don't know what to believe. Now... now I just want to go home. I'm sorry I got you into this."

"Not to worry." Virginia gave Camille a warm smile. "You didn't get us into anything. We're investigating a missing treasure. He's a con man. You had no way of knowing the truth. If Tom hadn't seen his face in the picture, and the Smithsonian Central Security Service computers hadn't recognized him as a fake, we all might have been taken in. The Pyramid Society keeps popping up as well. I think it's real, but I don't believe it is related in any way to the church. That has been bothering me for quite a while. I doubt the church had those men shot, who were after Natalie and me in the park. The Pyramid Society maybe did it, but we don't know who they are. Now, would you like to join us in our investigation? You have a certain amount of local knowledge and access that we don't. We could use you."

Natalie looked across the truck's cab at Camille. "I'm sorry about the subterfuge with my boyfriend. I needed something dramatic to get us out of there quick, and it was the first thing that came to mind that sounded like a plausible emergency."

Virginia shook her head. "You have to understand, she was an actress. Drama is her middle name."

"I see." Camille drove without speaking, then nodded. "After all this, you want me to help you?"

Virginia nodded. "Yes."

"I'd love to help. But my assignment from the Smithsonian is to work with the Vatican on the Roman artifacts found in the U.S."

Virginia tented her fingers and chuckled. "You should continue doing that, and play along with our so-called bishop. He might still be of use. We need to know more about him and what he's up to. We'll leave that to you."

Natalie rummaged through her backpack on her lap and pulled out a small glass with a paper napkin wrapped around it. "I lifted this. It has our fake bishop's fingerprints."

Virginia looked at the glass. "You're good. I didn't see you snatch it."

"I learned from the best."

"Huh?"

"Your husband. He's an amateur magician, remember?" She tucked the glass back in her backpack. "He taught me a few tricks."

"I hope that's all the tricks he taught you." Virginia settled back. "We'll call… Cousin Luigi when we get to the hotel and have him get the prints analyzed."

Camille pointed out the front window. "There's your hotel. Who's this Cousin Luigi?"

"A friend of ours here in Rome with a lot of contacts. Where are you staying, Camille?"

"I have a little, and I mean tiny, place a few blocks from the Vatican. It isn't much, but it is convenient."

"When we get to our rooms, I'll call Tom in Washington. We'll have you moved here with us. It will be safer for you."

As they pulled up in front of the hotel, Camille looked at the exterior. "I don't think my expense account can handle something like this."

"Don't worry," Virginia said, "Natalie and I will take care of it."

"Really? Okay. Thank you. When will I see you again?"

Natalie pulled out a small spiral notebook. "What's your cell number and the address where you are staying? We'll contact you as soon as we get things set up."

Camille gave Natalie the information.

"I have a better idea." Virginia pointed to the front of the hotel where the bell captain stood. "Pull in there and come up to our rooms. I'll have the hotel park your truck. We can make the arrangements while you are safely with us."

"If your boss agrees, I'll need to go get my stuff from my room."

Natalie leaned forward and glanced at Camille. "We'll go with you to gather your belongings."

Camille slowly nodded. "Okay. I have another question. How about the Vatican police car that will be taking you to the airport?"

Virginia smiled. "We'll take care of that, too."

CHAPTER 29

Camille brushed a strand of brown hair from her face as she sat on the veranda, overlooking the piazza del Popolo, while sipping a glass of white Zinfandel wine. Virginia sat on an upholstered chair in the living room with her feet curled under her, talking on the phone with Special Agent Tom Mason at the Smithsonian Central Security Service in Washington. Natalie sat on the sofa in the living room talking on her cell phone with Luigi.

After a few minutes, Natalie disconnected and sat back and waited for Virginia to finish her call. Then Natalie motioned to Virginia to join her. Natalie pointed to the drinking glass she had lifted from the restaurant with the faux bishop's fingerprints resting on the coffee table. "Luigi is sending John, his driver and right-hand-man, to do the fingerprint analysis. He'll be here in a half hour. How'd it go with Tom?"

Virginia rolled her neck from one side to the other to work out the kinks. "Okay. Tom agreed to move Camille here to our hotel."

"Great."

"Yes. He's arranged for her to continue her work on the Roman artifacts but under guard. The Vatican is going to assign police officers to protect her while she's in Italy. He's also sending Terry to assist us. He figured, since she is an anthropologist and an archeologist and worked with us before, she would be a big asset."

"When is Dr. Sorenson arriving?" asked Natalie.

"Terry is arriving this evening," Virginia said.

"Huh?"

"Tom has Terry in the air as we speak. She's flying to Rome directly from Austin, Texas, thanks to the Air Force."

"The Air Force? She hitched a ride on a transport?" Natalie asked.

"No. She's flying on an executive jet with a two-star general."

"A major-general, huh? Good for her. Where do we go to pick her up and when?"

"He has arranged to have Luigi's people pick her up and bring her here. She'll be here at the hotel by six. The SCSS got her a room across the hall from us. She and Camille will be sharing a suite like us."

"That's good. Did you say anything about the Vatican police car that's coming for me?"

"Yes. While I waited on the phone, Tom contacted the Vatican and Italian police authorities. There are no real Vatican police, or any other police vehicles, being dispatched to take you to the airport."

"So, I was to be kidnapped by a fake bishop? That's not Kosher."

Virginia laughed, "Looks like it, and the bishop isn't Jewish, either. But when the imposters arrive tomorrow morning, the Italian police will be here to arrest them."

Natalie pointed at the Veranda. "You'd better tell Camille about the changes."

They turned their heads toward the door as someone knocked. Virginia stood and pointed. "I'll brief Camille, you can get the door. It's probably John."

Natalie rose and padded barefoot across the plush rug to the door, unholstering her gun as she went. She stood on her toes and peered through the peephole and saw John, then opened the door. "Come in, John. I'm glad you're early." She looked at the large back case and bulky briefcase he carried and motioned him inside. "You bring a crime lab with you?"

John smiled. "*Sì*, yes. I brought everything I need to do the fingerprints." He walked into the living room and glanced around. "Wow. Nice. I think I work for the wrong agency."

Natalie pointed at the coffee table. "The glass is over there on the coffee table. Have fun."

John moved to the couch and sat. He opened the case and withdrew various pieces of equipment. Then he opened the briefcase. It held a large computer with unusual attachments.

Natalie watched as he slipped on gloves and picked up the glass. After examining it, he dusted it with a gray powder and examined the now visible fingerprints. He slipped a contrasting color cylinder into the glass, then positioned it. He used an optical device attached to the computer to scan each print. Then he rapidly typed on the keyboard and sat back. He pulled off his gloves. "Now we wait."

Natalie gave John a glass of wine and turned on the television while they waited. Nine minutes later, the computer chimed.

John leaned forward and pressed a key. "We have a couple of matches."

"We do? That was fast." Natalie jumped to her feet. "Wait, let me get Virginia." She hurried to the veranda and returned with Virginia and Camille. "Okay, John, who is our mysterious bishop?"

"Not so fast. One set is of the waitress at the restaurant, who was arrested when she was young for shoplifting. That was a long-time ago and her only offence. But two are for Victor Serrano. He is wanted by INTERPOL, Scotland Yard, and in the Far East and South America."

Virginia frowned. "Wow. What's he wanted for?"

"Art and antiquities theft, smuggling, art forgery, and sale of expensive stolen and fake merchandise. Scotland Yard is interested in him for the murder of an English baron. The English frown on that sort of thing."

"Funny. I remember that name," Natalie said. "Captain Steadman of the Georgetown, Texas police ran the name through the FBI and couldn't get a hit. I'd think the FBI would be linked to INTERPOL. How'd you do it? The Italian police or INTERPOL databases?"

John gave Natalie a sheepish grin. "No. I tried the CIA, MI-5, and MI-6 first."

"Oh. Nice work. What kind of information do they have about him? Like, where's he from, how old?"

John leaned closer to the screen. "He was born in New York City, New York in 1946. His father was a restaurant owner and an ex-Italian-prisoner-of-war during World War II and was held in a POW camp in the U.S." He ran his finger across the computer screen. "He was held at a prisoner-of-war camp in Arizona. His mother was a pre-school teacher."

Virginia plopped onto a chair. "Let me guess, his father was Franco Volpe." She frowned. "But his last name is Serrano?"

"You're right. Serrano is his mother's maiden name."

Natalie stepped closer. "Does your electronic crystal ball say if he was affiliated with a group called Grand Knights or Gino Giacopetti?"

John typed, examined the screen, then looked up at the women. "You ladies are good. Yes, there *was* intermittent and small money transfers between an account owned by Mr. Serrano and Grand Knights. It ceased about six months ago. It appears that Giacopetti was funding them, too. That has also recently come to an end. And the Italian authorities have intercepted a few untraceable messages between Serrano and Gino Giacopetti."

"Untraceable?"

"They figured out who sent them and to whom they were sent, but not where they originated. The signals were routed through multiple servers and satellites around the world. They couldn't say if they originated in Italy, the U.S., or Mars."

"Any idea what the messages say?" Virginia asked.

"Yes. To summarize them… Serrano told Giacopetti to… go to hell and stop looking for the treasure. Serrano said the treasure is rightfully his."

"No love lost there."

John gazed at the screen, scrolling down as he read. "This says both men seem to think they have a right to the treasure stolen during World War II and that your Lt. Cumo cut their parents out of their rightful shares after they stole it. Giacopetti told Serrano that he was messing with an operation that Giacopetti didn't want disturbed and to go home."

"An operation he didn't want disturbed. I wonder what that means," Virginia said.

"I don't know."

"Serrano, our fake bishop, is a world class crook," Virginia gazed out the window, then back at John. "He wanted to screw the church and Giacopetti out of the treasure. Poor Franco Volpe. His only son is not only not in the restaurant business but is an international antiquities thief and possible murderer."

Camille set her wine glass on an end table. "We know where he is, shouldn't we contact INTERPOL? I'd love to make the call."

Virginia rose from her chair and paced. "Serrano obviously doesn't know where the treasure is." She stopped pacing and grinned. "I have an idea."

"Oh, boy." Natalie shook her head. "Your ideas usually land us in a shootout or in some other serious trouble."

Camille gave Virginia a curious look. "What's your idea? If it takes him down, I'm in."

"Hold that thought. John, does Serrano have any ties to the Pyramid Society?" Virginia asked.

"Yes." John pointed at the screen. "Last week, INTERPOL pegged him as the leader of it. Goes by Giulio Cesare. It's the title of the society's leader no matter who the leader is. Like M is for MI-6 in James Bond movies. INTERPOL says there were rumors of it being part of the church. But that is *not* the case. The Pyramid Society was established in Europe in the early twelve-hundreds as a front to what we now call organized crime. An early version of the Mafia. It appears that at some time in the past, they did a few jobs for the church, but exactly what is not known. There are hints that it involved smuggling some people out of a country. The Pyramid Society has sometimes spread the word that they are part of the church, when it benefited them."

Camille looked confused. "This Pyramid Society has been around and committing crimes since the twelve-hundreds and no one caught them? How'd they accomplish that?"

John shook his head. "I don't know. They managed to stay under the radar. Probably by being crafty and using coercion, bribery, extortion, and murder."

Natalie waved her hand. "Not to interrupt, but why was it called the Pyramid Society?"

"The Pyramid Society was originally founded in Alexandria, Egypt and later migrated to Europe to be nearer their main clients. It now seems to be a one stop shop for stolen art and antiquities worldwide. If some rich person wants a particular, rare, valuable item, the society will buy it, steal it, or contract to obtain it, and deliver it for a handsome fee. If they can't get an item, they are not above forgery. They also dabble in extortion and the occasional assassination."

"A one stop shop. Where is it located?"

"INTERPOL doesn't know for sure, except that it appears to be someplace in Italy," John responded.

Virginia rubbed her forehead. "Does the magic machine of yours have anything on an Eric Bauer? He was suspected of being an Italian spy during World War II in Williamson County, Texas. I know, an Italian spy in Williamson County in the mid-forties? Sounds way off. Maybe he was spying on cows. A better question is what was he still doing on the ranch in 1994? Spying in the forties and ranching in the nineties?"

"Let's see." John typed and moved the computer mouse rapidly. After a couple of minutes he sat back and grinned. "Yep. The CIA has him listed as a priest who worked for the Vatican. That's it. Nothing else. Maybe he was looking for the treasure for the church."

"That makes sense. Excellent job, John. Thank you." Virginia rubbed her hands together. "Now to set Mr. Serrano up. Camille, I need you to act like nothing is wrong, and call the fake bishop and tell him you found some information we have about the location of the treasure and want to meet him. Ask if you can come to his office at the Vatican."

"If he isn't a real bishop, he either doesn't have one or will try to use one belonging to a real bishop," Camille responded.

"I don't think he'll risk using a real bishop's office. Make the call and let's see what he says."

"Okay." Camille used her cell phone to place the call. "Bishop Copello, this is Dr. Camille Pisciolo. I thought you might be interested in what information Virginia and Natalie have about the location of the treasure and your missing document. Can I come to your office?" She listened, then answered, "Okay, I'll meet you there tonight at eight." She disconnected.

Virginia dropped onto an upholstered wing chair. "What did he say?"

"He said to come to the Tiber River near the Mausoleum of Augustus, along the Lungotevere. He has a boat there we can use to go over what I have about the treasure. He will meet me at the street level and take me to his boat. He said to come alone."

"He has a boat there?"

"That's what he said." Camille's brown eyes widened. "You'll be there, won't you?"

Virginia nodded. "Of course. We will be close by to protect you."

"But I'll be inside a boat."

Virginia grinned. "We've snuck on boats before. We won't let anyone harm you."

John sat back. "So, he lives and works on a houseboat. Comfortable, off the radar, and moveable. Maybe it's the present home of the Pyramid Society."

Virginia pulled out a map of Rome from under a stack of books on an end table, and said enthusiastically, "Now that we know where he operates, here's the plan."

CHAPTER 30

At eight that evening, the sky was just turning dark. Virginia wet her lips as she leaned against a pepper tree, while watching the road and waiting for Camille to arrive. Fifty yards down the road, Natalie sat on a bench under an olive tree, playing with a camera. A cab pulled to a stop near the short wall above the Tiber, and Camille, with a black messenger bag strapped across her, climbed out. She moved to the wall and looked around.

After a couple of minutes, Serrano, dressed as Bishop Copello, came up the steps from the river. "Camille my dear, I'm glad you could make our appointment."

Camille cracked a smile. "I wouldn't miss it for the world, Your Excellency."

"Is the information in that bag you're carrying?"

She nodded. "Yes."

He turned back toward the river. "Let's go down to my boat and examine what you have."

"I… I can just give this to you. It's a copy." Camille glanced around. "Anyway, I'm meeting a friend soon."

"I understand, but I would like your take on the contents. Is your friend a gentleman? You could call and reschedule."

"No. She is a colleague, and she's on her way here to meet me."

"She's coming here?" Serrano stiffened; stress lines formed on his brow. "I told you to come alone."

"Yes, I know, but I'm nervous being out here alone at night." Camille turned toward the street as a cab approached and stopped. Terry Sorenson stepped out and walked to Camille.

Camille took a breath. "Bishop Copello, this is Dr. Terry Sorenson. She is the colleague I told you about. Terry, this is Bishop Copello."

Terry took Copello's proffered hand and shook it. "Nice to meet you, Your Excellency. Dr. Pisciolo told me she was meeting you here and was nervous about waiting out here alone. So, I offered to join her. You know, safety in numbers."

Copello's expression grew guarded. He glanced over his shoulder and motioned for another man, who had just come to the top of the steps to join them. "This is Father Armond. He will be with us, so there is no need for you to bother playing babysitter, Doctor Sorenson. Camille will be in good hands."

Terry looked around the darkening street. "I think I'll stick with Camille."

"But with Father Armond and me here, she will be quite safe," Copello said with an agitated voice. "We're just going down to my boat to examine some documents."

"Great. I don't want to be alone out here. I'll go with you. Then after that, Camille and I can go out for a late snack." Terry moved to the stone parapet and peered over the side at the simmering, dark water and the long, narrow riverboat tied to its mooring. "Is that your boat down there?"

"Yes." Copello's clenched his fists. "Since you insist on coming along, let's all go to the boat." He led the way down the steps in single file, with Camille following him. Behind her was Father Armond, with Terry coming last.

As Copello stepped on his boat with Camille, two speedboats shot out from under the Ponte Cavour Bridge with flashing blue emergency lights and sirens. They quickly came alongside Copello's river boat. *"Polizia! Direzione Investigativa Antimafia'!* Everyone stop where you are." Copello pulled a knife from under his jacket, turned, seized Camille, and pulled her closer to him.

Still on the steps, Father Armond spun around, reached under his jacket, and started to pull out a pistol, when Terry leveled her .38 special at him. "Not so fast, Father. Don't move or you'll be seeing God sooner than you planned." She watched Camille struggle, then slam her fist into Copello's throat. He released her and dropped the knife. Gasping for breath, he grabbed his neck and collapsed to the deck of the boat.

The six police officers rapidly boarded the boat. A plain clothed officer, with a badge clipped to his belt next to a holstered black semiautomatic pistol, hurried across the deck, then scurried up the stairs where Terry held Father Arnold at gunpoint. They quickly disarmed and handcuffed him. The Inspector smiled at Terry. "Nice work, Agent Sorenson. I'll take it from here."

"Glad to see you again, too, Inspector Tonelli. Looks like you made it here just in time."

The priest frowned. "Agent Sorenson? I thought you were some sort of doctor."

"And I thought you were some sort of priest." Terry grinned. "I'm a Ph.D. archeologist. But I'm also a special agent with the Smithsonian and we're helping the Italian police." She looked at the Inspector holding the priest. "He's all yours."

"Grazie." Inspector Tonelli pointed at two other uniformed officers now on Copello's boat. "They're Vatican police officers who joined us. This is going to be a long night." He stopped and stared as Virginia and Natalie came down the steps. They held out their badges. He chuckled. "I see you brought your own back up, *Dottore*. Hello again, ladies."

"Yep. We're a team. How's Camille doing?" Terry asked.

"I'll inquire." Inspector Tonelli unclipped a radio from his belt and called to the other officials. He then looked at Terry, Natalie, and Virginia. "Dr. Pisciolo is fine. A little *scosso*... shook-up, but otherwise good. We will need more statements tomorrow at the station. Can you come around ten?"

Virginia stepped down a couple of steps and smiled. "Yes. We will be there."

"Thank you for the tipoff. This may finally be the end of the infamous Pyramid Society."

"Let's hope so." Natalie watched the commotion on the docked riverboat. "What are you going to do with this guy and Copello, or more accurately, Victor Serrano?"

"They will be taken to the station and held. We will search the boat, their homes, and any offices we can find, seize their bank accounts, computers, investments, any safe deposit boxes, and phone records, then they will be formally charged."

"They won't get out on bail, will they?" Natalie asked.

"No. We'll hold them until our investigation is complete. The Vatican police will assist us."

"Good. We'll see you at ten tomorrow." Virginia looked at the men examining Serrano on the deck of the boat. "Is he going to be okay?"

"I don't know. One of the men down there is a paramedic and he's... wait." Inspector Tonelli listened to some rapid Italian spoken on his radio, then looked at the women. "Serrano's dead."

Virginia tensed. "What about Camille? Is she going to be held?"

Inspector Tonelli shook his head. "No. We watched the events that played out when we arrived. He attacked her with a weapon, and she acted in self-defense. With that, and what she and you three have done, there will be no charges against her. As I understand things, she's part of your team investigating the Pyramid Society and this fake bishop. He's really Victor Serrano?"

Virginia nodded. "Yes. We identified him from fingerprints, and then tied him to the Pyramid Society. INTERPOL, Scotland Yard, and other countries want him. They'll be happy now. If you like, I'll have our contact here in Rome forward the file on Serrano. It will be from an untraceable account and don't ask. You can say your expert Inspector work turned up the information."

Inspector Tonelli gave Virginia a sly, understanding grin "I see. *Grazie.* That would be helpful. The press will go *pazzo*... crazy with this. The press releases and press conferences will be *implacabile*... relentless." The Inspector gave a slight chuckle. "And the paperwork, *Mama Mia,* it'll take forever. I'll probably retire after it's done."

Natalie tilted her head and gave him a quizzical look. "You can't be over thirty-five."

"Like I said, *in Italia le scartoffie non finiscono mai.*"

"In Italy the paperwork never ends?"

"Sì. What are your plans now? Sightseeing? Shopping?"

Virginia shook her head. "Later. Now we have some more investigating to do."

"You do realize you are in Italy? Your... investigations... they should be coordinated with the *polizia.* What are you investigating now?"

"We're searching for a lost treasure that was stolen from the Vatican in the 1940s. If we get anywhere with it, we will contact both the police and the Vatican. We called your agency and the Vatican police when we uncovered Victor Serrano."

"Sì. Okay. Let's talk more tomorrow at my office." He turned and led the prisoner down the steps to the police boats.

Terry motioned toward the river. "Here comes Camille. I say we go out for a pizza and beer to celebrate this achievement."

Natalie put her hand on Terry's shoulder. "Terry my dear, pizza and beer? Really? This is Rome, Italy. We get *wine* and pizza."

Terry held her hands up in front of her in surrender. "My mistake. Probably no New England clam chowder either, right?"

Virginia laughed. "No clam chowder, and just for the record, no alligators."

Natalie and Camille frowned, then said in unison, "Alligators?"

Virginia sighed. "It's a long story."

"We have all night," Natalie chuckled.

Virginia looked at Camille. "How are you doing?"

Camille shrugged. "I'm okay, I guess. When he grabbed me and pulled that knife, I just reacted. I didn't mean to kill him." She held out her hands. "I'm still shaking. My stomach doesn't feel very good either."

"He attacked you with a knife and was going to use you as a hostage or kill you. The police said it was self-defense. It's your adrenaline level going down. The shaking and the queasy feeling in your stomach will subside in a while. With your upset stomach, do you feel up to a little snack with us?"

Camille nodded. "I think I'll need a lot of wine to quell my nerves, so yes, I'd love to join you all."

"Great. Now for that pizza and wine," Natalie said as she and the others followed Virginia up the steps. At the top of the stairs, they watched the two police boats moving down river and pass under the bridge. "I see they left some Inspectors and uniformed officers on the riverboat. Now, let's flag down a cab."

Camille rubbed her hands together. "I think that will be difficult at this time. There's a nice pizzeria, *Sicilia*, a few blocks away. We can walk." She pointed. "It's that way."

They crossed the Via di Ripetta and strolled down Via Tomacelli. About a block away from the Tiber, a Fiat careened around a corner and barreled toward them. Terry and Natalie dropped behind a large stone flowerpot with pink geraniums spilling over the sides and pulled out their pistols. Virginia grabbed Camille and shoved her into a doorway facing the street and pulled her down.

Rapid shots were fired from the vehicle as the car sped past. Sparks flew from the impact of the bullets on the flowerpot in front of Natalie and Terry, and from the walls of the building next to them.

Terry rose onto one knee and unloaded all six shots from her .38 special into the fleeing vehicle.

CHAPTER 31

Early the next morning, Virginia, Natalie, Terry, and Camille sat around a table having breakfast. Virginia finished her toast, sipped her coffee, then spoke. "That phone call earlier was from Luigi. He transmitted the information John discovered about our fake bishop and the Pyramid Society to the Smithsonian Central Security Service and the Italian police. The Italian and Vatican cops captured the fake Vatican police when they came to get you this morning, Natalie." Virginia looked at Camille. "How are you feeling after last night, Camille?"

"Good. After breakfast, I need to go to work."

"Do you feel up to it?" Terry asked.

"Yes. I wasn't prepared for what happened last night. I just reacted. I'm okay." Camille finished her orange juice. "I guess it's safe to take my truck."

Virginia shook her head. "We'll have the hotel limo take you and pick you up. That service is part of the rent we're paying and will be safer."

Camille smiled. "My co-workers will be impressed."

Terry ate her sausage biscuit. "What are our plans for today? Don't we need to go to the police station at ten?"

"Detective Tonelli called at six this morning. He doesn't need to see us today. He said maybe later. He'll let us know." Virginia sat back. "I think we should search the catacombs depicted on the quilt. Then maybe we'll have a better idea of what Gino Giacopetti is really up to and how to recover the treasure."

"What do you mean by what Giacopetti is really up to?"

"Gino lives the good life. He's supposedly from a rich and well-connected family and he collects art and artifacts. But there's a fly in the ointment. First, he was going to interrogate Natalie and me to find out what we knew about the treasure. Second, he tells Serrano to back off because of some operation he has going on. Third, Luigi can't find anything about this wealthy family he talks about. Then there are the shootings in the park and last night when men in that Fiat shot at you."

Hidden Threads

Natalie stretched. "He's the only party to this treasure hunt left, besides the church."

"Exactly. And since the church isn't trying to kill us, there's something else afoot."

"What?"

Virginia raised an eyebrow. "Maybe Gino Giacopetti's already found the treasure and doesn't want anyone else to get wind of it. He's protecting it and maybe using it to his advantage."

Natalie glanced out the window, then back at Virginia. "Possible, I guess. Okay, when do we go exploring?"

Camille held up her hands. "You're not going without me. I'll call in sick. I'll explain that after last night, I'm still a little shook-up."

"Good idea." Terry nodded. "Having Camille with us would be great. She has more background about the ancient Romans than I do. I'd appreciate her help. Where exactly are we going?"

"I'll be right back and show you." Virginia went to her bedroom and returned with the pictures and drawings of the quilt and a couple of maps. She spread them out on the table. "I marked the tunnels that are depicted on the quilt but are not on this map in red marker. There are a couple of entrances." She pointed at a spot on the catacomb map. "This area is not well frequented. We can enter here without much trouble. We then explore the tunnels and especially this one that goes either near or under Giacopetti's home."

Terry scooted her chair closer, bent over and examined the map, then straightened. "Camille and I can put together some equipment we may need if we find any of the treasure." She looked at Natalie and Virginia. "Are we going in armed?"

Virginia nodded. "We'll take an array of weapons. No telling what or who we may encounter." She glanced at her watch. "It is eight-thirty now. Let's meet back here at ten with what we are going to take with us. And remember, we are carrying everything ourselves and need to still blend in."

Terry and Camille pushed their chairs back and rose. "We'd better get busy. See you at ten." They hurried out of the suite.

At ten, the women reassembled in Virginia and Natalie's room. Virginia looked at the backpacks lined up in a row near the door. "Okay, gang, here we go." She eyed Camille, who seemed agitated. "Camille, what's wrong?"

"I'm the only one without a gun."

"Do you have much experience with a pistol?"

"Well, yeah—"

"We are going to give you some nonlethal weapons. You're more important to our team as an expert in things Roman and Etruscan than being a shooter."

Camille pushed her dark rimmed glasses up her nose and frowned. "Okay, I guess. But I can shoot. I was a—"

Virginia padded across the room and called the lobby, then walked back. "Our ride is ready."

Natalie frowned. "We're taking a limo and not looking conspicuous?"

"No. We're taking a hotel panel truck. The driver will let us out a few blocks from our target and then continue on his errands."

Terry smiled. "Nice. Let's go."

Standing in a park near a wooden building, Virginia consulted her map. "This catacomb was closed off years ago. The entrance is inside that structure. It was made so people wouldn't just go exploring and get hurt, lost, or destroy historical artifacts."

Natalie looked around and moved closer to the door. She examined the padlock. "Virginia, we need your expertise."

Virginia stepped to the door and examined the lock. "Keep an eye out." She pulled a small, black case from a pouch on her backpack. Crouching in front of the door, she used the lock picking tools and in a few seconds popped open the lock. She stood. "All right, now to get busy. Once inside, place your headlamps on and we'll go see what's under our feet."

They entered the small, dirty structure and found a partially rusted, cast-iron trapdoor in the middle of the concrete floor. It creaked as Natalie yanked it up and peered down into the hole. "That was easier than I thought it would be. Got a ladder here, but the tunnel isn't very far down." She climbed down the rusted iron rungs and stepped away from the side into the tunnel. "Dark, eerie, and dank but looks okay. Come down." Natalie took a few steps; then screamed. She turned, yanked a bone from a cavity in the earthen side wall, and said, "Be glad you're dead because I'd kill you for tearing my shirt."

Virginia, halfway down the ladder called to her. "What's wrong?"

"My shirtsleeve snagged a bone from one of the burial niches. I'm okay now. I think I want to go home."

"It's a little late to back out now," said Virginia. "Let's wait for the others."

Terry and Camille descended and regrouped with Virginia and Natalie a few feet into the tunnel. Virginia examined her map. "The catacombs are down this tunnel. There are two side passages. One leads towards Giacopetti's villa. Let's see what we've got."

Natalie felt the sides of the tunnel as they marched. "This isn't lime-

Hidden Threads

stone. What are the catacombs made of?"

Terry stepped closer to her. "The Catacombs of Rome, or *Catacombe di Roma*, are ancient, basically underground burial places in and around Rome. Rome sits on large areas of tufa or tuffs. Tuffs are locally present due to their formation from volcanic pyroclastic flows 600,000-300,000 years ago from the Monti Sabatini volcanic fields and from Castelli Romani, approximately 30 km from Rome. Tuff is relatively soft to dig into but subsequently hardens."

Camille said, "The complex system of tunnels, that would later be known as the catacombs, were first excavated by the Etruscan people that lived in the region predating the Romans. They were first excavated in the process of mining for various rock resources such as limestone and sandstone. These quarries became the basis for later excavation, first by the Romans for rock resources, and then by the Christians and Jews for burial sites and mass graves."

Natalie turned her head, her light hitting Terry's and Camille's faces. "You could have said it was soft rock that hardens."

Terry chuckled. "Right. Sorry about that."

"Don't be. That was interesting. And Virginia's husband and my boyfriend are both engineers. Ask them the time, and they'll tell you how to build a clock, then tell you the time."

"She's right." Virginia stopped. "We're headed downward. I think these things can be up to sixty feet or so underground."

Natalie took a breath. "Smells like damp loam and... rot."

After walking about a quarter mile, they found horizontal niches laid out in sequences, one above the other from floor to waist level. Most contained the remains of one ancient occupant, while others had more than one body. They noticed ancient graffiti etched into the walls in some places. A half-mile farther into the catacomb, they found an offshoot. Natalie and Camille ventured down the dark side passage.

Virginia and Terry continued in the main passageway. After another hundred yards, they found a side tunnel that went toward Giacopetti's villa. They entered the tunnel towards the villa and walked another fifty yards, then stopped at a cavernous area. Virginia's head lamp cast a beam around. The domed ceiling made the area seem bigger. Tables holding trays, chemicals, and glove boxes were arranged around the space, with metal cabinets and overhead lights. Gas cylinders were chained to metal stands near the tables with the glove boxes. At the far side was an electric lift. Virginia swallowed. "What the hell?"

Terry hurried to a metal table with two plastic trays on it. Through the thin plastic sheets covering them, she saw two elaborately illustrated documents. Terry removed the covers and examined the articles. "They are exact copies."

"Two of the same? Why?"

Terry removed her backpack and pulled out a lamp. "Let's see what this test tells us." She switched on the ultraviolet light and shined it on the first velum. The colors glowed under the UV light. Next, she shined it on the second document. Nothing. Terry pointed. "That one, the one that fluoresced, is the original. That one is a fake. A good one, but a fake."

Virginia stood silent then said, "Please explain, Doctor."

Terry leaned against the table. "The materials used in very old inks were mineral pigments and binders. Blue, for example, was ground Lapis Lazuli, vermilion consisted of cinnabar and Sulphur, green contained ground malachite or copper verdigris. White was lead with gypsum or calcite. They glow under UV light. Some change into spectacular colors. More modern inks are aniline dyes. They don't glow."

Virginia bent over and looked at the documents again. "Why would someone do this, except to sell it as the original? Wouldn't someone else be able to do what you did?"

"I suspect Giacopetti shows the original to the unsuspecting buyer and does this UV test, and then switches it for the fake while packaging it for delivery. It's the old bait and switch swindle. He can resell this thing multiple times. His buyers are not reputable museums or art galleries, they are rich guys with a thirst for antiquities and will keep these things for themselves because they know they are hot, and the cops would jail them for possession. As you know, it's big business."

"But this document looks to be from the early Middle Ages, not Etruscan."

"You're right. Let's look around."

Virginia and Terry looked at articles on various tables and in cabinets.

Terry held open a drawer on what looked like a metal workbench. "Lookie here."

Virginia hurried to the workbench. "Now that looks like Etruscan jewelry."

Terry pulled two pieces out and set them on the wood surface of the workbench. She pulled a small gray plastic box from her backpack and opened it. She withdrew a couple of small plastic dropper bottles and a set of directions. Next, she placed a couple of drops of a fluid on what appeared to be a gold bracelet. Nothing happened. She applied the same liquid to the twin bracelet. There was a slight foaming and greenish discoloration. Terry pointed at the specimen that had a greenish tint. "Fake. This one is an alloy of gold and copper."

Virginia looked around. "So, Giacopetti found the lost treasure and has been making fake copies and secretly selling them to sustain his lifestyle and preserving the originals for himself."

"Could be. He may have sold a lot of the originals before he came across this idea. Your army lieutenant sold off what he took to sustain his lifestyle as a rancher."

"Good point."

Virginia meandered to another table with a colorfully illustrated document on it. Next to it was a bottle of SP 70 sunblock. She motioned to Terry. "Have a look at this."

Terry set the artifacts back in the drawer, then scurried to the table and looked at the document. She shined her UV light at it, then pointed. "Look. See how most of this animal skinned vellum does not glow? But look over here at the corner. There, it does. Someone used sun block to stop the UV light from fluorescing the old pigments. Giacopetti may have been going to take this someplace and didn't want any officials to be able to determine it is the real thing and think it's a copy. It's an old trick."

"How has this been kept secret?" asked Virginia. "The Vatican has jurisdiction over Christian catacombs. They would know about this."

"When we came into this maze, Camille muttered something about this not being a Christian catacomb. And there is a faded Giacopetti family crest on the door to the shed we entered to get down here. He may own it."

"Oh. I missed that."

"I wonder how Natalie and Camille are doing?"

Terry put her tools away. "Giacopetti may have found the treasure, and this is just the workroom to manufacture and package the lookalikes. The actual remaining pieces are stored somewhere else."

They turned at the sound of the lift starting. The overhead lights came on.

Terry squinted in the bright light as she looked at the lift. "That's not good."

"You're right." Virginia motioned to Terry. "We'd better get the hell out of here and warn the others."

CHAPTER 32

Virginia and Terry jogged out of the room and into the tunnel entrance. They heard voices behind them. Virginia tapped Terry's shoulder. "Kill your light."

Terry switched off her head lamp and dove for the floor as the sound of a gunshot roared through the underground space. She whispered. "Virginia? Are you okay?"

Virginia's low voice responded from a few feet away. "Yeah. We must have set off an alarm back there. Now we need to skedaddle before more of them come looking for us."

A voice from a loudspeaker behind them said, "We know you are here. We have you trapped. Show yourselves or else."

Terry mumbled, "I don't like the sound of that. Trapped?"

"They must have found our break-in at the shed and may have people advancing on us from that direction, too. That could have been alarmed as well."

"We need to warn Natalie and Camille," Terry said.

"Yeah, let's go, but be careful; we can't use our lights."

They rose from the ground and, feeling the walls, slowly maneuvered down the tunnel. They heard voices behind them and saw brief flashes of light in the distance.

Natalie and Camille also heard men's voices coming from behind them. They switched off their head lamps and ducked into a short, rubble-filled side niche and waited. Three armed men with flashlights moved single file toward their location.

Natalie whispered, "We need to quietly take them out before they get too far and find Virginia and Terry."

"Okay. Let me try this." Camille reached into her fanny pack and withdrew a compressed gas cylinder. As the men passed, Camille stepped out and quickly drenched them with the DMSO and ketamine solution. The men stood stunned for a couple of seconds, then dropped their guns and fell to the floor. She looked at the unconscious men. "That worked well. I think we should tie them up."

"Man, you've got guts. Good job." Natalie stared the men. "They'll be out for quite a while. I hope you didn't give them enough to kill them."

"Me, too."

Natalie stood staring at the men. "I don't have any rope, do you?"

"No. But I brought these." Camille held a fist full of plastic zip ties. "I think these will do, don't you?"

"Zip ties? Hell, yeah. I'm glad one of us was thinking ahead. I've got some plastic gloves. We probably shouldn't touch them with bare hands because of your spray." Natalie took a few of the zip ties and bound the man closest to her, while Camille quickly restrained the other two. They picked up the men's guns and tucked them into their belts. Natalie looked down at the secured men, then at Camille. "We'd better find Virginia and Terry."

At the junction of the side tunnel with the main passageway, they found Virginia and Terry switching their lights back on.

"Glad you two are okay," Natalie said. "We had three armed men coming toward us from the entrance we used. Camille handled the situation like a pro."

Virginia eyed Camille. "What did you do?"

Camille grinned. "I used the DMSO and ketamine solution in the sprayer I brought. We tied them up, to be on the safe side."

"Good for you, but we still have a problem," Virginia said. "There are people coming from the chamber we were in, and they've already taken pot shots at us. Time to go."

Natalie pointed in the direction of the entrance. "I think it's safe to go back the way we came. The three men we encountered are tied up and either still asleep or dead."

Camille pointed in the opposite direction. "We can go farther into the catacomb that way and avoid the side tunnel. They'll think we'll try to retreat the way we came in and won't follow us. If I were them, that's what I would think."

"And when they find their friends? Then what?" Terry asked.

"They may believe we went that way and are now out of the catacomb." Camille took a breath. "I think we should leave, but I hate to miss the opportunity to see the rest of this place."

Virginia nodded and said, "We do need to find the treasure. Maybe it's down here somewhere, so I agree with Camille."

Natalie frowned. "It's risky."

"I know. But we've come this far."

"We'd better do something fast," Camille said. "I hear voices from that tunnel."

They turned and hurried further into the recesses of the main catacomb. After hastening another quarter mile, they came to a small chamber. Their lights swung rapidly around the space, illuminating numerous trunks, metal chests, and plastic cabinets with gas bottles connected via Tygon tubes containing scrolls, papyrus, and velum documents. Three chests stood open, and the gold contents reflected their lights. Resting on a metal table were a couple of old paintings. Off to one side were various sized empty metal boxes and crates, along with four flatbed pushcarts and two moveable A-frames with block and tackle chain hoists. Wide straps were rolled and stacked next to an A-frame. Three gray metal file cabinets stood near the A-frame.

Virginia stood in shock. "I think we found the remaining stolen Vatican treasure. Those file cabinets may hold the records of any sales over the years."

Terry tapped Virginia's shoulder. "Before you start to take inventory, I'd like to point out that this is a dead end. We're trapped, again."

Virginia sighed. "Yeah, but I have a plan."

Terry closed her eyes for a moment, then glanced at Natalie and asked, "Think we have enough ammunition?"

"I'm not planning on a war," Virginia stated.

"Good to know. What do you propose?"

Virginia slid her map from her pocket and unfolded it. She pointed. "I remember passing these small side niches. We set a trap here in the cavern, then retreat to these niches. When our pursuers go by, we let them come in here and trigger our trap. That should neutralize a few of them. Then, as the remaining men try to get away, we take them out as they pass us."

Natalie looked at the map. "Or, once they pass and get here, we hightail it out of the catacomb the way we came in."

Terry looked at the map with a thoughtful expression. "Can I make another suggestion?"

Virginia nodded. "Of course. What did you have in mind?"

"We set your trap, whatever that is, and we hide in the niches until the men pass, like you said. As they get… get involved with the trap, we go to the room you and I found, take the lift up to the villa, and leave while the men run through the catacomb looking for us."

Natalie frowned. "May not be the best idea. There are probably more men there. Then what?"

"We would have the element of surprise on our side. They have men down here so, maybe they'll think the lift is carrying their own people," Terry added. "We take them down, then leave."

"Surprise doesn't stop bullets."

"True, but they won't be expecting us, and we are a determined group of women."

"It's insane," said Camille. "Like Natalie said, we don't know what we'll be walking into. It could be a room full of armed men."

"But it just might work." Natalie reached behind her and touched her backpack. "To add insult to injury, after we get to the villa, we can use the EMP devices and knock out the electrical power. That'll add a little more… surprise. Maybe enough that we don't get captured or killed."

"I like it." Virginia looked at Camille. "You have anything to add?"

"No. I like the going to the villa idea. But if Giacopetti is there, with more men with guns… it will turn ugly in a hurry, and we'll be outnumbered and most likely outgunned. And one more thing, if we do this, we can't hurt the artifacts."

"Agreed. Let's get busy," Virginia said. She looked at the women. "What?"

Natalie shook her head. "We aren't mind readers, Virginia. What's the trap we're setting up?" She turned toward the tunnel and listened. "We'd better get busy, and fast. It sounds like our nemeses must have found their unconscious buddies. We may have company soon."

Virginia turned around. "I feel a breeze."

"Maybe another way out?"

Camille pointed. "No, just a ventilation hole in the ceiling."

Terry hurried to the area beneath the vent and looked up. "It's a decent size. There had to be one around here to help ventilate the catacomb. There are probably a number of them throughout the catacomb system."

Virginia rushed to the vent. "Can we climb out?"

"No. It's not quite big enough, and there is nothing to hang on to. And remember, we're about sixty feet underground."

"You know that, but the guys after us may think the distance to the surface is shorter, so we can let them think we're slowly climbing out. It would be a good way to lure them into our trap."

CHAPTER 33

The four women worked fast.

Terry and Camille moved a stepladder under the vent hole. Terry stood at the top of the ladder with bits of torn fabric and positioned them on the ladder and into the vent hole. She scraped the sides of the vent to resemble someone using their back and feet to ascend the hole. Satisfied, she climbed down, tossed some dirt on the steps of the ladder, then sprayed the sides of it with the DMSO and ketamine solution. "Hopefully that will be convincing. And when they encounter the solution on the ladder, they will be out of the game."

"The light won't be good up there, so I think it'll work," Camille said. "I just hope they aren't smart enough to realize someone couldn't climb out."

"I agree. What are Virginia and Natalie up to?" Terry glanced around and saw light beams from headlamps flashing around the small cavern.

Virginia called out. "We're done here. How are you two doing?"

"Finished," Camille replied.

"Okay, let's get out of here."

Terry and Camille rushed to Virginia and looked around. Terry frowned. "Where is Natalie? Is the trap ready?"

"It is now," called Natalie as she hurried to the others. "I'd love to stay and watch but… let's go while we still can." She followed the others down the catacomb to a short, side recess with rubble on the floor and in the entrance.

The four women climbed over the rocks and hid in the alcove. Five minutes later, six large men with pistols and assault rifles stormed past them. The leader shouted something in rapid Italian.

Natalie leaned close to Camille and whispered, "What did he say? I couldn't make out any of it."

"It's an atrocious Roman dialect of sorts. Not the pretty Florence or Tuscany Italian. He shouted to try to bully us. It's the usual BS guys with big bodies and small brains use to try to intimidate people. I wish I could see their faces when things go to pot on them."

More shouting came from the direction of the small cavern, then rapid bright flashes, a series of explosions, and loud screams and chaos. Then only a couple of moans and groans.

Terry looked at Virginia. "What did you do?"

"Camille was right when she said things were going to go to pot. We set up the flash-bang grenades, positioned the DMSO and ketamine canisters, and sprayed part of the area with the SRH stuff."

"Oh, God! You didn't! You used the SRH?" Terry gave Virginia a questioning expression. "How the hell did you get it into Italy?"

Camille looked confused. "What's SRH?"

Virginia chuckled. "A few years ago, on the *Trail of Threads* case, Terry and I were in the jungle in Central America and discovered a compound the natives used as a weapon. It caused your bowels to empty suddenly, rapidly, and painfully. It incapacitates you in a hurry. We couldn't pronounce what the natives called it, so Terry and I named it the *Shit Releasing Hormone* or SRH. It has come in handy a few times. A chemistry professor friend of Andy's, at the university where he works, figured out how to make it in the lab and provided me with some for the trip."

Camille smiled. "I can just picture what things look like in there right now. Not pretty. The smell would be pretty bad, too. You guys are mean... I'm glad I'm on your side."

Virginia looked out at the tunnel. "Now would be a good time to move out."

Virginia hurriedly climbed over the rubble, with the others following. She bolted down the catacomb and turned into the side tunnel that connected to the work area. The large spotlights were now on, illuminating the cavern. They quickly stepped around the tables, over electrical cables, gas tubing, and cabinets to the now open lift. She then motioned for them to climb into the elevator, closed the door, and pressed the up button. Virginia took a breath. "I hope there isn't a welcoming committee up there."

The lift started to move up. Natalie moaned. "Now you think of that?"

The elevator slowly rose and jerked to a stop. Virginia turned. "Get down. Someone may be ready to shoot. Natalie, you toss a couple of the flash-bangs out. Terry, you spray the DMSO solution into the area, and I'll toss in a small EMP device. Make sure all *your* electronics are off. Otherwise they'll be fried."

Terry raised an eyebrow. "How small is small for your EMP gadget?"

"About fifty yards... give or take a couple."

Camille tapped Virginia's shoulder. "What can I do?"

Virginia looked at the pistol in Camille's belt. "Where did you get that?"

Camille patted the semiautomatic in her belt. "Compliments of the guys

Natalie and I took down."

Virginia bent down and pulled a .38 special from her ankle. "Take this one, too. A revolver is more reliable, and I know this will fire. You don't know how good a condition that one is in. If someone is either shooting or going to shoot at us, use the revolver. Don't hesitate, just aim, and fire. Okay?"

"Yes."

"One more thing. First close your eyes and cover your ears, or you'll be temporarily blind and deaf because of the flash-bangs."

Camille took the pistol. "Okay. Thanks."

The elevator door hissed open into a brightly lit room with three men inside. One holding a radio started to turn and said, "What was keeping you? I tried to… oh, shit!"

The crouched women rapidly exited the elevator. Natalie tossed the grenades, Terry cut lose a spray of the DMSO solution, and Virginia threw a small black box into the room. The room went dark. The blinding flashes from the grenades were like bright arc-lamp strobe lights as they went off. The noise was deafening. There was a flash and report from a gun across the room. A bullet slammed into the rear of the elevator. That was quickly followed by two shots from Camille's revolver. Then nothing.

The women waited ten seconds. Virginia used her headlamp to illuminate the room. The three men were on the floor. Two were unconscious. Blood trickled from their ears. The third was stretched across a chair, moaning but otherwise not moving. Virginia noticed two bullet holes in his chest.

Camille used her flashlight to look around. "Our entrance wasn't very subtle, was it? What do we do now?"

Virginia looked at the man Camille had shot. "Nice shooting."

"I was a sheriff's deputy in the Bay Area of California while doing my graduate work. Got a lot of practice."

"Now you tell me?"

"Sorry, just—well, I'm new with all this and didn't want to seem like a braggart or something." Camille swung her light at the men. "Any idea who they are?"

Virginia nodded. "Hired goons. Gino Giacopetti isn't in this bunch, and he wasn't in the catacomb either. We need to see if he is here someplace and subdue him, then get out of the villa. Someone may have heard the gunfire, and I don't want to explain things to the Italian police." She pointed at the area near the downed men. "Stay clear of that space. The DMSO solution is still on all the surfaces."

They walked around the men and went out into a dark hall. The heavy window drapes were drawn. The villa was dark. No signs of any other lights but theirs.

Camille swallowed. "Might be a good time to just vacate the premises.

We can locate Giacopetti later."

Terry tilted her head. "Good idea. I hear sirens."

Natalie shined her light on the sweeping stairway. "Here's a way down."

Camille glanced back into the room. "How about the man I shot?"

Natalie frowned. "Do you care? He tried to shoot us."

"Yes, but he's just a... a man doing his job. He isn't behind all this, and he may be still alive."

"What? Were you a medic as well as a deputy sheriff?" Natalie asked.

"Matter of fact, yes."

"Okay. Let's go see how he's doing," Virginia sighed. "We can take him along if need be or leave him for the police."

They turned back toward the room, when the front door of the villa burst open, and a voice called up from the first floor. "Police! Anyone in here show yourselves now!"

Natalie pulled out her last flash-bang grenade. "Just our luck. They got here fast. Must be a donut shop close by. I could—"

"Let's not antagonize the fuzz any more than we have to," Virginia whispered. "We need to go out the way we came in, disappear like Ninjas in the night."

"How? The elevator is fried." Terry murmured, "I hear more police cars arriving."

They returned to the room with the elevator and closed the door. Natalie swung her light around. "No other doors."

Terry rose from beside the man Camille had shot. "We don't have to worry about him. What's the plan?"

"Over here," Camille said. "I found our exit."

Virginia shined her light toward Camille. She stood next to an opening in the wood paneling. "Good job. How did you find that?"

"I've been in Rome long enough to know these old villas usually had secret passages to allow the owner to escape burglars and to clandestinely visit their mistresses. I figured if there was one it had to be on this wall or the one opposite since the elevator is on the back wall and the door leads to the hallway." She swung her arm toward the opening. "Shall we go?"

Virginia turned at the sound of people pounding up the stairs. "Natalie, toss that toy of yours out the door and get back here."

"Okay." Natalie hurried to the entrance, cracked the door open and tossed her last flash-bang grenade into the air and rushed back to the hidden passage as it went off.

With the four women inside the passage, Camille closed the concealed door.

Virginia shined her light in both directions. "Now, which way is out?"

CHAPTER 34

Virginia shined her light in both directions. Then she pointed to her left. "This way. Looks like a ladder over there."

The women followed Virginia down the narrow passageway and stopped at a wooden ladder affixed to the wall studs.

They stood at the ladder, when Natalie sneezed. "Sorry. It's the dust."

Virginia shook her head. "I hope no one heard you but us."

"Me, too."

"It is dusty and has a… unique… smell," Terry said.

Camille wrinkled her nose. "That odor? Probably the fragrance of dead rats and a lot of garlic."

"Dead, garlic-seasoned rats or not, this'll at least get us to the first floor. Maybe we'll find a secret exit from the villa there." Terry quietly climbed down the ladder to the first floor. The other women joined her. Terry looked around. "If there is an exit on this level, it may lead us directly to the police; they're both inside and out. Could there be another way… like a tunnel to someplace away from the cops?"

Camille waved her lamp from ten feet to their right. "There's another ladder here that goes down."

Virginia wiped a cobweb from her face. "Let's go down and see what we've got."

They descended the ladder to the basement level. Virginia noticed the passageway went only one direction from where they were. "Can't use these concealed entrances back into the villa. Too many cops. Looks like our options are limited. Let's follow the tunnel and see what kind of dilemma we've gotten ourselves into."

Camille took the lead. After a couple of turns around corners, she stopped and pointed. "There is another passageway, and it goes away from the villa. The one that ends down there ends at a wall."

"Don't waste valuable time. Go… we're right behind you," said Natalie.

They continued through the side tunnel, until they reached a wall with a rusted steel door set in concrete and stone. Virginia pressed her ear against the door and listened. "No noise. Shall we give it a try?"

Virginia and Terry took hold of the big wheel in the middle and tried to turn it. Nothing happened. It was rusted in place. Virginia leaned against the door. "Nuts. Stuck. Not what we need right now."

Natalie pulled a small spray canister from her backpack. "Excuse me." She stepped around the women to the door and sprayed the wheel's shaft, locking bolts, and anything that looked like it could move. Then she stepped back. "Okay, try again."

Virginia sighed, then with Terry's help, tried to turn the wheel. After three tries, the wheel creaked and slowly rotated. They rotated it four times, when it stopped. The round bolts slid back into the door. It moved slightly. Light streamed through the small slit on the edge. She glanced at Natalie. "What did you do?"

Natalie held up the canister. "WD 40."

Virginia chuckled. "You brought WD 40 with you? Why?"

"Yeah. Well, I wasn't planning on it. I had used it on a wheel at my ranch and just stuffed it into my suitcase and forgot it until we got here. I tossed it into my backpack when we got to Rome."

"Good job." She carefully eased the door open and peered outside. Faint light streamed in through small rectangular widows set high in the basement walls. "We're in the basement of a building." Virginia stepped through the portal, followed by the women.

Camille glanced at the massive stone support columns, wooden rafters, battered trunks, crates, and shelves with various dust-covered articles on them, then pointed at a set of old, cracked and discolored statues leaning against a support column. "By the looks of those saints and the surroundings, I think we're in the basement of a large church. It's musty down here." She moved toward a sagging wooden set of shelves, then frantically wiped her face. "I hate cobwebs. They give me the creeps."

"Let's get out before some padre catches us and calls the cops," Terry said. "There are stairs over there."

They hustled to the worn stone staircase and climbed up. Virginia listened again at the door, and hearing nothing, she eased it open. They were in the church sanctuary behind the main altar. "Okay, let's try to look normal and walk out of here."

Terry gave a soft laugh. "The way we look right now is more like street bums. And we certainly don't belong in this part of the church."

"You can't wash up," said Natalie. "Let's just try not to attract too much attention."

Camille stopped and pulled out her cell phone. "Got some bars. Before we go any further, I'm calling the Vatican. They need to know where the treasure is before it gets lost again or tied up in Italian bureaucracy."

"Good idea," Virginia said.

They waited as Camille softly spoke in rapid Italian to someone on her phone. After a few minutes, she disconnected. "Okay. The Vatican police, along with people from the museum, are racing toward Gino Giacopetti's villa and to the entrance to the catacomb we used."

"How did you explain what we did?"

"I didn't. I called a special number and gave them a detailed tip off. The Vatican has no idea we called this in."

Terry patted Camille's shoulder. "You're becoming as devious as we are."

"Thank you." Camille looked at Virginia. "Now what?"

"We get out of here, go back to the hotel, and call the Smithsonian Central Security Service to report what we found," said Virginia. "Then we plan our next move."

Terry shook her head. "What's our next move, and am I going to like it?"

"Trust me, you'll love it. We're going after Gino Giacopetti."

Terry groaned. "I had to ask."

Natalie stepped back from the edge of the altar base and whispered. "Only a couple of parishioners and a priest out there. Good time to boogie."

The four women strolled out from behind the high, main altar, into the large nave, past wooden pews, Gothic columns, side chapels, large, high, stained-glass windows, and Byzantine mosaics. The lone priest gave them a questioning look, smiled, and then returned to talking to a woman. They walked down the side aisle toward the main doors, when they heard a commotion behind them. Virginia stopped and turned. She let out a frustrated sigh. "Now what?"

An elderly, short, round nun in full habit was hurrying toward them waving a bright burnt-orange baseball cap. "*Toilette per signore. Uno di voi ha lasciato cadere il berretto.*"

Camille smiled. "She says one of us dropped their hat."

"That's mine," said Virginia. "It must have fallen out of my backpack. So much for not being noticed." She walked to the nun and took the hat. "*Grazie.* How can I thank you, Sister?"

Camille translated "*Come posso ringraziarti, sorella?*"

The nun just shook her head. "*Non necessario mia figlia.*"

"She said it—"

"It isn't necessary, I got that." Virginia removed her wallet from her backpack and pulled out a twenty-dollar bill. "Please tell her this is for her troubles and the church. It's the least I can do."

Camille translated and insisted the nun take the money. Then she asked the nun for her name.

The nun smiled at Virginia. In a slow broken English she said, "My...

nome is *Madre*... Mother Isabella. *Grazie per la vostra generosità.*"

"It is no problem. Thank you for my hat."

Mother Isabella looked at the cap with a puzzled expression, then said something in Italian.

Camille smiled, "She said it's a funny color."

Virginia held the hat up. "It's from the University of Texas."

Mother Isabella's eye widened. *"Le università con la mucca con le grandi corna?"*

Camille laughed. "She asked if it is the university with the cows with the big horns."

Virginia pointed at the Longhorn symbol of University of Texas on the front of the cap "Yes. The cow is a Texas longhorn."

Camille translated. *"Sì. La mucca è un longhorn del Texas."*

"Texas? Sì, tutto è più grande in Texas, giusto?" asked the smiling Mother Isabella.

"Yes, everything is bigger in Texas," said Virginia. "Even the cows."

Mother Isabella chuckled, then turned and said as she walked away, *"Faresti meglio a sbrigarti, la polizia è nel tunnel. Li bloccherò."*

Camille's brown eyes widened. "She said the police are in the tunnel, and we need to hurry. She'll try to stall them."

"Now she tells us," Natalie said. "Maybe you should have given her a fifty and the hat."

"Maybe, but let's get out of here fast," Virginia said.

They quickly walked to the front of the church and out the huge, dark, ornately carved wooden doors. They stopped in the street. Virginia looked at the people around them. "Let's split up. Natalie, you and Terry wind your way back to the hotel. Camille and I will take a different route. If by some chance the cops are looking for us, they would be seeking four women. We won't make it easy by all being together. Change your appearance a little by using the hats you brought and tie the souvenir stuff we brought onto the backpacks."

"Will that be enough?" asked Terry.

"It should. With the number of people and tourists around, a little change can be more than enough."

Camille nodded. "You're right. I remember that from my sheriff's training." She put on oversized red sunglasses. "These should help as well."

"Same idea we used in Hollywood," Natalie stated. "Cosmetic changes can be huge."

They did the modifications to their appearances as they parted and walked in different directions. Turning the street corner, Virginia glanced over her shoulder and spotted two confused police officers standing on the steps of the church, looking around while Mother Isabella berated them. Virginia and Camille disappeared into the crowd.

CHAPTER 35

Sitting around the living room of Virginia and Natalie's hotel suite, eating pizza and drinking beer, the four women watched the news on TV with Camille translating the announcer's words. "The Rome and Vatican police, acting on an anonymous tip, complaints of noise, and power problems from the neighbors, raided Gino Giacopetti's villa and the catacombs beneath the villa. The discovery of Giacopetti's incapacitated henchmen, part of the Vatican treasure, which was stolen in the 1940s, a dead body, and his business of selling the artifacts and illegal copies, had resulted in arrest warrants being issued for Giacopetti."

Virginia sat back on the sofa. "Well, it seems we did a pretty good job today. But Giacopetti is in the wind. We need to capture him."

Camille sipped her beer. "Why? The police now know of his activities, seized his bank accounts, and are looking for him."

"The Vatican investigators have been looking for the treasure for over seventy years and never found it, and now, even though they know who he is, they probably won't find him. He's smart, crafty, and probably has money stashed someplace, just in case something like this happened. But we, on the other hand, are dedicated, have resources, and do not have other cases to work on. And he pissed me off."

Natalie finished her slice of pizza and reached for another. "I'm game."

Terry nodded. "Me, too." She eyed her slice of pizza as she bit into it. "This is really good. It must be the cheese. I think we should investigate more if for no other reason than for the food in Italy."

Natalie sat back, eyed her slice of pizza, and sighed. "You're right, this is good. Now, Virginia, where do we start?"

Camille's cell phone rang. She answered, and after a brief conversation, hung up. "That was a friend of mine at the Vatican Museum. He said the police have confiscated the treasure in the caves and related items and moved them to the museum for inventorying and authentication. There are a number of fakes included."

"At least they've been taken to a safe place," said Terry.

"There's more. They found records that gave the history of Giacopetti's sales of both the real artifacts and the fakes. The problem is, they are in some sort of code."

"We need to get a copy of that history," said Terry. "It may give us an idea as to where he might go."

Natalie dabbed her mouth with a napkin. "Even if we get it, we'd need to crack the code first."

Camille grinned. "A copy is being emailed to me tonight. I'll send it to you all when I get it." She looked at the other women. "Don't ask."

Virginia stood and moved the whiteboard, that the hotel had provided them a couple of days earlier, to a position in front of the sliding glass patio doors. "Okay, let's do some brainstorming. What do we know?"

"Giacopetti's a crook," said Camille.

"He's a con man," added Natalie. "And the cops are after him."

Terry mumbled, "He knows the catacombs pretty well."

"He uses codes to safeguard his clients' IDs," added Natalie.

Virginia copied everything on the board then added, "He is smart, likes money, is a showman, likes attractive women, he's shrewd, and probably has money hidden somewhere."

"He may still be somewhere in Rome," added Natalie. "I wouldn't be surprised if he doesn't have a couple of backup places to hide until the heat blows over."

Camille grew pensive. "He can travel throughout Europe without going through immigration, so we'd never know if he slipped into another country. He may even have multiple identities."

"Okay." Virginia added Natalie and Camille's comments to the list. "What can we surmise from all this?"

Terry chuckled. "He'll live well in some country without extradition."

"You're probably right. But what if we leak to the press that a number of the artifacts he sold were fakes?"

Camille looked stunned. "That might get him killed."

"But it might cause him to panic and do something stupid," said Virginia.

"But we may not know he's done anything rash," said Natalie. "What if we let the word out, among the population of Rome with less than stellar reputations, that we, some unscrupulous ladies, are in the market for some of his artifacts? You know, we have rich, discreet buyers in the U.S., and we still need to fill some orders. A man with his ego might jump at the chance for a last score, especially if he still has some of the treasure or a few of his fakes. He'd definitely like a chance to kill all of us. This way, he comes to us."

Virginia smiled. "I like it. Not the killing us part, though."

Camille took a sip of her beer. "I know just the people to start with."

She pulled her phone from her pocket and went to her suite to make the calls.

An hour later, Camille returned to Virginia's suite. "I called some devious and somewhat callous contacts in Rome's underground art and antiquities trade. They'll get back with me when they have something to report."

Terry tilted her head and asked, "Why would they call you? You're not a crook."

Camille plopped onto an upholstered chair. "They know I'm honest, but in more than one instance I bailed their sorry asses out of trouble. A couple of times with the cops, but mostly with rivals who were bent on killing them. They owe me. I told them I have a friend who knows these… designing, unethical women who travel in the illegal arts world. And if I could use these deceitful women to catch Giacopetti and make him either disappear or turn him over to the police, it would enhance my stature at the Vatican Museum and the Smithsonian and get him out of their… businesses. They also would get a generous reward, and I'd owe them a favor."

Natalie finished her drink. "They bought that?"

"Yeah. They are not the brightest crayons in the box, but they understand *generous reward* and they don't like Giacopetti. From what they said, he has screwed most of them over a time or two. So, add a favor from me, revenge, along with greed, and Giacopetti doesn't have a friend in Rome's underworld."

Virginia smiled. "I like it. When do you think we'll hear from any of them?"

"Maybe tomorrow. Not sure, really." Camille looked at her phone. "Giacopetti's coded list is here. I'll forward it to all of you now."

Virginia eyed the message on her phone. "Thank you. I don't know about you guys, but I'm tired. I think we can wait until tomorrow to try and crack the code."

Terry stretched. "I think after everything we've been through, we need a night on the town. A little R&R."

Virginia sighed. "So much for rest. Camille, you know Rome better than us, got any ideas where we can safely go tonight for some fun?"

Camille sat back and grinned. "Oh, yeah."

Natalie glanced out the window. "We'd better go out prepared for trouble. I'm sure none of us are on Giacopetti's Christmas card list."

Virginia glanced out the dark patio window. *I hope this little R&R of Terry's doesn't get us killed.*

CHAPTER 36

Having had dinner earlier at *Trattorio da Bucatino*, the women exited *Conte Staccio* nightclub at eleven that evening. They strolled down *Via di Monte Testaccio*. "So much for being party animals," Virginia said. "It's early by the standards of the people at that nightclub, but I'm tired."

"Me, too," Camille said.

Virginia scanned the area. "Don't look back, but we're being followed."

"I knew we attracted too many lonely Italian men's attention," said Natalie.

Virginia chuckled. "Your evening ensemble would attract dead men."

Terry glanced backwards. "They're gaining on us."

"There are three of them and four of us. And they don't know we're armed," said Camille.

Virginia tried to flag down a cab. No luck. "Looks like we're on our own." She spotted a black panel truck heading in their direction. "This may not be good."

The truck screeched to a halt next to the women and the side door slid open. Two men jumped out as the three men following them rapidly approached. One man, dressed in a dark blue turtleneck sweater and jeans, grabbed Virginia's blouse. She made a quick and powerful jab into the man's throat. He stumbled back grasping his neck and trying to breathe.

Natalie stepped close to the next man out of the van and kneed him in the groin. He tumbled to the ground, moaning and holding his crotch.

The three men, coming up to them from behind, slowed and gazed at the fallen men. Terry approached the closest of the trio and sprayed bear strength pepper spray into his face. He turned screaming and ran.

The last two men held out their hands palms up and quickly backed off, then turned and retreated into the night.

Camille watched them disappear. "Hell, I didn't get to spray them with the SRH stuff. You guys had all the fun."

Natalie looked at Camille. "Fun?"

Camille pointed at the man holding his groin. "At least you got to impede his love life for a while."

Natalie turned to see the man she kneed starting to rise. "True." She moved closer to him and pushed him over. "Who sent you?"

He glared at her but didn't respond.

Camille stepped to the man and said something in Italian. He just shook his head and tried crawling back into the van. The man Virginia hit was still on the ground and looked pale and was still trying to catch his breath. Camille knelt next to him and repeated her question in Italian. He tried to say something, but it came out garbled. She stood and turned to Virginia. "I asked him who sent them. They weren't very cooperative."

Virginia nodded. "I noticed."

"Let's get out of here before the police come."

They hurried down the street, toward the Tiber River. Once there, they headed in the direction of their hotel and watched for a cab. As they approached the *Piazza del Cavalieri di Malta* on the *Lgt Aventino,* another utility van quickly rounded a corner and abruptly stopped next to the women.

The doors suddenly slid open and a man jumped out, holding a Heckler & Koch MP5A2 9mm Submachine Gun on them. He waved the gun. "*Raccogliere,*" he said.

Not a good idea to try something with that machine gun aimed at us. Grabbing for it will get someone killed. Virginia nodded. "I don't need a translation. We're getting in." She and the others climbed into the van. The man with the machine gun took Terry's pepper spray.

They sat on the floor, guarded by the man holding the machine gun. Another man drove as the vehicle sped through Rome. After a short ride, the van approached a dilapidated building. The door slid open, and the van entered a building. They were inside what appeared to Virginia to be an abandoned automotive garage. The women were forced out of the van. Virginia noticed oil stains on the concrete, the remains of a car lift, and pieces of a broken compressor against the far wall. An old faded pinup-calendar was pinned to a corkboard near a grimy, cracked window and dirty workbench. A banged up gray cabinet stood at an angle against the far wall. A rusty wrench lay on the floor next to a battered empty toolbox. They were prodded toward the rear and then told to climb down a wooden ladder. The space they were now in was a bricked chamber with a large metal plate set into the floor in the center of the room with an iron ring attached. Attached to the iron ring were chains. While still being covered by the man with the submachine gun, the women were pushed down against the side wall and the chains attached to their wrists. The men then went back up the ladder and shut the door. The sound of a bolt being slid followed. The only illumination was from a single dim bulb suspended from the ceiling.

Terry fumed. "I hope the hotel has a good dry-cleaning service. My dress is a mess."

Camille rattled the chain. "We're chained up and locked in a... a musty, dirty, brick vault... it may have been an old cistern, and you're worried about your dress? We need to get out of here." She turned as Virginia slipped the belt from her slacks, removed a Velcroed pouch, and pulled out a couple of small metal tools. "Virginia, what are you doing?"

"Getting us out of here before someone else decides to visit us." Virginia picked the lock on her chain and opened the locks for the others. She removed the heel of her boot and extracted a small blob of what looked like Play-Doh.

Camille frowned. "Plastic explosive? C-4?"

"No. SEMTEX. Nice thing about this stuff is shock won't set it off, so it was safe in my heel."

"Where did you get that?"

"From Cousin Luigi."

"Who?"

"I'll explain later." Virginia removed something from the other boot and wound wires together. She then rose to her feet and went to the ladder. She climbed, pressed her ear to the trap door, and listened. "Sounds like two men. One standing on the trapdoor," she whispered. Virginia pressed the SEMTEX into position. Next, she inserted a small rod and connected it to an inch square device. She jumped down and hurried to a far corner. "Get over here and cover your ears." Fifteen seconds later, a resounding explosion blew the door into pieces. The escape path was now clear.

Virginia recovered from the sound of the blast and climbed the ladder first to scan the situation. "May have used too much SEMTEX. Oh, well." Blood, bone, body parts, and gore of the man standing on the door when the detonation happened were spewed around the garage and ceiling. The second man lay a few feet away against a wall. His head was bloody, mangled, and resting at an unnatural angle. Pieces of the wood from the door stuck out of his chest, abdomen, and legs. One arm was twisted in an abnormal direction. He wasn't moving. She climbed out, followed by the others.

Natalie turned all around, looking nauseated. "You made quite a mess."

Camille glanced around. "Yuck. If I hadn't been a sheriff's deputy and a paramedic in my past life, I'd be sick. But this has made me squeamish."

"The smell of carnage and grease is enough to gag a maggot." Terry pointed at the van parked near the rear of the garage. "If the keys are in it, let's take it and vamoose. No need to wait for their friends or the police to come."

Camille scurried to the vehicle and looked inside. "Keys are in the ignition. But I'd suggest we use gloves, in case the cops find it after we're done."

Natalie looked around the space. "If there aren't any in that metal cabinet, then we're out of luck." She hurried to the cabinet and opened it. She pulled out some clean, white shop rags. "These will have to do." She tossed them to the others.

Virginia climbed into driver's seat as the others clambered into the van and drove across the open space, stopping at the closed overhead door. Terry jumped out, pushed the up button on a control box next to it, and scampered back into the van as the door rose. They sped out into the dark Roman evening as the sounds of sirens could be heard approaching.

Natalie settled on the floor in the back and against the side of the vehicle. "Someone must have heard the explosion. I'd love to know who was responsible for our kidnapping."

Terry chuckled. "I bet Mr. Giacopetti won't be too thrilled about what we just did."

Virginia drove back to the hotel and parked the van a block down the street. They left the van idling with the keys in it and strolled to the hotel.

Camille glanced back at the van as they walked away. "I hope someone steals it."

As they entered, the gentleman manning the front desk called Virginia over. "Signora Clark. You have a message."

She went to the counter. "Who's it from?"

He looked at the envelope. "It says, 'Your Cousin Luigi'."

CHAPTER 37

Before dawn, a dark blue BMW slowly drove by the abandoned garage, where numerous police and fire vehicles crowded the street in front. Emergency beacons illuminated the neighborhood. Giacopetti peered out the rear window. "What the hell happened? Where are the women?"

His driver shook his head. "I don't know, *signore*. Giovani said on the telephone that they captured the four women and secured them with chains in the chamber below the floor. We have heard nothing since then."

Giacopetti waved his arm. "Yes. And now we know why. He said the women took out the first group and walked away." His face reddened. "They just walked away from five tough men. Giovanni said he captured them right after that and had them chained and locked up. Now we have this mess on top of the disaster at the villa and catacombs. Are the women dead in there?"

The driver turned a corner and drove toward central Rome. "According to the *polizia* scanner, someone in a building down the street heard a loud explosion and called the *polizia*. The *polizia* discovered one man dead with multiple injuries and the other… ahh… scattered all over the walls, ceiling, and floor. Giovanni maybe? The door to the basement was blown open, but they found no trace of anyone else in the building. The women are gone. The van used by Giovanni to capture the women was stolen, and this garage was abandoned, so as not to be traceable to you, *signore*. The van is still missing."

Giacopetti slammed his fist against the seat. "The women did this, then… then just drove away with the truck?"

"*Si.*"

"I want those women captured and brought to me. I will kill each of them slowly and painfully!"

"*Signore*, maybe it would be a good idea to move to your country retreat and let this cool down first."

"Those… those damn women found my operation in the catacombs and my villa and now the police have everything that was there… including all my records. They have severely crippled my operation. It has worked well and undetected for decades. Even the church, with all its resources, couldn't find it. Now four brazen American women waltz into Rome, and in a few days destroy everything? I can't believe it! I want them all dead!"

The driver's cell phone rang. "Ciao?" He listened then disconnected. "*Signor* Giacopetti, that was a contact of mine. There is more bad news."

"More?" Giacopetti tensed. "What now?"

"The *polizia* have warrants for your arrest."

"This will change our plans a bit. We'll have to move our operation again."

"That's not all. The women you want have sent the word out among certain parties that they have buyers in the United States for some Etruscan and early Roman artifacts, especially yours."

Giacopetti turned red. "They did what?"

"They put the word on the street that they want your artifacts, *signore*."

He closed his eyes and took a deep, calming breath. "Well, how about that. This could work well for me."

"But there are those who know you have been crippled and are no longer your allies."

Giacopetti's temper flared. "Meaning?"

"Others, besides the police and the women, want to dethrone you, sir. Your rivals wish to see you fail. They will take the artifacts and cut you out. Really cut you... out."

"So, we kill the women and anyone who tries to steal from me," Giacopetti said through gritted teeth. "Any idea who these parties are?"

"Just two so far, *signore*. *Signor* Franco on the east side, and *Signor* Cappelli."

"They are *pericoloso*... dangerous. But at least we know who our enemies are. Do you know where the women are living, while in Roma?"

"No, *signore*."

"That's too bad." Giacopetti started to cool down. "Okay. Take me to our apartment, Joe. At least it isn't in my name, so it is untraceable. I need to relax and work things out with a nice glass of vintage vino."

CHAPTER 38

Virginia entered her suite, followed by the other women. She sat on the loveseat, opened the message, and read it. "Camille, we may have signed Giacopetti's death warrant."

Camille sat on an overstuffed chair across from Virginia. "Why?"

"According to Cousin Luigi, two criminal organizations are now after Giacopetti. To make things even worse for him, the police have warrants for his arrest."

"So, if we don't capture him first, the police will get him, or his competitors will kill him. Problem solved."

Virginia nodded. "Pretty much. Us capturing him wouldn't do him much good, either. We'd turn him over to the police. So, his selling us the artifacts probably wouldn't be much incentive for him to come to us."

"Oh, he'd come to us." Terry plopped down on the couch near the window with a glass of wine. "Probably because he wants to kill us."

Natalie sat next to Terry on the couch and sighed. "Nice to know we're wanted."

Camille looked horrified. "Someone wants to kill us, and you three... you're so calm, like this is normal."

Terry sipped her wine. "Yeah, but they don't have alligators in Rome."

"Huh?"

"Don't get her started with the alligators," said Virginia. "It's a long story."

"It tried to eat me," complained Terry. She leaned forward and looked at Camille. "We were in the jungle of Central America, on the *Trail of Threads* case, fleeing from upset natives and a crazed drug lord that we pissed off, when we encountered the alligators."

Virginia sighed. "You shot it."

Holding her glass in a tight grip, Terry drank the rest of the wine. "I still see his toothy grin in my sleep."

Camille's eyes widened. "Are you people for real? Crazed drug lords? Upset natives? Alligators? People shooting at you and trying to kill you?

Getting captured by men with machineguns and you blowing people up? I take it you all routinely attract trouble like bees to honey."

Natalie chuckled. "Yeah. We do. Keeps life interesting."

"Do you three have normal lives as well?" Camille rubbed her temple. "Like with no one wanting to kill you?"

Virginia set Luigi's note down. "Yes, we are usually normal people with real jobs, friends, and families, without mad killers chasing us." She pointed at Natalie. "She even owns a ranch."

"Good to know. Did your... Cousin Luigi say anything else in his message?"

"He said the people after Giacopetti work for *Signor* Franco and *Signor* Cappelli. Know them?"

"Yes. I know of them. They are a couple of gentlemen who traffic in stolen art, artifacts, rare books, cocaine, fentanyl, and other nasty drugs in central and southern Italy." Camille brushed a strand of her brown hair from her face. "From what I learned working at the Vatican Museum, they have operations with others, like a consortium, in Greece, France, Egypt and Spain. Franco and Cappelli are not the kind of men you want mad at you. They are well connected. Prosecutors have never had enough evidence to convict them, and witnesses disappear before any trials." Camille stood and hurried to the minibar, poured herself a tall drink, and drank half in one gulp. "I thought being a deputy sheriff was stressful. After meeting you all, that job was a cake walk. Virginia, you just blew a man to bits and killed another tonight, and here we sit, discussing things like nothing happened." She turned to Terry. "You're right, Terry, no alligators in Rome, but I guess things can get worse."

"They probably will." Natalie frowned. "We have a copy of Giacopetti's coded customer list, right?"

Virginia looked around the suite. "Yeah, it's here somewhere." She climbed to her feet and went to her bedroom. After a couple of minutes she returned with a stack of papers. "Here is the printout. It was in the safe."

"Good. While we are all here, why don't we start unraveling the code?"

Terry put her wine glass down on the coffee table. "Because it's late and we've been through hell and back tonight, I vote for another drink, a good night's sleep, and start fresh tomorrow. Since we have Giacopetti gunning for us, it might be wise to stay close to home for a couple of days."

Camille nodded. "I'll vote for that."

Natalie yawned. "You had to mention sleep, didn't you? Okay, I think that was a good suggestion. Lock those papers back in the safe, Virginia. We can start on them tomorrow."

Hidden Threads

Natalie woke. It was still dark. She pulled her nine-millimeter Ruger semi-automatic from under her pillow and glanced toward the sound and faint light coming from the living room. She swallowed. *Now what?* She got to her feet and slowly moved close to the doorway and peered around the molding. The light was coming from a desk lamp. She spotted Virginia in her pajamas, sitting at the desk in the far corner surrounded by papers, printouts, her laptop, and pictures. A yellow pencil stuck out of her hair. Natalie lowered her weapon and padded across the room. "Virginia, what are you doing? It's four o'clock in the morning. Even the pigeons are asleep at this hour."

Virginia turned around. "I'm sorry if I woke you. I tried to be quiet. I had a thought about the coded list during the night and wanted to get on it while the thought was fresh in my mind."

Natalie eyed the mess around the desk. "Any luck?"

"Yes. I found the key to the code."

"You did?" Natalie stared at Virginia. "How?"

"It's in the quilt."

"What about it? There aren't any numbers or letters on it, and it's in Texas." Natalie glanced at the papers on the desk. "You got the answer from the pictures?"

"No, not from the pictures. From the actual quilt, and yes, there are. There is the name block on the back, but that wasn't where I thought they were. I called Andy—"

"You called your husband in the middle of the night?"

"He's seven hours behind us. I called him at three our time here in Rome. It was eight last night there. I had him heat the diamond sections of the quilt with a hair dryer."

"And?"

Virginia beamed. "He got the messages that were written in invisible ink between the lines in the fabric. The key's a steganographic code hidden in the quilt. Andy wrote the key down and emailed it to me."

"Good for him. But you'd better lock all this up and get some sleep. In the morning, at a reasonable hour, we all can start to decipher Giacopetti's coded customer list."

Virginia turned off her computer and started to gather up her documents and pictures when Natalie said, "Wait. How did the key to the code get into the old quilt in Texas, when the list belonged to Giacopetti here in Rome?"

Virginia picked up the papers and headed for her bedroom and the safe. "The same way the catacombs got in it. The treasure had to be hidden when it was stolen. Lt. Cumo could only take part of it, so the rest was left with a co-conspirator. That had to be Giacopetti's father or grandfather. The thieves made the code, so they could keep track of the treasure and communicate. Cumo put it into the quilt for safe keeping."

Natalie followed Virginia to the safe. When the files were secured inside, Natalie asked, "After we decode the lists, what then?"

"We can give them to the police, and then go get Giacopetti."

"All we need to do is walk down the street. His thugs are pretty good at trying to capture us. Then we can make them take us to him."

"Only next time, we go out properly armed and alert."

At nine in the morning, Natalie opened the door and let Terry and Camille in. A breakfast buffet, supplied by the hotel, was near the window. They found Virginia sitting at the table, munching on an almond croissant and smiling.

Terry gave her a confused look. "Why are you so happy?"

"Got the key to the coded list of Giacopetti's clients last night," Virginia said.

"Great," said Terry as she placed a croissant and a slice of mango on a plate, then sat at the table. "Where did you get it?"

"It was in the quilt. I figured the code key was there and asked my husband to look. He found it and sent me the key."

"So, when do we start to work on deciphering the list?"

Virginia finished her croissant and sipped her coffee. "We don't need to. I emailed the list and the key to… Cousin Luigi. He's got the… company's computer working on it. We should have the results by noon."

Camille sat with her dish filled with fruit, almond croissants, bacon, and scrambled eggs. "Okay. I really need to ask this. Who is this Cousin Luigi and who does he work for? What company?"

Virginia glanced at Natalie, then sighed. "Luigi is our contact here in Rome and is a friend of mine with… a lot of resources… and a great restaurant."

"Great restaurant? Nice." Camille leaned forward. "Resources? Like?"

Natalie drank her orange juice. "He provided our special weapons."

"Those special, silenced pistols, the DMSO compound, and your EMP toys?"

Virginia nodded. "And other things."

Camille sat wide-eyed. "Does he work for the SCSS like you guys?"

"No. We operate pretty much on our own. When we're in Italy, he provides things we may need, and expertise as required, like now. His computer will decipher the code a lot faster than we can."

"I see… I think." She shrugged her shoulder and started to eat her eggs. "This cousin is what? FBI? CIA? Interpol?" she mumbled.

"Camille, this is one of those times it's best not to know." Terry rose and went to the buffet for more food, then returned to her seat. "So, what's on the agenda for today?"

"While we wait for the decoded list, we need to figure out how to draw Giacopetti out, find out where he is or where he will go, and if he has any more of the treasure stashed somewhere," Virginia said. "We've already got the word on the street that we are interested in certain antiquities. But maybe there's more we can do."

Natalie drank her coffee. "I left my crystal ball in Texas."

"We don't need a crystal ball. We can start with the neighbors of his villa. Get any information they may have, descriptions of his vehicles and any other data we can gather."

Camille frowned. "The police would have already done that."

"Yes, but people sometimes remember more later. Some are nervous and reluctant talking to the police." Virginia said. "Then there are those who may have known he was a crook and done favors for him and are afraid to talk to the police. We're not the Italian police. We are just women who are interested in what happened."

"Okay, but they might not talk to some American women they think are just looking for gossip. The Italians can close ranks pretty fast."

Terry nodded. "Camille has a point. We could use some sort of cover story."

Natalie smiled. "Virginia, you need to make another call to Cousin Luigi."

Virginia's laptop made a ringing sound. She rose and rushed to it and looked at the message on the screen. "Luigi just sent Giacopetti's decoded client list and some other data that was included in it. I'll print it out and we can take a look at it. Maybe it will give us other places to start."

Natalie sipped more coffee. "Or get us killed."

CHAPTER 39

Virginia opened her computer and examined the downloaded files. "These are the lists of Giacopetti's customers, what he sold them, the addresses, and the sale prices. There are symbols next to some. That may indicate the item sold was a reproduction. There are also some other notes that need deciphering."

Terry looked over Virginia's shoulder. "Should we take this to the police?"

"And say what? Hello, Mr. Policeman, we're Americans, and we illegally broke into a locked, privately owned catacomb and home, shot a man, and stole this list, decoded it, and are now giving it to you out of the kindness of our hearts?"

"I see what you mean." Terry straightened. "We'd be so tied up in so much red tape, you could make a quilt out of it or be held in jail until we're ninety, while they took their time sorting it all out. Shooting a man probably won't win us any favors either. They'll ask about the explosion last night, too. Very inconvenient."

"We have that inspector, Inspector Tonelli, with the Rome police we used to shut down the fake bishop's Pyramid Society operation," said Natalie. "We could contact him. At least he knows we work for the SCSS and likes us."

Camille sipped some coffee. "I have an idea."

Virginia turned and looked at her. "What do you have in mind?"

"I've been at the Vatican for some time, and the Vatican police are supposed to protect me at my lab there, right?"

"Yeah."

"They know me. What if I take the new information to the Vatican police?"

"They'll ask you where you got it as well," said Virginia. "Either we give it to them officially as SCSS agents and hope we don't get into hot water for operating on their turf, or we—"

"We could do what we did before and give it simultaneously to the

Hidden Threads

Rome inspector as well as the Vatican police agents we contacted as SCSS agents," added Terry. "Since the officers we used before know us and are happy about us helping them take down the Pyramid Society and the bogus bishop, they may not ask too many questions. We can tell them they can say this information was the result of *their* investigations and leave us out of the picture."

Natalie finished her breakfast. "That's a good idea. We share the decoded list with officers we know at both agencies. Then what?"

"Hold that thought," said Virginia. "I've got the Inspector Tonelli's email address. I'll send him the information. Camille, can you email the Vatican police?"

"Yes. I'll get my laptop." Camille rose and hurried to her suite. A couple of minutes later, she returned and set the computer on the coffee table. "Okay, email me the documents, and I'll forward them to the Vatican."

A half hour later, after sending the list to the police, the women sat staring at the decoded documents. Natalie sat back, rubbing her eyes. "I had to ask what was next, didn't I? I should know better than to say 'then what'. Now I'm seeing double. Tell me again what we're looking for."

Terry looked up. "Anything to give us a clue as to where Giacopetti may be or where any more of the treasure might be located."

Virginia leaned closer to her list. "Found something."

"What?" asked Camille.

"Giacopetti has an apartment he owns... do they call them apartments or condos in Rome?"

"I don't know. But either way, where is it?"

"It's about three blocks from here." chuckled Virginia. "He's three blocks away, and he doesn't know where we are. Funny."

Terry shook her head. "Real funny. Too close for comfort. Does that say anything else of interest?"

Virginia nodded. "Yeah. According to this, it's in a building that has a garage big enough for... something... can't make the rest out."

Camille smiled. "Give me the location of the new address, and I'll forward it to the Rome and Vatican police."

"Okay. That'll save us from another shootout."

"Or having Virginia blow the place up," Natalie said.

Terry frowned as she scrutinized the documents in front of her. "Oh, boy. Looks like he's got another place near the Coliseum. It may be a storage space. At least, I think that's what these figures indicate."

"Does it say where exactly?" asked Virginia.

"No. But according to this, and it's in Latin, the actual *Maria Magdale-*

na... Mary Magdalene documents are there along with some fine Etruscan and Roman jewelry, art, and some other old religious paintings. There is supposed to be a live, *invitationem solum*... invitation only, auction for them... sometime... It's hard to translate." Terry opened her calendar and flipped to the present month, then said, "Uh-oh, it's tomorrow. *Cash vel aurum solum*... Cash or gold only. Using Latin suggests he wanted to keep this even more secret. I don't think he wants *Signor* Franco and *Signor* Cappelli crashing his party."

"We already checked with the Vatican," said Camille. "They have the original Mary Magdalene papers."

Terry wet her lips. "We'd better have them verify they are the originals. From what we learned in the catacombs, Giacopetti is a great forger. Lt. Cumo and his gang could have stolen it, and then the gang put a copy back somehow."

"Or he could be selling a fake copy," said Camille.

"Yeah, but from what we now know, it could also be the original."

Virginia stood, walked to the sliding glass doors to their balcony, then turned. "We need to notify the Vatican. Camille, we'll leave that to you. Ladies, keep searching for anything that gives us a hint about the location of that storage place."

After lunch, the women started rereading the documents. Virginia paused. "There is going to be an auction for the Mary Magdalene documents and the other things. But if Giacopetti is going to be conducting it and the cops raid his apartment-will it really happen? If I were him, I'd take up temporary residence close to, or at, the auction site. But even with that, I don't see anything here that pinpoints the location, other than it's close to the Coliseum, or helps us get into the auction. And, to attend, we'd need the exact location and invitations, or we'd have to somehow break in and try not to get killed."

Camille pushed her glasses up on her nose. "I like the 'not get killed' part. Can your Cousin Luigi help?"

Virginia bit her lip and thought. "I don't know. I can ask." She sat back in her chair and dialed Luigi's phone number. When he answered, she asked him for help locating the auction and gave him the information they had. After hanging up, she turned to the others. "Luigi said he'll have some of his people start to check into it. He said they'd check the dark web as well. That's something I don't know how to do."

Terry stretched. "We've been at this all day. I don't think there is any more we can do for now. Want to go sightseeing and have a nice dinner out?"

Camille's cell phone rang. She answered it, listened. then hung up. "That was my friend at the Vatican Museum. He had the curators retest the Mary Magdalene documents. They are not the originals. The Vatican Mu-

Hidden Threads

seum is up in arms and wanted to know how I knew they were fakes. I told them to talk to the police." She glanced at the others. "We must get those documents back."

Virginia nodded. "As soon as we know where and exactly when the auction will be held, we'll go get them and capture Giacopetti."

Camille looked worried. "Can't we just tell the police?"

"Yes, but Giacopetti is well connected. Even with an arrest warrant out for him, he's likely to slip through the legal system," Virginia said. "Even if Italy is twice as good at prosecuting criminals as the US, some people can use influence, blackmail, murder, and money to escape justice. And he'd probably know about any police raid before it happened."

"So, what would we do with him if we capture him?"

Natalie chuckled. "We could throw him into the Mediterranean with concrete shoes."

"Nice idea. Or we could turn him over to the Vatican or Luigi," said Virginia.

"Your so-called cousin? What can he do?" asked Camille.

"You'd be surprised. Maybe Luigi would follow Natalie's idea and pollute the Mediterranean with Giacopetti's body." Virginia's cell phone rang. She answered it, took down a few notes, then disconnected. "That was Luigi. We have a place and time for the auction. As we already know, it's by invitation only and it is a live auction. No computer bidding. It's probably going to be well guarded. And with Giacopetti's connections, he'll know when and if the police try to raid it."

The women looked disappointed.

Natalie's expression turned to one of curiosity. "I know that look, Virginia. What dangerous, outlandish, and crazy idea is formulating in your devious mind?"

Virginia smiled. "Cousin Luigi has managed to obtain invitations for the four of us to go to the auction."

Natalie shook her head. "I had to ask."

Giacopetti sat at his ornate desk in his lavishly decorated apartment, reviewing the materials for the upcoming auction. He started to rise, then froze. He sat back down and examined the list of attendees for the auction again. He spotted the names of four women who his secretary had recently added. He sat back, stared at the ceiling, and thought. *Can it be? Has my luck just changed for the better? Could these be the four women who have caused me so much trouble? Now that I know who they are, I'll have my guys ready to take them out once and for all. But I'll wait to see how the bidding goes. Maybe they'll buy most of the goods and the Mary Magda-*

lene documents. If so, after I have their money, I'll dispose of them and resell the items to the next highest bidder. I can make a killing. I remember two of them from my villa party. What were their names? He ran his hand across the back of his neck, then ran his fingers down the list. *Right... Virginia Davies Clark and Natalie North. But who are the two new ladies? Who do these women work for? Are they really brokers for antiquities trying to cut me out, or do they work for some law enforcement agency? Law enforcement people don't flagrantly break laws like these women did, so what exactly is going on?* His thoughts were interrupted by a text message marked urgent. He picked up his cell phone and read the message. *So, the police are going to raid my apartment tonight.* His grip on the phone tightened. *I bet those women are behind this. Time to relocate my headquarters yet again.*

He made a call. "Mario, I need to see you immediately."

CHAPTER 40

In the early evening, the four women climbed out of the cab a block away from the address Luigi had given them. They were dressed to impress. Virginia and Natalie's outfits left little to the imagination. Terry wore a figure hugging, fire engine red pants suit, while Camille had on a tight red top and black slacks. Her dark brown hair brushed her shoulders in a wave. Despite how they were dressed, they walked a block north of the building where the auction was to be held and examined the area for escape routes, security cameras, and the types of buildings. They continued to search the areas to the east, south, and west.

Finally, Virginia stopped and looked at her watch. "Okay, we've got the lay of the land. We need to proceed. Giacopetti has our names on the invitation list and knows we're coming. Consider this a trap we're walking into. Everyone knows the plan, right?"

Natalie chuckled. "Bid on the items like we mean business, capture Giacopetti, and get out without getting killed." She looked at Virginia with a raised eyebrow. "I think it still needs a little tweaking."

Virginia shrugged her shoulder. "Think of the plan as fluid. Look and act sexy. Most of the bidders are probably men, and we should be able to cause enough distractions to keep any attacks at bay for a while. Giacopetti won't want to cause a scene with his… guests present."

"You hope. Don't forget, he has guards."

"Do we stick together or split up to search for the treasure?" asked Camille.

"There is safety in numbers, so we stick close and to the plan. Keep your playthings handy."

They strolled down an alley to the bright-green door, under a spotlight, on what appeared to be an abandoned warehouse. Nine high-end cars were parked in a row down the alley. A rather muscular man in a dark suit stood to one side of the portal with a clipboard. He smiled as they approached. They handed him their invitations. He checked them off the list on his clipboard. He pointed. "Right through that door, ladies. Have an enjoyable evening. It should make for an interesting *sera...* evening."

"The interesting part bothers me," Natalie whispered.

As they entered the building, Virginia watched him make a call on his cell phone. "We've been announced," she muttered.

They walked down a drab, dimly lit corridor toward a brightly lit area. Entering the main arena, Camille gasped. "Look at all the Etruscan artifacts and old paintings. And to think this is what's left of the treasure."

Terry pointed. "I bet the Mary Magdalene documents are in that glass case." She walked to the display and touched it. "It's acrylic. No breaking it with a hammer," she mumbled to herself. She bent over and examined the documents.

As she straightened, a man carrying another clipboard approached. *"Mi scusi.* May I be of assistance?" he asked.

Terry twisted a strand of auburn hair, then opened the small purse slung across her shoulder and pulled out a compact blacklight. *"Sì.* My associates and I are bidding on the items here this evening."

He nodded.

"I'd like to verify this document's authenticity by using a blacklight. Can you open the case and let me take a quick look?"

The man's eyes caressed her body, then he smiled. *"Sì.* For such a beautiful lady, no *problema,* but I must remain here with you." He pulled out a set of keys, unlocked the side door to the cabinet, and opened it.

Terry stuck her blacklight into the plastic box and switched it on. No glowing. She reached inside and carefully scraped the surface then shined the light again. Nothing happened. She stood back, returned her light to her handbag and grinned. *"Grazie."*

The man smiled. *"Prego.* Will there be anything else, *Signorina?"*

"No, you've been most helpful." She watched him relock the cabinet.

Camille ambled up to Terry. "Is it the original?"

"No glow, so not the real deal."

"What! You mean it's a fake?" Camille said a little too loudly.

Other men in the immediate area turned and looked at Terry and Camille. One gentleman with carefully styled gray hair approached. "You said the Mary Magdalene documents are... are forgeries? How do you know this?"

Camille brushed a lock of hair from her face and said, "I'm an anthropologist specializing in the Etruscan and Roman periods, and my friend here is a renowned archeologist. She just examined the documents."

The man stared at Camille. "If what you say is true, then how about the rest of the items here?"

"Haven't a clue. We didn't bring metallurgical test equipment."

"Are you two *Signorinas'* bidders?" he asked.

Camille's expression grew guarded. "Yes." She pointed. "We're with those other two ladies. They are the ones with the money, we're the technical part of the team... *consulenti.*"

"I see. *Grazi.*" He turned on his heel and hurried to talk to the group of men he was with.

Terry shook her head. "I think we just screwed the pooch. Better warn Virginia and Natalie." Camille and Terry hurried to the other women, who were examining Etruscan and Roman jewelry, and told them what had happened.

Virginia looked across the room at the man Camille had spoken to, who was now engaged in a heated discussion and waving his arms at a man with a tablet computer. The man started to rapidly type on the tablet. "Not good. We kicked the hornet's nest a little too soon." Virginia flexed her fingers. "I think we'd better retreat and notify Luigi to have the police raid the place before Giacopetti disappears again with the loot and orders us sacrificed to Mt. Vesuvius."

They started back for the door, when four tall men with lean hips and broad shoulders, walking with a slow, cocky swagger—affected by heroes of old westerns like when they saunter into salons filled with bad guys—approached and stood in front of them.

Virginia watched them draw near. *You've got to be kidding me. Their imitation of John Wayne is pathetic. That's what they get from watching too many old US westerns.*

One of the men spoke in broken English. "You *signorinas* will accompany us, *per favore.*"

Cold fingers brushed Virginia's heart. "We were just stepping out for a breath of air. Kind of stuffy in this old building."

His facial expression remained stoic. "This way, *signorinas.*" The men surrounded them and herded them toward a side corridor.

Natalie pointed toward the main hallway. "The entrance is that way."

"Your exit is this way," he said.

Virginia stopped. "Why are you taking us this way?"

"*Signor* Giacopetti's orders. Now move, *per favore.*"

"Humph." Virginia, followed by the others, strode to the end of the hall—painted institutional vomit-green like so many government buildings—to a door with chipped brown paint. A man opened the door and motioned for them to step outside into a walled-in, dirty, utility area and parking lot, illuminated by one spotlight high on the building. An empty beer can rolled away from the door. Brown leaves spun in a gust of wind in a corner.

After the door closed behind them, one of the men stepped closer to Natalie and quickly pulled out a knife. When he started to thrust the knife toward her, she used her forearm to block it, then she grabbed the man's wrist, whipped his arm behind him, and wrenched the elbow upward to a point where his shoulder painfully dislocated. The knife tumbled from his grip. He dropped to the ground, screaming and cursing.

Another of the men grabbed a length of thick, iron rebar and raised it to strike Terry. She snatched a broken piece of Masonite from a mound of trash next to her and flung it and some dirt into his eyes. He dropped the rebar and staggered back with blood streaming down his face. He tripped and fell, striking the back of his head against the concrete curbing in the area. Blood started to pool around his head.

Camille knelt, picked up the rebar and swung it with all the strength she could muster, clubbing the man near her across both of his knees. He screamed, collapsed to the ground, and rolled around, grasping his broken knees.

The fourth man stopped and looked at his companions on the ground. His face darkened as he turned toward Virginia. He pulled out a pistol, started to aim it, then stopped. He arched a speculative eyebrow. Curious, he watched her pull a lipstick out of her purse, smile, and then aim it at him. "What are you doing?" he asked.

"A girl needs to look nice before she kills someone, don't you agree?" She pressed a small button on the side. Two wires with prongs at the ends shot out and into the man's chest. Virginia immediately pushed the black bottom of the lipstick holder, shooting 12,000 volts into him. He shook violently. She pushed the button again. His body quaked, then he fell quivering to the ground. He stopped moving. His gun skidded a short distance away. Virginia pulled the little canister out of the holder and reloaded it. "Trouble with these macho types, is they have big egos and small brains." She kicked the gun across the yard.

Camille knelt and felt the man's throat for a pulse. She looked up at Virginia and shook her head. "How many volts and amps does that thing of yours put out?"

"Something like the electric chair," answered Virginia. "I think we should rejoin the party."

Terry looked at the men on the ground. "After all this, you want to go back in the lion's den?"

"You bet. Giacopetti won't be expecting us."

"You got that right."

They reentered the building and walked down the corridor when Virginia noticed a door with a padlock. "I wonder what's in there?"

"Let's find out. We can't get into any worse trouble." Natalie aimed her laser watch, pushed the side button, and watched the beam cut through the hasp. The lock fell to the floor.

Camille shook her head. "Nice accessory. Can I get one?"

"I don't know. I'll ask Cousin Luigi." Natalie turned the knob and opened the door. She reached around the doorjamb, found the light switch,

Hidden Threads

and illuminated the room. "Bingo!"

Camille entered and rushed to a table with an open portfolio containing what appeared to be old pages of a hand printed document. "Terry, bring your lamp and let's see what we've got."

Terry hurried to the table and used her ultraviolet light. The document's printing glowed. She bent closer and studied the first lines. "These are the original Mary Magdalene documents."

Natalie stood a few feet away, examining a crate full of gold jewelry. "This is the only box with anything in it. The other two over there are empty."

Virginia scanned the room. "I bet this is what Giacopetti is holding back as a future source of funds to support his lifestyle. We should put a serious dent in his plans."

"What do you have in mind?" Natalie asked.

"Camille. Take the portfolio with the authentic Mary Magdalene documents and go out the way we came in. Natalie, go with her, in case you meet any resistance."

"And if we do?"

"Neutralize it, permanently. I'll call Luigi and have him meet you. Once you two are safe, have him send in the police."

Camille swallowed. "Will... Cousin Luigi get here in time?"

"He's two blocks away with the police," Virginia said.

Natalie pointed at the crate of gold jewelry. "What about that?"

"It's too heavy to take out the front door. Terry and I'll hide it, then rejoin the auction."

Camille finished closing the portfolio, stopped, and listened. "Sounds like ruckus in the big room. We'd better get moving." She and Natalie hurried out.

Virginia punched the go code into her phone and sent it to Luigi. "Luigi's been notified. He'll pick up Natalie and Camille just before the police arrive. Terry, ready to go cause more damage?"

"Yes." She pushed the crate. "It's heavy, but not as bad as I thought." She examined the base. "Rollers. We could push it out the rear door and leave it out there with the men we injured."

Virginia chuckled. "Good idea. If Giacopetti comes looking for it and finds the lock destroyed and the room empty, he'll have a heart attack. When the police come, they'll find the treasure, the men, and hopefully Giacopetti, all in one location." She helped Terry push the crate out the rear door into the utility yard still strewn with prostrate bodies of injured and dead men.

Virginia and Terry reentered the auction, where the clients were in an uproar about being sold counterfeit goods. Word that the Mary Magdalene documents were fakes had spread through the crowd. Virginia spotted Giacopetti standing on a raised platform trying to calm the group.

He spotted Virginia and Terry. Glowing with rage, he yelled, "You two again!" He motioned towards three huge men, who Virginia thought looked like linebackers for the Green Bay Packers. "Get them," Giacopetti screamed.

CHAPTER 41

The men pulled semiautomatic pistols from under their jackets as they pushed their way through the angry bidders. When they got within ten feet of the women, they raised their weapons. Virginia yanked a canister of the SRH compound from her purse and fired it into the faces of the two closest men. They wiped their faces, then froze. The men's stomachs rumbled audibly, then one man murmured, "*Dios mio.*" The 'Shit Releasing Hormone' spray went into effect. They dropped their guns and fell to the floor in excruciating pain as their bowels quickly and loudly emptied. Agonizing intestinal spasms continued. The smell quickly overpowered the room. Virginia watched as the third and fourth men, whom she hadn't sprayed, staggered, then fell. She glanced at Terry.

Terry winced and pointed at the men Virginia put down. "That's disgusting. The smell is... overpowering."

"Yeah, I used the whole canister of the SRH on them. Probably overdosed." Virginia pointed at the two unconscious men. "What did you do?"

"I used my last canister of the DMSO-ketamine solution. They'll be asleep for about six hours." She eyed the two men Virginia had sprayed. "At least I didn't make a mess."

Virginia watched as the bidders ran for the exit. She spotted Giacopetti rushing at her, waving a Roman short sword. She dropped the empty canister of the SRH liquid, but before she could get to her gun, shots rang out. Giacopetti fell, his sword skidding across the floor. She slowly turned. Inspector Tonelli stood behind her with his gun aimed at Giacopetti. She took a calming breath, then said, "Nice to see you again, Inspector. You were just in time."

"What happened?" He wrinkled his nosed. "That smell. It's nauseating."

"You'll want to hose those men down before you take them out of here," Virginia said. "You don't want to mess up your police vehicles or ambulances." She pointed to the two sleeping men. "They'll wake up in about six hours." She watched as more police officers stormed into the room and visibly reacted to the smell.

"Do I want to know what you did?"

"No. But rest assured, these men will fully recover. Oh, there are more of Giacopetti's thugs out back. You'll find more of the stolen Vatican treasure out there, as well as in here."

Terry pointed at the acrylic case. "The documents in there are fakes. Giacopetti was going to sell them as the originals."

"I see. You ladies were busy tonight." Inspector Tonelli walked to Giacopetti, knelt, and pressed his finger to the carotid artery, checking for a pulse. He shook his head. "More damn paperwork. Let's step outside. With the poor ventilation, the stench in here is unbearable." They passed police officers and medics entering as the Inspector rushed Virginia and Terry outside. They stood on the sidewalk a few steps from the entrance and watched more emergency personnel arrive.

"That's better." Tonelli pointed at a large police van with barred windows. "We captured the bidders from the auction as they rushed out. Maybe we can recover more stolen Vatican artifacts and art, and who knows what other things we'll find at their homes and offices."

Terry glanced at the van. "It looks like the stolen Vatican treasure case is over, and these collectors of stolen art are now in custody. Not a bad evening's work."

Inspector Tonelli eyed Virginia and Terry. "One more detail. We're also investigating an explosion and multiple homicides at an abandoned garage across *Roma*. You ladies wouldn't know anything about that, would you?"

Virginia raised an eyebrow. "An explosion in an abandoned garage? Why would we know anything about that? We don't have a car."

"Because one of the dead men had a history with Giacopetti. The second person was... unidentifiable," said Inspector Tonelli.

Virginia looked stoic. "Why?"

"He was splattered all over the garage by the explosion."

"I see. We were all at our hotel last night when that happened," Virginia said.

"I didn't say when it happened."

"Oh." Virginia shrugged her shoulder. "They were probably doing something dangerous, and it blew up on them. Making drugs possibly? Making meth can be very dangerous and explosive."

"Possibly. You have no idea what was going on and were not involved. Right?"

"If you say so," Terry said.

"Okay. You ladies were officially not involved in that incident."

"I'm glad that's settled," said Virginia.

An officer walked up to Tonelli, whispered in his ear, then left. "I just learned the real Mary Magdalene documents were to be auctioned tonight. What we found were fakes. Do you have any idea where the original Mary Magdalene documents are? They were not with the items in the rear yard." asked Inspector Tonelli. "The Vatican is extremely concerned."

Virginia and Terry exchanged glances, then Terry spoke. "They are on their way back to the Vatican in the protective custody of an excellent visiting Smithsonian anthropologist."

Tonelli's face brightened. "Dr. Camille Pisciolo has them?"

Terry nodded. "Yes."

He quickly glanced around, leaned toward the women, and spoke softly, "Do you know if the lovely *dottore*... doctor is... is married?"

Virginia's eyebrow shot up. "You're interested in Camille?"

"*Sì*. She is warm, witty, spunky, adventurous, intelligent, *bello*... beautiful, sexy, energetic, full of life, and has big brown bedroom eyes. She is a special lady. Remember, I interviewed her at length at the river when we arrested that fake bishop."

Virginia gave him a soft smile. "She's not married. In case you're wondering, she's staying at our hotel. You might want to come there tomorrow for some... follow up questions... in private, of course. Oh, one other thing, she was a sheriff's deputy in California while studying for her Ph.D. in anthropology."

"*Sceriffo*? She was a sheriff?" He beamed. "*Grazie.*"

"But remember this, if you cause her any physical or emotional distress, we will come back to Italy, and you will feel pain like you've never felt it before," Virginia said, then winked.

"Female *mafioso*. Just what I need." He chuckled. "I believe you, and I'll keep your comment in mind, but rest assured I have only the very best intentions. I will treat her like a *principessa*. What are your plans now?"

Virginia laughed. "A hell of a lot of paperwork."

Three days later, Virginia, Natalie, and Terry were stretched out in their bikinis on a resort hotel beach in southern Italy. Natalie sipped her banana daiquiri. "With the remaining Etruscan artifacts and the Mary Magdalene documents back safely at the Vatican and the bad guys either dead or going to prison, we can now relax. It's great that Tom and the Smithsonian sprang for a couple of days R&R for us."

"Especially after all that paperwork." Virginia lowered her sunglasses and looked at the view. "I wish Andy could be here to enjoy this."

"Yeah, I miss Jeff. He'd love it here," Natalie said. "Maybe he and I can come here on vacation."

"We need to fill in Captain Steadman, with the Georgetown Police, about all this, for no other reason than to satisfy his curiosity. He will hound us until we give him the details."

"As will our beloved museum director, Dr. Doverspike," said Terry.

Natalie shifted on her lounge chair. "To think we got all this from a quilt."

"Quilts can be quite informative, as well as works of art," Virginia said. "Look at some of our other adventures."

"Right. We have had some real humdingers of cases involving quilts."

Virginia adjusted her sunglasses. "Gail Knight was happy we finally solved her treasure and ghost problem, and we were able to find out about the people from World War II who were involved. The Smithsonian is notifying the families. This should provide closure for her and the families."

"I miss Camille." Natalie sighed. "She was great."

"Me, too," Terry said. "I wonder how she's doing?"

Virginia picked up her iPad and looked at her email. "You're going to love this. According to her last message, she's enjoying our... or I should say *her* Inspector's company at his family's winery in Tuscany. She says his mother is teaching her some family recipes. I'm sure she's in good hands."

Terry chuckled. "I bet you're right. She might have thought he was just a nice but poor Rome police officer, but who knew his family was in the wine business. If his mother is teaching her family recipes, then Camille is a big hit with mama. That's important to Italians. Any mention as to the size of the winery?"

Virginia scrutinized the messages. "Yeah, she remarks in this email that it's three thousand acres, and the business does millions in sales all over Europe and the US. There's also a large olive grove on the property, and she says they sell olives and olive oil. I'd say she hit the jackpot."

Terry finished her pina colada. "Does he have any single brothers?"

"No. Two sisters."

"Nuts." Terry watched a man sitting near the bar: black hair and eyes, skin so bronzed he might have been part Indian. The coppery shade was not restricted to his face and hands; his shirt was open all the way to his belt, displaying beautifully rippled muscles. His arms were folded. His ankles crossed. He looked completely relaxed. He smiled and nodded at her. Tangled sheets and long, hot nights immediately leaped into her mind. "Ladies, things are looking up."

Virginia's cell phone played the Pirates of the Caribbean theme song as the ring tone. She put down her margarita and answered it. "Hi, Andy. Yes. We're done with our investigation and will be coming home in two days. I can't wait to tell you about it." She listened. "Sounds wonderful. Say hello to Jeff for Natalie, she can't wait to see him. I'll call you tonight with the travel details. Love you." She disconnected.

Terry adjusted the top to her bikini and said, "That was short and sweet."

"I didn't want to go into the details and answer an hour's worth of questions over the phone."

"Now I'll get a call from Jeff," said Natalie. "I'd better have another daiquiri. He'll want the juicy details, too."

"Anything else from our friends in Washington?" Terry asked.

"Nope... well... don't miss our flight home."

Natalie finished her banana daiquiri and waved at the waiter to bring another. "I think Camille will be semi-retired shortly and learning the ins and outs of Italian cooking and the art of wine making. She was great and fit into our little group. It was like she'd always been with us. Like I said before, I miss her. But I'm glad she's found someone who thinks the world of her."

Virginia nodded. "Inspector Tonelli thinks of her as a princess. As he put it, *his principessa*. And with a huge family winery, I guess he can afford to make her a princess."

Terry smiled. "Camille will make a great 'Italian' wife and wonderful mother. She doesn't need more of our type of adventures. From what I've learned about her, she'll be running the winery before long." She leaned back, staring up at the cloudless, azure Italian sky. "And now we know someone we can visit in Tuscany who will be in the wine business. I wonder if we could get a discount?"

Virginia tapped the screen of her cell phone. "Camille just sent a copy of the Tonelli family recipe for spaghetti sauce. It's an attachment. She says it's great."

ADDENDUM

Dr. Camille Pisciolo's Spaghetti Sauce Recipe

Ingredients
- 2 cans tomato paste
- 1 large or 2 small cans tomato puree
- 1 TBE spoon garlic powder
- ¼+ cup sweet basil
- 1 pound 97% lean hamburger
- 1-pound HOT Italian sausage
- 1 cup sliced mushrooms
- 1 large bell pepper
- Extra Virgin Olive oil, as needed

Cooking
- Chop bell peppers and brown in olive oil and remove from pan
- Cut sausages in half and brown in the olive oil and remove
- Brown and chop up the hamburger
- Return peppers and sausage to pan and add the two cans of tomato paste.
- Add 6 tomato paste cans of water (3 cans of water from each can of paste)
- Add tomato puree
- Add garlic, basil, and mushrooms and stir
- Simmer for 4 hours over low heat and thicken. Add water, as necessary.
- Serve over pasta with a salad and Italian bread

Dr. Camille Pisciolo's Meat Balls and Meat Loaf Recipe

Ingredients
- 1 Lb. ground beef
- 1 Lb. ground pork
- Salt and pepper
- Parsley flakes
- Garlic powder
- ¾ to 1 cup grated Romano cheese
- 3-4 cups Italian seasoned breadcrumbs

Instructions
- Mix all ingredients, knead thoroughly.
- Let stand minimum of 1 hour.
- For meat balls, form into balls and drop in hot Camille Pisciolo Spaghetti Sauce Recipe spaghetti sauce made without the meat.
- For meat loaf, form as a loaf in a baking pan and cover with canned or homemade tomato sauce and bake at 350 until done.
- May also be made into patties and fried.

ABOUT THE AUTHOR

Dr. David Ciambrone is a retired aerospace and defense company executive, scientist, professor of engineering, and a business and environmental consultant and is now a best-selling, award-winning author, living in Georgetown, Texas, with his wife Kathy. He has published twenty-five (25) books: four (4) non-fiction, two (2) textbooks for a California university, and nineteen (19) mysteries and has two (2) new mysteries in work. He is the author of the Virginia Davies Quilt Mysteries.

Dave has been a speaker at writer's groups, schools, colleges, libraries, quilt guilds, writer's conferences, and business/scientific conferences internationally.

Dr. Ciambrone also wrote three newspaper columns and wrote a column for a business journal.

Dave is a member of Sisters in Crime, the San Gabriel Writer's League, the Writer's League of Texas, Mystery Writers of America, the International Thriller Writers Association, The Beacon Society, and DFW Sherlock Homes Society.

Dave was appointed a U.S. Treasury Commissioner and to the management board of the Resolution Trust Corporation (RTC) by President Clinton.

He is a Fellow of the International Oceanographic Foundation

Visit David at

Author's Website:davidciambrone.com

Facebook:facebook.com/david.ciambrone?fref=ts

Twitter: twitter.com/mysterywriter5

LinkedIn: linkedin.com/pub/david-ciambrone-sc-d-fiof/11/ab5/bb3

Amazon: amazon.com/author/davidciambrone

Progressive Rising Phoenix Press is an independent publisher. We offer wholesale pricing and multiple binding options with no minimum purchases for schools, libraries, book clubs, and retail vendors. We offer substantial discounts on bulk orders and discounts on individual sales through our online store. Please visit our website at:
www.ProgressiveRisingPhoenix.com

If you enjoyed reading this book, please review it on Amazon, B & N, or Goodreads.
Thank you in advance!

www.ingramcontent.com/pod-product-compliance
Lightning Source LLC
LaVergne TN
LVHW010258260326
834688LV00044B/1356